NS

drowned

drowned

NICHOLA REILLY

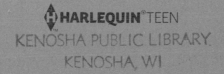
HARLEQUIN®TEEN

Recycling programs
for this product may
not exist in your area.

ISBN-13: 978-0-373-21122-7

DROWNED

Printed in U.S.A.

For my sister Jen

One

The Way the World Ends

I write things on the sand so I won't forget them. Things I like.

Darkness.

Dreams.

Clam.

Buck Kettlefish.

Things I want.

A warm dry place.

A long night of sound sleep.

I watch the waves come and erase the words from the shore. Erased from existence. From possibility. It's almost as if the waves are taunting me.

For thousands of tides I am sure people thought about how and when the world would end. Maybe they wondered whether it would happen while they were alive, or if their children, grandchildren, or maybe even their great-great-

great-great-grandchildren would be the unlucky ones to be there when the world crashed down around them.

But I don't have to wonder.

I know it is going to happen soon, and maybe in my lifetime.

Every morning I wonder if I will see the sunset. Every breeze is like death breathing down my back.

The sun burns like fire among black smokelike clouds on the horizon, making my eyes squint and burn. High tide is approaching, the waves slowly coming closer. With every breath, every heartbeat, they rise a little more. Soon almost everything will be underwater.

I stand and shake the sand out of my mat, then roll it up and affix it to my knapsack. I've gotten pretty good at doing all these things one-handed. My clothes are wet, and my lips taste like salt. I'm not sure why I'm yawning because I had a pretty good spell of sleep. Nearly half a tide. Half a tide where, at least in my mind, I was somewhere warm and dry, somewhere that didn't smell like crap or rotting fish.

I plod along with the others, away from the steadily rising waters. It's chilly but at least my tunic is only slightly damp; it doesn't stick to my skin. Nothing is ever dry here. It's either sopping wet or damp, and damp is a blessing.

It's time once again for formation. We all know the tides. We must, or we'd pay for our ignorance with our lives. It's time for all of us, all 496 of us, to trudge to the platform that stands maybe sixty of my feet above the ground, at the center of the island. At least, at last total, there were 496 of us. I don't like to count because our numbers are constantly falling. We all know this, which is probably why nobody looks at or speaks to anyone else. Better not to get too familiar.

When someone disappears, we all assume the worst. Because the worst is usual.

The only person who does look at me is Mutter. His face is dark and leathery, and his beard is scraggly and foul, greenish-gray, filled with old, dead things. He has his own scribbler scars, but at least he has all his limbs. He is useful. He sneers at me, disgusted. "Waste of space," he hisses as I find my spot on the platform. "Scribbler Bait." I wipe away the sand with my bare foot. The number two is scratched there.

Number two is my spot, for now. It's near the dry center of the circular formation, where things are safer. There are 496 circles arranged around it, spiraling out from the center. The circles are small; there's barely enough room to stand. There used to be thousands of circles, one for every person on the island. But the only thing constant about the island we call Tides is change.

Children get the central spots. When I reach my sixteenth Soft Season, when I am an adult, I will be given a new spot based on the importance of the job I am given. Mutter is right, though. I don't have any special skills, and my deformity makes it difficult for me to pull in the nets or do the things fishermen do. I'd barely make a good scavenger, the lowest of the low. People call them Scribbler Bait.

"I saw a scribbler on the platform last night," Xilia whispers to no one in particular. She is a scavenger, too, and quite mad. But many of those who occupy spaces on the outer edge of the formation are crazy, because they brush with death every time the tide comes in. And nobody can deny that the scribblers have been getting braver. That's not the name we always had for them. When I was young they were called spearfish, because they'd often spear fishermen as they brought in the nets. But then they started coming onto the sand when the tides receded, sunning themselves. They'll attack us on land, ripping through our flesh with their spear-shaped noses, then feasting on our blood. They're getting smarter, too, because after a while they began burrowing under the sand, hiding from us, and springing out whenever a human came too close. They make long, winding paths in the sand with their sinewy black bodies—like scribbles, my father had said. My father started calling them scribblers, and everyone followed him, as they usually did.

I've never seen a scribbler on the platform before. The thought makes me shudder. The platform, however small and inadequate, is our safety. But I know our safety is eroding. It has always been so. A thousand tides ago, the platform was twice the size it is now at high tide. There was room for twice as many people. Now we are under five hundred. I know this because there are fewer than five hundred spaces. The largest number that's still visible, though it is nearly half eaten by the tides, is 496. At least, that was the number the last time I had the energy to look.

I sigh and throw my things down on my spot. The spot is so comfortable and familiar to me that I feel as if the imprint on the stone conforms perfectly to my feet. Sweat drips from my chin. My eyes sting from the glare reflecting off the white concrete. Little Fern, who is seven, comes hopscotching up to space number one, scrawny as a sprig of seaweed, two white-blond braids framing her sweet smile. She has a little stick in her hand, something she's never without. When she steps next to me, she touches the stick to my elbow. "Your wish is granted," she says with great flourish.

If only. If only the stories I told her about fairies were true. There are so many things to wish for.

I was space number one until Fern turned five, when we all moved over a space to make room for her. Before then, she occupied the same spot as her mother, who was a fisherman before she died many tides ago. They used to give mothers spaces in the center of the formation when they had children, but then things became so dire that some women had babies just to get a better spot. I was told Tiam's mother had, and my mother had, though I can't remember ever squeezing next to her on her spot. Two babies in a season was a virtual baby boom. So they put an end to that practice after I was born. Now nobody has children. It just means more people. And there are already too many people.

After all, when a baby is born, it just means that when that child turns five, we'll all have to move one space to the left. The person at the very end of the spiral is out of luck. Space is something people have been known to kill for.

I'm grateful for Fern, though. She is the only one who still smiles at me. As for the others, we are not friends. We do not trust or like anyone, even our own family members—if we have any of them left, and most of us don't. We all know what is coming, and we've all lost enough to know that caring for another person doesn't make things easier.

Which means I have a big problem.

"Hey, Coe."

Just like part of the formation washes away in every tide, part of me is lost every time I hear his voice.

"Hi, Tiam," I say, staring at the sandy ground. Looking up at him, at those liquid sapphire eyes, will just make the pain worse. Besides, I already have every inch of his face memorized. Him? If I hadn't been required to assume the space next to him for the past ten thousand tides, if there weren't slightly under five hundred of us, I doubt he'd know my name.

Fern waves her wand some more, granting wishes to the air. I wonder how obvious it is that most of the wishes I have in my head involve Tiam. It's not that I want to wish about him. It just happens.

Tiam drops his stuff in space number three. For as long as I can remember, he has been beside me. When I was young he used to hold my hand to keep me from being scared. He is never scared.

I move as far away from him as I possibly can, which isn't far enough. The spaces are only maybe two of my feet in diameter, so now that we are older, we rub shoulders. Even though I try to wash up every day in a tide pool, I know he can smell me. I have the luck of having the job that makes me reek a hundred times worse than the normal, forgettable stench that most of us carry. Mine seems to bury itself deep under my skin. No matter how much I bathe, it never completely goes away.

If he does smell me, though, he never lets on. In twenty tides or so he will reach adulthood, and I'm sure he will have a good spot in the formation. A spot for the most valuable people. He is smart enough to be a medic, strong enough to be a builder, brave enough to be an explorer.

He is everything I am not.

Tiam always comes to the formation at the last moment. I think it's his way of laughing at nature, while the rest of us cower before it. He says, to no one in particular, "So, what is the news?"

I know that isn't directed at me. I spend most of my free time alone, so I don't ever hear any news. But formation is the time to catch up on the latest gossip. Burbur, in space four, who is one of the most respected royal servants, says that she heard the king coughing in his sleep while making her normal rounds in the palace. Tiam raises an eyebrow, and everyone murmurs, "Ah, really?" Finn, a fisherman, whispers that the food brought in during this morning's harvest was "pitiful," and people shake their heads and say, "Is that so?" This goes on for a moment as I wonder whether or not to submit the only piece of information I have gleaned in the past hundred tides. Finally I clear my throat.

Tiam and the rest turn to me, clearly surprised that I'm contributing. "Xilia said she saw a scribbler on the platform last night," I offer weakly.

Someone, Burbur I think, huffs. Another person snorts. Tiam says, "You mean the Xilia who sees scribblers in her soup? In the eyes of her enemies? Floating among the clouds?"

Laughter isn't heard often on the island, but at this, people burst into fits of loud guffaws. I shrink into the center of my space. "Point taken," I mumble.

He leans over so that his warm breath grazes my cheek, and immediately I stand spear-straight. "Sorry, Coe, I don't mean to make light of it," he whispers. "Xilia says things just to scare people. And the last thing we need is for people to be more afraid."

Tiam the peacemaker. He is so like my father, it's scary. And it's hard to feel offended when he whispers in such a gentle way. I can't feel anything other than my heart thudding against my chest, the heat rising in my cheeks. I nod. "I know. It's okay."

"We've lost another!" someone shouts. From here I can see a body being hoisted into the air and carried in the hands of the others, toward the edge. It will be tossed over. That is the law. We spend much of our lives on the platform, squeezed together so tightly that the air tastes rancid, and one can barely raise a hand to wipe the sweat from his brow; so it's not uncommon for people to pass out while standing in the scorching heat. It's a woman, but I can't see who. I can only see the dirty bottoms of her feet as she is carried farther away from me. I look at Tiam, who is frowning. He doesn't approve of this law.

I know the sea is close when the wind picks up and I can feel its mist in my face. The people on the outer edge begin to scramble and shout, and we collectively sway along with the waves, breathing in as each one comes, out as it recedes. The sea is not close. Not yet. The newly risen sun, still veiled in those smoky clouds, will have nearly begun to sink from its high point in the sky by the time we are done here. But Fern

already has her hand in mine, and it's sweaty and trembling.
I do my best to calm her by stroking it lightly.

Tiam grins past me, at her. "Hey, Bug," he says. "Try this."

She turns to him, eyes wide. Tiam is balancing on one foot
like a crazy man.

Fern and I stare at him.

"Try this," he says, patting his stomach and rubbing his
head. "Bet you can't do that."

"You'll get in trouble," I warn, but I know people make
special allowances for Tiam. Fern giggles and squeals. Tiam
always knows how to make everything better. He knows how
to make those tense moments in the formation pass quickly.
"You are *such* a crabeater," I mutter, trying my best to sound
gruff, as if I couldn't care less about him.

The waves are close now. I can hear them crashing against
the platform, smell them. My wet hair, and the hair from the
woman behind me, whips my face. Skeletal limbs press against
me. People hug themselves and moan. We all tremble as one.
The scribblers at the edge are hissing, sensing the human flesh
that is so near. During the worst of it, I always look up at the
calming sky, at the seagulls gracefully arcing overhead. But
today there are storm clouds above. A jagged edge of lightning slits those clouds, followed by the rumble of thunder.
All of nature rages around us. We are powerless here.

But Tiam does not care. He spins in circles, touching the
tip of his nose. While the rest of the formation huddles together, wishing their space were bigger, Tiam acts as though
the space is a mile wide. His antics get riskier and riskier as
the moments drag on, so that one can barely take notice of

the waves crashing around us. He causes such a commotion that all the people at the center of the formation, the important people, stare at him. I try to nudge him to stop, but he doesn't care.

"Hey, Bug," he says. "Let's race. Ready?"

I exhale, relieved. I know this game. They've played it every tide since Fern was three. Fern smiles and waits for him to count down from three. Then they both take huge gulps of air and hold it. I count slowly. *One-one-thousand. Two-one-thousand.* Their faces strain; Fern's cheeks turn the color of the sunset. I'm up to seventy-five when Tiam opens his mouth and the air explodes out of him. Fern holds hers until 103. A new record. When she finally gives up, she grins, triumphant. She is always triumphant. And in that triumph, the ocean disappears, if only for a few moments.

The tide begins to go out, and the rest of us let out the collective breath we'd been holding. For most of us, it will *never* be a game, not while the unpredictable and merciless sea rages around us.

Tiam picks up his bag and starts to stroll off. For me, that is always the saddest part of every tide. Despite being the farthest from the edge, he always manages to be one of the first down. He'll climb down when the water is still at the base of the platform. There are ropes attached to the side of the platform, and Tiam and some of the stronger and braver men use those to go up and down. They'll hang from them as the tide goes out, tempting fate as scribblers nip at their ankles. Another game. But I have no choice but to use the ladder. I am always among the last to descend. There is now only one ladder to the platform. This ladder is our salvation. It has been patched and rebuilt a thousand times, often after someone has fallen to his death. It has ninety-seven rungs, some rotting metal, some driftwood, all of which bow and creak underfoot. I know this because I have counted them every day of my life. When I was younger, there were two ladders. Now entering and leaving the platform eats away much of the tide, especially for those in the middle of the platform, who must arrive first and leave last.

When I finally reach the top of the ladder and descend, I can tell something is different. Everyone seems focused in the direction of the castle. By the time I make it to the ground, I've found the reason.

At the base of the formation, standing there in a cheerful pink robe that glistens as it billows in the breeze, is the king. He and the princess are standing right below the platform, watching as each person descends the ladder. They spend each tide in the castle tower, which is where they live. The tower is the only part of the castle that isn't underwater during high tide; it's slightly taller than the platform, so when the rest of the world goes beneath the sea, only those two things remain. The tower, though, is not exactly stable. It seems to sway a bit whenever there's a stiff wind, which is why only the king and princess and their guards have ever been up there. I always wonder if it will come crashing down during a storm, and then where will we be, without any rule?

The fact that they have left the castle at all is astounding; I haven't seen either of them in a hundred tides. The king and the princess sit in their quarters in the tower atop the castle, overlooking all of us, watching us struggle in formation like insects in a rainstorm. But here he is, frowning, tapping his foot on the concrete and pulling on the end of his manicured beard.

His eyes are focused on Tiam. I bite my tongue for him. Tiam doesn't belong in any single group, preferring to hover among the fishermen, the scavengers, the builders. In a world where sameness is much preferred, he's always been one to do things his own way. He's always acted like a lunatic in formation, but maybe today is the day he finally gets punished for it. I watch him stroll blithely toward the king, my heart skipping beat after beat at the thought.

Don't look at him. Don't look at the king, I try to transmit to Tiam telepathically. But he's so bold. Commoners are not allowed to view royalty. To do so is cause for immediate demotion of one's standing in the formation. I'm already pressing my chin to my chest in reverence. I furtively watch as he raises his eyes to the king's shoulders…his chin—*no, don't do it!*—and finally his eyes. By then there are bloody teeth marks in my tongue. I draw in a breath and wait for something terrible to happen.

But it never does. The king's voice is soft. "So, it's nearly high Hard Season. Your sixteenth, eh, Tiam?" he asks, quite jovially, adjusting his cape. His cape is blazing as pink as the sunset, easily the most beautiful thing I've ever seen, so it hurts to know I can't gaze upon it directly.

Tiam tilts his chin up. He responds as if he were talking to any adult. Polite, not groveling. "Yes, sir."

The king nods. "Good, good."

The king is a good man. He is taller than all of us, and regal. His beard is trimmed, red as the sunrise, and shiny and luxurious as his silk robes. Wallows have ruled the world for as long as any of us can remember. We don't study history anymore, but from what I understand, the first Wallows were just regular people, like us. When the floods came, they opened their land and their castle to those who had been displaced. The one part of history that always rings in our ears is how the Wallows graciously allowed others to inhabit their property. The Wallows are most kind and benevolent, for it was their selfless act that allowed us to live.

King Wallow has ruled since before I was born, and I think we are lucky to have him. The people of Tides listen to him. In a world such as ours, it would be so easy for chaos to reign, for people to disobey the rules for their own survival. But the king has made sure order prevails. He has dealt with all the troublemakers. He has kept us safe.

I'm standing there, still awed by his presence at the formation this soon after high tide, but in a second I begin wishing I'd run far away. Because in that second the king turns to me.

My eyes drop immediately to the ground, along with my stomach. "And you..." He seems to be fishing for my name. But even though there are only 496 people in this world, it seems to elude him, as it does most everyone.

"Corvina Kettlefish," I manage.

"Ah." He pauses, as if he's never heard the name before. I am sure he has, but there's no reason he should remember it from thousands of tides ago, when I'd been his daughter's playmate. Though I do not meet his eyes, I know that in the silence, he's taking in my straggly hair, dark and menacing as the ocean, my odd, ruddy skin, mottled with freckles and blisters. I hear him sniff loudly, and cringe. "What is that horrid smell?"

"I, um…" I sputter dumbly. People are constantly sniffing around me, wrinkling their noses and waving their hands in front of their faces. I don't want to explain. It's mortifying enough talking about my duties when Tiam and the entire island aren't audience to it.

Princess Star blinks and fans her delicate pink hand in front of her pretty nose. She's not of this world. Everything about the princess is pretty or special. The rumor is that many tides ago, a few seasons before I was born, she appeared suddenly in the tower as a gift from the gods, a sign that our world would be safe forever. She is light, goodness, hope.

"No mind," he says, with a dismissive wave. "How many Hard Seasons have you seen?"

I stare at the ground and whisper, "Fifteen. Next will be my sixteenth Soft Season, Your Majesty." Soft Season's nearly two hundred high tides from now. Most people look to Soft Season's coming with anticipation, as it's the time when the ocean is not as menacing. I, however, cringe when it approaches. Every time it comes, it means I am closer to being cast to the outer edges of the formation.

There is a pause. Then, finally, a laugh, which disintegrates into a disgusting, phlegmy cough. As Burbur had said. Coughs are always reason for concern here. The medics have no way to treat them. They don't have a way to treat most illnesses and afflictions. Seaweed compresses or saltwater gargles are the usual prescription. But most people who start a cough never get better.

"Goodness' sake," he mutters, staring at my arm, and I scramble to hide my deformity. But it's too late. "More Scribbler Bait."

I'm used to being called Bait. People know me as that, instead of Corvina or Coe. That I'm used to it is the only thing that stops me from running away without being dismissed. Star interrupts. "But, Father. This is the one, I thought."

My mind whirls. *The one?* Can she be talking about me? It's hard to believe that someone so ethereal and special ever thinks about *me*.

King Wallow coughs loudly again. Then he clears his throat, and his eyes settle back on me. They are full of disgust. "She is... I don't think... Just look at her."

Star says, "Then, who?"

King Wallow walks away, with Star at his heels, almost floating like the angel she is. "Let us decide on that later. But if you ask me, she's nothing but useless." They leave me with Tiam, my face burning.

Two

Prayers to Broken Stone

Once it's no longer underwater, I walk slowly back to the moldy sleeping compartment, taking deep breaths to calm myself. The compartment is the only place on the island, save for the craphouse, where I can spare my skin from the sun. It's a vast rotting building of concrete and metal, coated in barnacles and rust. Many people hate the mold and confinement of this place, and choose to rest outdoors. But I prefer the cool darkness, the steady dripping sounds, the familiar smell of decaying metal.

Xilia is kneeling at the side of the formation, where she has propped up her idols. One is a skinny plastic female doll with white-blond hair. The other is a fat naked baby doll with chubby cheeks and dimples, and a soiled cloth body. There is also a red furry creature, bald in spots, with bulging white eyes. She has an honored place for each of them. "Come, pray with me, Coe," she beckons.

I kneel beside her for a moment, just to be polite. Xilia is the only one who prays, or at least the only one who prays openly. I think everyone else has their own gods they pray to, in the darkness, in whispers, so that nobody can hear them.

I pray, too, silently. I pray that when death comes, I can accept it with dignity. That's the only thing left to pray for these days. All other prayers have gone unanswered for so long, they seem like asking for the moon.

"Oh, gods, thank you for sparing us this tide, for you are indeed great. Protect us from the savage sea. If the next is to be our last tide, please deliver us safely into your kingdom."

"Amen," we say in unison.

Xilia inspects me. "I think it will be the next tide," she says. "I will be gone on the next one, for certain."

Xilia says this every tide. Yes, she's crazy, but I think she does it to prepare herself. I, too, think about that tide every day. The tide that will sweep me away. I try to remember to be strong when the end comes. "It could be," I say. After all, every tide *could* be.

Xilia told me once what it is like at the outer edges of the formation. I've never been there, never had to see what it is like as the water climbs up to meet you. First, very slowly, the craphouse goes under, and then our sleeping compartment, and then the lower floor of the castle, until all you see is its cheerful seashell-pink roof under the churning, blackish waters. Then, as far as you can see, the only thing visible is the tower and the top of the formation. Usually there is a good five of my feet between the highest tide and the edge of the formation, but during high Hard Season, it's less than one. During Hard Season, waves often smash against those on the outer edge, pushing them toward the center of the formation, and so people in the middle will push back, making those on the edge fall in. Certainly, they may swim, try to climb back up again, but nobody will help them, and if they're too weak to climb up themselves (which most of us are), then the scribblers will get them. For those on the outer edge, every second of high tide is a battle, every wave may be the end. It is a maddening game. Which is why I indulge Xilia. I know I will be in her place one day.

Once inside the compartment, the smell of mold comforts me, as does everything about being in this dark, closed space, where nobody can see me. The wrinkles I have from squinting flatten out, and my eyes adjust neatly to the darkness. I have my own duties to complete, but the words *Scribbler Bait,* along with what Princess Star said to me, keep ringing in my ears. *The one?* What could she possibly mean by that?

The princess is all things I am not. I sometimes catch my reflection in a tide pool. My skin is freckled and has brown scabs from the sun, as it blisters easily. Unlike all the others, my skin turns a hot red during the evening. It's not a pretty pale pink like the princess's; it's wildfire. I also have mottled scribbler scars everywhere, on my cheeks, my shoulders—and deep ones on my torso, as if someone tried to reach in and steal my ribs. My hair is a mangled nest of dull black, blacker than the ocean, coated thickly with salt and sand. I stopped trying to comb my fingers through it so long ago I can barely remember when it wasn't like this. I'm smaller than most everyone, only a head or two taller than Fern. Then there are my eyes. They're wide-set, slanted strangely and coated in strange thick black lashes. Plus they're pink. Pink! I'm always blinking like crazy in the sun because the sun hurts my eyes so much that I can't keep them open. Everyone else on the island is blond or reddish-haired, tanned, tall and strong, with light blue or brown eyes, and blond, barely noticeable lashes. But the worst thing is my stump. The place where my right hand once was is red and raw and shines grotesquely in the sun. I wear the same tunic fashioned together with old pieces of cloth and plastic and even kelp, and I know I smell like a rotting fish, at best. When my mother named me Corvina, she must have known who I would be. Named after a smelly, slimy, disgusting fish.

Tiam used to be a very popular name here. It was once considered to be a lucky name, for it pays respect to the goddess Tiamat, who rules the sea and controls its chaos. But people don't believe in luck anymore, since all of ours has been bad, so I'm probably the only one who knows its meaning. I doubt even Tiam knows. But Tiam is the closest thing to a god I've ever seen, and so I often wonder if our names control who we become.

Star, too, is heavenly and pure, like her namesake. I am not allowed to look directly at her, but sometimes I sneak glances when her back is turned to me. It's impossible not to. Her hair is clean and bright and shines like the early sunlight when it breaks over the horizon. She wears robes of colors more brilliant than I'd ever known possible, and her sinewy limbs are always adorned with pearls and other jewels. Her skin is even and soft as the clouds.

This is the one, I thought, she'd said. She said it as if I were a fish she was selecting for dinner, as if we hadn't been play-mates as children. I've been told that long ago, when I was young, the princess, Tiam and I would play together in the castle. We had the honor of entertaining the princess because we were the only children on the entire island. Maybe Star, like I, does not remember those times. I do not remember my early childhood; I've pieced it together from what Ana and others have told me.

I stretch my mat on the wet sand and lie down. The com-partment was just underwater, so I hope the endless dripping of water from the roof and down the walls will lull me to sleep. Instead I keep thinking of what Star said, and how the king laughed at me.

I roll over and draw in a breath. Tiam's outline is there, in the doorway.

He never comes to the compartment to sleep. He's always out, building something, scavenging, making himself useful. When he does rest, he does so outside. He is so unlike me, preferring the wide, open outdoors to closed, dark spaces. If given the chance, I'd live my whole life in a closed, dark space.

The small hopeful part of my brain tickles with the thought that maybe he came looking for me. But the last time he did that was probably when I was a child and he was looking for someone to build sand castles with. Then I notice he has two buckets of rainwater in his hands. He's replenishing our drinking jugs.

I watch his strong back, glistening with sweat, as he pours the two buckets into the big red container at the corner of the compartment. It's dark inside the compartment, and he is too busy to notice me. I try to think of a time when he wasn't busy, when we were kids and used to race down the beach at low tide. He always won.

"Coe," he whispers, startling me.

"Yeah?"

"Come scavenging with me," he says. "I want to try the west side."

At first I think I must have misheard him, that he must have been asking someone else. Why would he want me to scavenge with him? But the longer I lie there, waiting for the person he was asking to get up and walk, the more I realize that his eyes, even in the darkness, are focused directly on mine.

"Okay." Heart beating madly, I stand up, roll up my mat with shaking hands and put it into my bag. For him, my duties can wait a little longer. I heft my bag onto my shoulder and when we walk outside, the sun temporarily blinds me. The storm has passed, and the clouds have burned off. Tiam slings his bag and his scribbler-nose spear over his back and jogs quickly ahead. I hurry up behind him like his shadow, watching with envy how much the sunlight loves him, faithfully reflecting every tiny platinum hair on his tanned back and making his skin glimmer like gold.

"Don't listen to Wallow," he says to me. "Don't listen to any of them. They underestimate you."

"Right," I mumble.

"You're better than any of them. If brains were muscles you'd be stronger than all of them."

I turn away from him to hide my blushing. Why is he telling me this? We used to confide in each other as children, yes. But for so many tides, as he's been planning to enter adulthood and assume his new role, we've been like strangers. It was something I accepted; I found it inevitable that he'd pull away and eventually stop talking to me altogether. Because I'm strange-looking and don't have any usefulness in this world. It's true; I do know a lot more than the rest of them. But it's all about useless things. My dad was also that way. He taught me everything he knew about the past, about the way things used to work. Before he left on his Explore so many tides ago, he gave me a thing called a "book," one of his very prized possessions. Two of them, actually. One is a collection of stories called *Fifty Famous Fairy Stories*, and the other is a journal that was kept by some of our ancestors. The first entry was shortly before the floods began, and the last was thousands of tides ago. Now there is no more paper and nothing to write with; it must have been around the same time those things started becoming a luxury that we lost the language with which to write at all. On this book, the graying pages are so scribbled upon that not a single space remains on them. Some of the entries are in such tiny print, I have to squint to see the writing. I read from them whenever I have the rare chance of being alone, since if anyone knew I had them, they'd insist I add them to the kindling pile. I have just about every word memorized. But nobody here has use these days for fairy tales or facts about ages past. Nobody has use for me. Especially not someone like Tiam.

"But brains are *not* muscles," I say. My father might have been the only one with intelligence to rival mine, but he also had brawn. Thinking about my father again, I feel sick. I'd gotten good at existing without thinking about him, at denying what must have happened to him. "That was the first time the king has talked to me. Ever," I say.

"Really?" He seems surprised. He scratches his chin.

"I think they have something under the folds of their robes."

He raises his eyebrows. "You do?"

"Yeah. They're being awfully sneaky."

After a moment he says, "Well, you're the smart one."

I squint down the shoreline. We're alone. The thought sends a chill down my spine, as it's an unspoken rule in Tides never to go off alone with anyone. People who do have a way of disappearing. The king may keep order in this world, but in a world where space is at a premium, even the most useful of people aren't safe. And we do not have the luxury of mourning anyone, much less the people stupid enough to put themselves in danger. "Why did you ask me to come with you?"

"You're right. Something's going on," he whispers. "I need to tell someone. If I don't, I'll burst. Can I trust you not to tell anyone?"

He's placing his trust in me. *Me.* I feel my face getting hot. *Trust no one* is the first rule of Tides. It is not easy, depending on people without placing trust in them, and yet that is what we all have learned to do. But when he looks at me, his face serious like that, I could agree to anything. "Yes," I say, shivering.

"King Wallow is dying."

"No!" I blurt, covering my mouth. I think back to the way he'd hacked and sputtered while talking to me, and the greenish tinge to his skin, and know that Tiam is right. "How do you know? What will we do?"

"I was called to the palace late last night. But—"

"You were? When?" My mouth hangs open. I hadn't seen him leave, but of course, I was in the compartment, where he rarely goes. Still, I'd expect to hear some whisperings of something as big as this during formation. "Did you get in trouble for something?"

"No. I—"

"What is it like? Is it beautiful? Is everything made out of pearls?"

"Don't be silly. You've been there before."

"I was a child. I don't remember it." I sigh. The truth is, I remember very little from before my accident. I was very young, and I am sure it was traumatic, so I blocked much of the memories surrounding it out. What do I remember? I have hazy, dreamlike memories of my father taking me by the hand, bringing me on long walks around the island. Of following Star down vast hallways as she giggled, and her bright red braid bounced between her shoulder blades. Of a giant bed, bigger than the island, covered in nothing but pink seashells, though that certainly must be a dream, for it is far too ridiculous. Because every other direction holds the black, murdering sea, the cheery, sunset-colored castle is easily my most favorite scenery on the island. Sometimes I dream about lying down upon that ridiculously huge bed, being surrounded by all that gorgeous free space. But the castle is very much a secret. Only the king, the princess and their dozen and a half servants and guards are privy to what goes on inside. "Is it true the staircases glisten like the sun?"

"Sort of. Just after the tides go out, and everything is still wet, I guess."

"And is there a bed in there…a huge one…made of seashells?"

"No. What? Never seen anything like that before. Anyway, can I please finish?" he asks with a flustered laugh.

"I'm sorry." I bite my tongue, even though I really wish he'd help me build the vision in my head. It would give me something nice to dream about.

He continues, "King Wallow has no heir."

"Oh. But he has Star."

"No *male* heir," he says. "No one to assume the throne."

"That's a stupid rule, that the ruler has to be male."

He shrugs. "It is. But regardless, Star is not fit to rule. She has no understanding of what it is to lead, and I doubt that she would want to."

My father told me what life was like without a king. Before King Wallow assumed the throne, there was a gap, as well. King Wallow had been only ten when his father died. The world had been thrown into absolute chaos. People fought constantly. They murdered people in their sleep, just to make sure they had a spot on the platform. The one thing I remember of my father, more than anything, was him pressing his forehead to the king's ring before leaving on his Explore. He would do anything for our king. He believed in the power of his rule; that it was good, or at least necessary. But with no one to assume the throne? A shiver runs down my back. "So what are you saying? That—"

"He wants me to do it," he interrupts. "To be king."

"Oh." I'm silent for a moment, trying to take this information in. I'm not sure if I *can* take it in. Tiam... The boy I grew up next to... He is many wonderful things. But not a king. Not *my* king. "But you're...you're not...royalty."

He shrugs. "But how does one become royalty in the first place? The Wallows weren't always royalty. You know that. There was difficulty, and they rose up and took the lead."

I don't know what to say, so I say nothing. All of the thrill that I'd felt about being his confidant evaporates. I'd foolishly hoped that telling me his secret would bring us closer. If he's a king, *the* king, there might as well be an ocean between us.

"What do you think?" he asks cautiously.

I look at the ground. Then I start to laugh. I can't help it. He studies me, confused, until I explain. "I'm sorry. But you as a king? This is only your sixteenth Hard Season."

"King Wallow assumed the throne on his sixteenth season," he points out.

"But still...why *you?*"

His voice is hurt. "The king said it's not the first time they had to choose a commoner for the throne. He said he'd had his eye on me for this since I was a child. Supposedly, when I was a child, I narrowly evaded death. I was cast out into the ocean, and survived. This impressed him. It was a sign from the gods, he said, like Star. You know he's always given me special allowances. I think he's always seen himself in me. Plus, I'm more of a king than anyone on this island. I mean, would you rather Vixby, or Mutter…" He names the two maddest men on the island.

Immediately guilt seeps in. "No. I mean, I know you can do it. But I just… I've known you forever. And I've never thought of you as a king." I pause for a moment, squinting, imagining him sitting up on a throne above the formation in a brilliant pink robe, looking down upon us. I wonder if I won't be allowed to look at him anymore. I guess that doesn't matter. It might even make things easier, since I already have trouble looking at him without blushing. "Yeah. You would make a pretty good king."

"You think?" Now he seems doubtful.

"Well, sure. You're right. You're the best choice there is." I can tell there is something he isn't telling me. "Why? What are you thinking?"

"Not much. Just that there are a lot of things I would change."

"Like what?"

"Like wearing those ridiculous pink robes and stuff." We both laugh at that. "And the palace. It's…well…it's not right. It's totally not fair that they get the best of the salvaged items. I'd have teams of people go into the royal stores and figure out if there is anything we can use. It's not fair that only a select few get to go down there. And maybe we could build up the platform, make it higher, bigger…."

"Maybe," I say, trying to keep the doubt out of my voice because he sounds so adorably hopeful. But we both know they've tried to bolster the platform, make it bigger and wider and stronger. Every effort has failed. The materials that wash up on shore are inadequate, and on top of that, there's only slightly more than half a day between high tides, which isn't enough time to get anything in place. The ocean that surrounds us is blacker than night, except for the whitecaps that foam above it. It is always rough, always vile and menacing like poison, never smooth or glassy or pleasant to look at. There is a strong undertow only a few feet offshore, so we've lost just as many fishermen to the ocean's pull as to the scribblers. When it came to bolstering the eroding platform, the builders would make progress, only to have it undone by the waves a tide later.

"I think I can help us. As king, I mean. I think I can do good. Only..."

He looks troubled.

"Only?"

"I'd hate to be the last king of Tides." He pauses. "That's what I'll be, right?"

"I don't know." But of course I do.

"You know everything. You're the smartest person in the world."

"My father is," I say.

We walk along the shore in a long moment of silence. There's pity in his silence. I know he thinks, the way everyone else does, that I'm pathetic to believe Buck Kettlefish is still alive. But he, too, knew that we didn't have much time. It was the reason he volunteered for the risky Explore. Once every one thousand tides or so, the builders put together a raft to be used during the Soft Season, when the ocean is slightly calmer, to be used for an Explore. They build it on the platform. Every tide the ship is kept safe in the dry center of the formation, and we in the spaces surrounding it will gaze upon it in its various stages of completion. Finally, when it's done, one soul will be selected, usually by lottery, since it's a death sentence. Nobody ever comes back from Explores. That is why everyone was shocked when my father volunteered.

"Okay," he says. "You're the smartest person *on the island,* then."

Which isn't saying much, I think. A truly smart person might have the answers, might be able to save us. I bite my lip. "Yes, I think you will be. The last king, I mean."

After a moment, he stops, picks up an oyster shell and pries it open. It's been roasting in the sun for a while, so the contents are dry and rotten. He dips his index finger inside and, with an "aha!" pulls out a nice-sized, perfectly round pearl. He's been gathering them forever, and has the best collection on the island. He must have thirty or so by now. He reaches into his pack, pulls out a small box and drops it inside with the others. I always wonder what he expects to do with them. Maybe make a string of them to give as a gift to the princess. It's not as if any commoners would wear them; they're just not sensible.

But they sure are pretty. There is a picture of a girl in a long gown in *Fifty Famous Fairy Stories,* with hair braided upon her head and beautiful white pearls adorning the hollow of her throat. I sigh, imagining a string of them around my own neck. I don't know why I constantly think of such impractical things when I am around Tiam.

We walk along to the west side. There's not a single soul

anywhere to be seen, and so when a seagull squawks above us, it's eerie and foreboding.

Tiam is thinking something else as he watches two birds soar over us. "I wish we could live up there, in the clouds. And fly, like them."

Tiam wishes a lot. I guess I do, too. But his wishes are so creative. He doesn't think like everybody else. He's not only strong, he's smart. Yes, he would be a good king. "We used to," I mumble.

He laughs. "Yeah, right."

"We *did*," I insist. "We built machines that could fly like birds and carry people inside them. But that was a long time ago. Like thousands and thousands of tides ago."

"Really?" He sighs. "That was the Golden Age of Man, right, that you told me about?"

I nod. I'd explained to him that every civilization, every race, has its Golden Age. Ours was so many tides ago, all we have are rumors and stories about its grandeur. Back then, every human was clean and beautifully dressed. Children had fat, rosy cheeks and so much land of their own that they could run across it until they were out of breath and still have more to conquer. Every dinner table was piled high with so much food of all colors and tastes, more food than anyone could possibly eat. People went to social gatherings and did things called dancing, music, art, because they enjoyed it, because it made them feel good and because they didn't have to fight for what they needed. They had everything they needed at their fingers. They never had to wrestle for food or dodge scribblers or clean out a craphouse.

I'd told him that every civilization also has its decline. Some go quickly, others erode away slowly. Our decline started quite suddenly, with the floods that covered the earth. Nobody knows why it happened, because it wiped out nearly everything. It made recovery impossible. Now what little is left is just fading away, bit by bit, like the last embers after a fire has been stamped out. Humanity is fighting, and has been fighting for a long time. But we've been losing for too long. We used to think that we could get back some of that lost rosy-cheeked grandness, but nobody believes that anymore. We're almost at the end. I don't think anyone can deny that.

He smiles at me, only for a moment. "You're amazing," he says into the wind.

"Sure," I mutter, blushing more deeply.

"It's true. The things you know. It's just sad that, well…" He looks away, but I can complete the sentence for him. *It's just sad that you are so deformed.* He smiles irresistibly, which makes it impossible to hate him. "Forget it."

I quickly change the subject. "So what does *you* being king have to do with me?"

"With you?"

"I mean, why did the king pick today to talk to me?"

"Oh. I…don't know," he says, a peculiar expression on his face. Either he's picturing himself sitting on the throne wrapped in pretty robes or he knows *exactly* why the king was talking to me.

The west side is the side of the island that gets hit the worst by the tides, but the best things wash up there. It's also the part of the island that's most often ridden with scribblers. Before, they were easy to avoid. Since I learned they've been burrowing under the sand, I, like most people, have been afraid to come here. But having Tiam with me gives me courage. Or maybe it's that I'm already so nervous around him that the thought of being speared by a scribbler doesn't sound so bad.

There's a greenish slime on the sand where the waves once were, and bits of dead insects and jellyfish. In the same instant we see something triangular and reddish poking up from the ground, like an arrow pointing to heaven. We run to it, and Tiam picks it up. It's just a small, narrow piece of plastic. There are some letters on it. "What does it say?" he asks me.

I am the only one who can read; if my father and I were gone it would be just another lost art, like dancing or painting pictures. Buck Kettlefish taught me, and I learned, because I'd always wanted to be like him, and that was the only way I could manage. I try to keep it hidden, though, because the king forbids anything that doesn't contribute to our society. Tiam is the only one who knows I can do it. That secret has been safe with him for many seasons. "R-U-N. It says 'run,'" I say.

"Run? From what?"

I shrug. "It might be part of a bigger word."

"Hey, hold out your wrist," Tiam says. I hold out my hand, and he ties it around there. "Looks good," he says.

I admire the way it shines. If I squint just right, it's just as bright as a string of pearls. Then again, pearls would look silly on me. I'm not royalty like Star. Royalty! "You can't. You know you need to bring anything we find before the king first."

"Nah. They won't miss that little thing."

I'm not sure, but I'm so used to hiding my right arm from them that I suppose it won't be hard to hide my left one, too.

"Besides, *I* may be king in a few weeks' time," he says, a hint of disbelief in his voice.

"Yes, Your Most Grand and Benevolent Majesty," I say, offering up a curtsy. But I'm unable to keep a straight face.

"I prefer Your Holiness," he says, and we both start to laugh again. Then his face hardens. "There is one other thing. Something the king wants me to do."

"Oh?" I say, studying the ground. And for the first time, I notice them. Long, winding scribbles in the sand. Fresh ones. They end right before our feet. How could we have been so stupid not to have noticed? Well, for me, whenever I'm with Tiam, I seem to forget everything, including simple things like how to walk and breathe. But was his head so in the clouds at the thought of being king that he didn't see them? "Tiam," I whisper.

He studies them. "Don't worry. If they were under the sand, you'd see a small circular mound there. They hide with their heads poking up a little, and that's how they can find us."

I'm about to exhale, relieved, when I catch sight of the area behind him. There is, unmistakably, a mound right behind his foot. Two of them, actually. "Um, like those?" I whisper, trying to point. That's when I notice that there are nearly a dozen more, all within jumping distance of his foot.

He swallows. "R–U–N," he says softly, and I don't have to be told twice.

I'm three steps into my dash back toward the sleeping compartment when I hear the hissing of the scribblers behind us. Or...in front of us? "Tiam!" I whisper, stopping short. "Look."

There are more mounds ahead of us, and I can see their small black faces, dotted in sand, protruding from the ground, as if they're ready to attack. If they can be called faces. They have no eyes, just horrible mouths with huge ragged teeth and a nose sharper than the royal guards' metal spears. Tiam comes to a halt beside me, kicking up sand, then reaches behind his back and in one swift motion pulls out his spear. When one slithers out, he is ready. He slices it in half in midair with one quick, expert swing of his weapon. When two more spike out of the sand, he easily does away with those, too.

He's so busy fighting, and I'm so bewitched by his moves, that we don't notice the one snaking its way up behind us until I take a step back and feel a sleek form skirt against my foot. It rears back to attack me, and before Tiam can turn and notice it, I'm already beating it down with my backpack. I hit it again and again and probably more than necessary, because by the time I get full control of myself again, it's been beaten flat, mutilated beyond recognition, its green insides spilled generously upon the sand. I stare at it for a moment, breathing hard, then turn to Tiam, who has fallen silent. He's staring at me.

"Wow," he says. "You are deadly with a backpack."

I shrug and hide my stump behind my back as I inspect the dead animal. "I just really hate those things."

Three
Paralyzed Force

When we hike up the beach toward the sleeping compartment I can already hear Ana's shrill voice.

I want to hide. Instead I watch Tiam's and my shadows growing on the side of the platform as we trudge through the sand toward it. His image on the concrete is strong, with a square jawline, muscular arms, broad shoulders tapering in a perfect V to his waist. I, on the other hand, look like some odd mythological creature, with a crazy, shapeless nest of hair that makes my head look massive in comparison to my small, sticklike body. Tiam: Beautiful. Coe: Frightening.

"Coe! Coe!" Ana shouts as she comes around the platform to meet me. "Where have you been? There's poop everywhere in there, and as usual, you're nowhere to be found!"

I sheepishly grab my shovel and head to the craphouse. Tiam apologizes to Ana and says something about how he thought I was done with my duties, or else he wouldn't have asked me to come. He knows as well as I do that with Ana, it's better to make peace. Tiam's role as peacemaker will probably serve him well as king. King! I shudder in disbelief at the thought and stare down at my crusty old shovel. Tiam: In Charge of the World. Coe: In Charge of the Craphouse.

Ana has hair red as fire and a temper to suit. She's been through thirty-five or thirty-six Hard Seasons, making her one of the oldest people on the island. She is also one of the most important people who doesn't serve the royal family. She is the cook and manager of housekeeping. Those titles would suggest that she has some talent in making meals and organization, but she has neither. She's very good at stretching a piece of fish to feed several dozen hungry mouths, and she's even better at barking orders. She was also my foster mother, and Tiam's, too. She's good at this job, at making sure no one laid a finger on me whenever Buck was busy tending to the fishing. Even now, she runs the sleeping compartment so militantly that it's the one place I don't fear closing my eyes. People listen to her, respect her.

The job of Craphouse Keeper, Ana told me when I assumed it when I was five, "always falls to the youngest person in the world." But Tiam never had to shovel crap, and neither did Memory, the next youngest person in the world. And Fern is now the youngest, but when I pointed that out, Ana just shook her head and barked, "Be grateful." It seems that either I am the greatest Craphouse Keeper in the world or they think shoveling crap is the best job a one-handed nobody should be entitled to.

By the time I get up my courage to steal a glance at our

future king, he's already strolling down the beach, his back toward me, scribbler-nose spear in his hand. Looking for treasure, I guess. He never stays still for long, so I don't know why it hurts me that he didn't take the time to say goodbye. I trudge around the compartment and down the path a ways to another smaller compartment of rusting metal walls, bolted into the ground. I pull open the door and climb inside the dark building.

It smells, obviously. At first, the stench was unbearable, but now I guess I've grown accustomed to it. There's a constant drip-drip-dripping here, just like in the sleeping compartment, as this building is also underwater when the tide comes in. Though my arm ends about a hand's length below my elbow, the stump is useful for many things. I've gotten pretty good at using my stump to support the shovel when I dig in and using it to heft over my shoulder, even without fingers to grip it.

I guess I *should* be grateful there's only one of these to clean. We used to have two craphouses, but the other washed away, so now we have only one for 496 people. Well, the royals have their own, supposedly, in the palace, but I've never been there. One craphouse for 496 people is pretty, shall we say, crappy, considering that the craphouse is one of the few places on the island where a person can be completely alone. Some people, like Mutter, who hates everyone, will brave the stench and stay in there for half a tide, just so he doesn't have to see anyone. Others will pee in the tide pools or defecate wherever they please, and though that is illegal, no one says anything. There are far worse offenses in our world.

There's a little seat with a big hole in the center of the room, and though I fill it with sand before the tide comes in, sometimes excrement will come loose and end up everywhere when the tide goes out again. So I'll need to shovel it back into place, then add in more fresh sand, make sure the seat is clean.

I try to imagine myself in the castle, wearing long pink robes that stay dry, as I shovel the wet sand and excrement. I've come to realize that the only way to make it through this job is by daydreaming. I imagine myself sleeping on that giant seashell bed and feasting on good food and smelling like something other than seawater and crap.

The only problem is that my daydreams often wander to Tiam, and thoughts like that can kill a girl.

By the time I'm done and step outside into the sun again, there's a line of three people waiting. Luckily it's no one who's going to give me trouble, like Ana or Mutter. Fern is there, legs together, hopping about. The other two, Mick and Vail, twins who are fishermen, look through me.

I fold my crap-crusted shovel in a tattered cloth and pack it into my bag. Then I start over to the east side, where the tide pools are. But I notice that, strangely, the shores are empty of people. On such a small island, when the shores are empty, it means only one of two things: the tide is coming in, or an assembly has been called. It's impossible that the tide is coming in; the horn announcing low tide hasn't yet blared. When I walk to the sleeping compartment and see Tiam peeking through one of the rusted holes in the metal, I know that Ana has called an assembly. The king does not like these, but he is never around to dissolve them, and so they go on, maybe once every hundred tides or so. When I approach, I can hear voices inside, raised in argument. Keeping my distance from Tiam as I know my stench is unbearable, I whisper, "What? Something bad?"

He turns to me, his face serious. "I guess. I don't know." He throws up his hands. "If only I could be *in* there."

We can't because we're not yet adults. When we've reached our sixteenth seasons, our voices will matter. Right now, we're forbidden from assemblies. But that hasn't stopped us from watching everything from the outside; the walls of this place are so full of holes, we might as well be present. I can still remember my father striding among assembly. Back then, I didn't understand much of what they were quibbling about, but still, Buck Kettlefish was a force. He always had a voice, and a strong one. People listened to him. Now they are looking for someone to listen to, but nobody has presented themselves yet. Maybe Tiam, when he is of age, will be that person.

I peek inside. They are just finishing up discussing the king's visit to the platform, obviously, because his cough is the big topic of discussion.

"Something's going on. Why was he there?" Vixby grunts, and the group begins to bubble with speculation.

Ana says something I can't quite hear, and then, "And if the death of the king is imminent, we must make preparations…"

Someone talks of Star, but Ana says, "Star is too young to be of any help in this matter. We cannot rely on…"

"But you are to be king," I whisper to Tiam.

He says, "Quiet. No one knows that yet."

"Well, they *should*. Why else would you have been called there yesterday evening?"

Ana says, "Do we have any nominations?" and a sickening feeling wells in the pit of my stomach. No, this is wrong. There is nobody in assembly that's fit to rule us. Nobody.

"Are you going to tell the king? He needs to announce his plans, and soon," I urge.

He doesn't answer, just continues to stare through the peephole, so I do the same. Finn strides up to the front of the room. Vail is another. Ana asks for more, but there are no more. Standing there, Finn and Vail shift awkwardly. I try to think of Finn ruling the world. He's a good person, I suppose. Another fisherman, he'd been one of my father's closest allies. He's quiet, does what he's told. But a leader?

"But what about you?" I ask Tiam.

"I don't know," he says. Then he turns to me and smiles. "Don't worry, little Coe. I'll think of something."

Assembly ends. People disperse, hanging their heads as they leave the compartment. I walk to where Melame Wiggins has positioned himself. Melame minds the tide pools. That's his job. He's in charge of making sure they're clean, and that no scribblers are near.

We wash in the tide pools. Freshwater, which we get from the rainstorms, is only for drinking, since it can burn the skin off commoners if they come in contact with it too often. Sometimes we don't even have enough for drinking, so we ration it and we're often thirsty. Our skin is always coated in salt and sand. I taste salt constantly on my lips, and sometimes they blister and burn. Sand constantly grits in my clothes and between my legs, creating raw welts on my skin, but I'm used to it. What I can't stand, though, is stinking the way I do.

This tide pool looks clean and new, as if not too many people have washed up in it yet. Melame, as well as a few others who are lounging in the pool, see me coming. They all start to get out, which is ridiculous, considering I've never bathed near *anyone* before.

Melame positions himself between me and the tide pool. "You have no place in this pool," he grumbles.

"You should know by now that I've never bathed in your tide pools," I mumble.

He wrinkles his brown face. "Sheesh. You stink."

"Does that surprise you?" I snap back.

I walk toward the southern shore, where I find another tide pool. It is small and free of scribblers. I sink into it slowly, cautiously, and scoop water into my hand and wash it over my arms and back. For thousands of tides I've been the vilest person on the island. As if Melame and the others expect that to change.

If you walk at a leisurely pace, the island itself, when the tide is lowest, can be crossed four or five times in a tide. From one end, you can just barely see the ocean at the other end. It is small, and getting smaller every day. The castle stands in front of me, in the distance, about a stone's throw from the platform, in the direct center of the island. There's a bit of a breeze but not enough to sway the tower. I wonder what the princess does in there all day, alone. I wonder if she's just as lonely as I am. As I'm about to lean my head back against the sandy bank and stare up at the sky, I catch a glimpse of Tiam in the haze on the horizon. He's carrying his spear over his shoulder and strolling along the shoreline with Rickman, the head fisherman. Rickman, a man who never cracks a smile, like most of the people on the island, is making a weird noise I can't quite make out. He's laughing. Nobody on this island laughs unless they're with Tiam. I guess it isn't just me he puts at ease.... He's like that with everyone.

I sigh. No wonder the king chose him. He gives the people of this island life, a reason to hope.

My brown-and-green tunic billows around me, floating on the surface of the water. I sink my toes under the cool sand and tilt my head to the sky, trying to think of some common bond we have. Well, we once had Ana. She clothed us, fed us, kept us out of danger. I can't say she ever cared for us because caring for another person is just not done here. People have to watch out for themselves, above all else, or they'll die. Ana did what she had to do. It was her job.

We both were born to mothers who had us just to get a better spot in the formation. At least, this is what Ana told me. She didn't have me out of love, because love is far too dangerous. People don't do that here. She had me out of fear. Tiam's mother did, too. I wonder if he can remember his mother. He never speaks of her. The only real memory I have of mine is her pink eyes, but sometimes I think that might be wishful thinking. Maybe I wouldn't feel so utterly alone if I had *something* in common with someone, even a dead someone.

I'm not sure why I still care about her, since she certainly never cared about me. Supposedly, one afternoon, when I was three, she left me out alone, making sand castles. By the time

I was found, I'd lost my hand to the scribblers, and almost my life. I think they executed her for that, which is what they do to murderers here. Sometimes the king will make examples of wrongdoers, so that chaos won't reign. The king also wanted to cast me out, too, because I was so badly injured. But somehow, I survived. I am sure Buck had a lot to do with convincing them. Anyway, this is what I've pieced together from the little I've heard. Nobody talks much about it. As I said, nobody cares about the past. We just have our memories, and I don't have many of those.

Sometimes a foolish, girlish thought pops into my head. If Tiam and I had a baby, what would it look like? Would it have his blue eyes, or my icy pink ones? His heartbreakingly beautiful smile, my crazy black hair? And then I remember that's selfish, impossible and just plain insensible. My mother might have been stupid and selfish for trying to save herself by bringing me into this world of pain, but she was right not to care about me.

Love *is* dangerous.

The scribblers got her, I think. When they execute someone, they simply throw them in the ocean. They'll thrash about, but the guards will not let them back ashore. The guards will stand there and wait until the person falls beneath the waves. Sometimes the scribblers will get them. Sometimes they drown first. How is that for irony, that in a world governed by the ocean, not a one of us knows how to swim more than a few clumsy strokes? We don't, can't venture more than waist-deep into the ocean for long, for the undertow is vicious, and the scribblers are many. I've seen a few executions in my life. Well, I've heard about them. I don't watch them. I'm not like some who enjoy watching people, even bad people, suffer.

As I'm just getting comfortable, massaging the knots out of my limbs, aching eyes shut in the blinding brightness of the sun, I suddenly feel a rush of cold water over my head. Salty fish entrails slip over my nose and cheeks, landing in big bloody chunks in my lap.

I jump up. You'd think by now I'd have learned *never* to close my eyes.

Mutter is holding the bucket and scowling at me. "You think that taking a bath will clean you, Bait? Why don't you go back to the crap, where you belong?" Vixby stands behind him, laughing.

I start trying to scoop the fish pieces out of the water, but it's fruitless. Now they're spreading across the surface of the entire pool in a greasy mess. The boys strut back down shore, toward the other fishermen. Or maybe they're men. When men here reach past their eighteenth Hard Season, they all start to look alike, so it's difficult to tell age. It's true that I'd often thought that when the king was weeding out the troublemakers, Vixby and Mutter would be his next choice. But they weren't always this difficult. They used to be the quiet ones who just went about their duties, pulling in lines, bringing in fish, standing in their circles in formation like good citizens. But gradually, they began acting out. Calling people like me Bait. Squabbling over their places in the formation. People say it's the sun. But I think it comes with the gradual realization that this life has no purpose. It's not as if there's good in this world anymore. It's just day after day of misery, of waiting to die. Every day you wonder what the point is, or if there even is a point, and the longer you go on, the more life seems like a game you're meant to lose. Mostly it drives people to harmless things, like Xilia, who talks to herself and sees apparitions everywhere. But every once in a while it will drive a person to worse. "They're harmless," I say out loud, as if saying it aloud will make it true.

Suddenly a shadow descends upon me. I brace myself for more cold water, but instead, the brave person just slinks into the water next to me. It's Finn. I stare back at him in shock and begin pulling my ragged dress down over my scars. No one has ever ventured into a tide pool with me. He says, "Depends on who you are."

"Um. What?" I ask, confused.

"Whether they're—" he nods his head toward Vixby and Mutter "—harmless really depends on who you are. And they don't like you very much."

"But I didn't do anything."

He proceeds to scoop water into his hands and splash his face. The water slides among the fine hair on his jawline. Finn has been around three Hard Seasons more than I have, and I think he's rather nice to look at, for now. But as I said, after a certain age all the men begin to look alike. He's getting to that age where all the expressive, interesting parts of his face will be covered with knotted hair. Eventually, the men on this island all start to look like monsters, like the hairy animal from the *Beauty and the Beast* story in my fairy-tale book. Each time I'd read that story, I'd always imagine Vixby or

Mutter or one of the other men, roaring from behind their mask of matted, dirty fur. They are altogether frightening.

Finn, though, is different. He was also one of Ana's children. He's always been the quiet, unassuming type. Even though he's a fisherman, he's not one to astound with his abilities; he just does what he's supposed to do. Where Tiam knows how to attract attention, Finn deflects it. He's steady and reliable, and was always right behind my father whenever work needed to be done. My father had mentored him, so I'd often see them together. Which is probably why I'll often turn in formation and see him, several rows back, watching me. In the compartment, he'll usually find a place near me. He's rarely talked to me, though. I suppose I could find it unsettling, but I guess I just need to believe that someone, anyone, cares about me even one-tenth of what my father did.

"Sometimes you don't have to *do* anything," he says softly. "You just have to be. That's what scares me."

"Scares *you?*" My eyes widen. I lap up the attention eagerly. It's so sad; we're not supposed to care for each other, and yet I can't imagine that anyone on this island is so damaged that he doesn't want to be cared about. I feel as if I thirst for it each day, like water; and like water, it is always in such short supply. That's probably why I jump at Finn's expression of concern.

"Well, yeah," he says with a small laugh. "I don't want you to get hurt. You need protection. Especially with your father...away."

I don't answer. I know everyone assumes I need protection because of my arm, because my size and ruddy skin and bad eyes make me so different and unsuited for this world. And maybe I do. The way he pauses when speaking of Buck Kettlefish tells me all I need to know. He thinks my father, my protector, is dead. No one has said as much, but I guess that's the consensus. People know that it's high Hard Season now, and he left at the beginning of my fifteenth Soft Season. He's been gone for 539 tides. Not that I keep count or anything.

"High Hard has been pretty gentle so far," he says. "That's good."

I nod. High Hard is the most damaging. We lose most of our numbers during high Hard. But it's been pretty easygoing so far. Though bad things always seem to happen just as we're exhaling with relief. Just as we're letting down our guard.

"How are you doing, by the way?" he asks.

"Um, I'm doing…fine," I sputter, the words feeling foreign on my lips. But am I? I suppose every day I am still alive is a good day.

He gives me a sad smile. "Don't lie. I know how much Buck means to you. So if you need anything, someone to talk to…" He looks away, his face reddening. "Well. I'm here. Okay?"

Someone to talk to? About what? My breath catches in my throat. I don't understand his offer. Nobody ever offers such things. But even as the proposition tangles up my brain, it also opens some small, hopeful part of me, a part that has longed for this kind of attention.

"Thank you," I say, voice faltering.

"Coe, I know them. I fish with them every day. So I worry about you. We've lost enough people for stupid reasons. I don't want you to be next," he says, sliding out of the water and walking down the shoreline, toward them. The words *I don't want you to be next* hang in the air after him, making me shiver. Sure, Vixby and Mutter have taunted me since my father left, but it's never been anything too life-threatening.

I sit up. "Finn, do you know something I don't?" I call after him.

He shrugs, but I already know the answer. Of course he does. Everyone does. He spends his time with other fishermen. I spend most of my time alone. No, you're not supposed to trust anyone, but isolation can get you killed just as fast. I used to find out what I needed to know from Buck. Now it's not just my deformity and my size that make me vulnerable.

When I am done washing, I walk past the fishermen and think I'll take refuge for a while near the platform, away from the sun, where the small bit of shade there will give my stinging eyes a rest. I relax, closing my eyes there until at once I hear movement. I open one eye for a moment and see four pairs of feet marching toward me. Guards. They always walk in tight formation, purposefully, unlike most of us, who listlessly meander about. I wonder what on earth they're out for, but I know it's probably nothing good, and for a split second, I feel sorry for whoever they're after.

That is, until they stop at my feet. I open the other eye and then sit spear-straight. Four of the eight palace guards are staring down at me. I try to choke out some words, but nothing comes. I've done a good job at making myself invisible. The palace guards have never approached *me*. *What would they want with a Craphouse Keeper?* I think, but at the same time I

remember Princess Star inspecting me this morning in formation. *This is the one, I thought.*

"Are you space two?" one asks me. "In the formation?"

I nod, still mute.

The first one looks at his mates. "She's the one. Get her."

My hand tightens into a fist, though I'm not sure why. I
wouldn't strike any of them; I'm not suicidal. There are four
of them. I've never seen this many of them together at once.
I'm not quite sure why half of all the king's guards have been
summoned to retrieve *me,* the defenseless one-handed Scribbler Bait. I swallow. "What is this about?" I finally find my
voice, as two of them reach their gloved hands under my
arms and hoist me to my feet. They don't answer, just lug me
along as if I'm a beached fish they found on the shore, spray-
ing sand as they march. I try to walk, but they're moving too
fast, dragging me inches above the ground so that my toes
leave ruts in the sand. My face burns with a combination of
humiliation and fear as the others watch me.

Of course, no one steps in to help me. Where is Finn's
protection now, when I need it? I can't see him anywhere.
On the shoreline, I see Tiam casting out a drop line, tanned
back to me. He turns at almost the second I wish he would,
as if he hears me screaming for him in his mind, and then he
breaks into a run.

His long legs propel him across the sand so that he's standing in front of them, spear drawn, in a matter of seconds. I
expect that the next words out of his mouth will be, "What
are you doing?" or "Leave her alone." Instead, he says, very
evenly, "Don't hurt her."

The men have metal spears, weapons that could slice him in half with one swing. They move around him, and he grinds his jaw. He doesn't look as if he's planning to attack, but maybe he's going for the stealth approach. In case he's about to lunge, I hold out my hand. "It's okay," I tell him. "Just… My bag. Where's my bag? Can you watch it for me?"

I really don't know if it's okay, or if I'll ever have the chance to see my bag again. But I know attacking the guards is simply stupid, even if he is going to be king one day. His eyes bore into the guards for a moment. "Don't be afraid, Coe," he mouths. Then he walks toward the base of the platform and picks up my sack, pulling the strap over his head so that it joins his own on his back. He never looks at me, just stands like stone as they drag me off.

I watch Tiam, standing motionless. *Don't hurt her.* He knows. He knows where they're taking me. Why they're taking me.

We move beyond the sleeping quarters, the craphouse. Meanwhile, all the people we pass look at me as if seeing me for the first time. And then I look up and see the castle towering over me. The castle. I know I'd played there as a child, but my memories all seem like dreams. I can't remember ever being this close to it. It's towered over the island for so many days of my life, in its shimmering splendor, just like the moon; lovely to look at, impossible to visit. I've always thought of it as this fantastic mirage in the distance, that if I ever got this near, it would disappear. But here it is, enormous, a hundred times bigger than our sleeping quarters.

The guard slides open the door, and I find myself kissing

the floor. But something is strange... There's no sand there. It's the color of sand, but smooth and cold. I quickly straighten and bring myself to my knees, then gasp.

The room is bigger than anything I can imagine, the color of a seashell, with sloped ceilings that glimmer like a pearl. There is no furniture, only a pink mat on the floor. Princess Star is sitting there, cross-legged, a bowl in her lap. She's wearing a lace thing over most of her face, but I can see her jaw working. She's chewing on something. "Keep her over there," she calls across the room as I avert my eyes. "I don't want her near me until she washes."

Near her? Why would I go near her? "I've washed," I say softly.

She laughs. "I can still smell you from over here. You'll have a freshwater bath."

Freshwater? Freshwater! My heart catches in my throat. I value my skin too much to have it burned off my body. Is this some kind of punishment? "For...for what?"

"To be my lady-in-waiting, of course." She pulls the lace veil back from her face and studies me. "Or do you like cleaning the craphouse?"

"I'm... Me?" Surely she is mistaken.

"Yes. Governesses are for babies. And I'm an adult. This is my seventeenth Hard Season. My father said I could choose one servant. And you come highly recommended."

"Me?" I sputter. Who would recommend me? "But your governess. What will become of Kirba?"

"Look at me," she instructs, ignoring my question. Kirba has seen more than thirty Hard Seasons and is one of the cldest on the island. Surely, though, Star will have compassion for the lady who raised her. Hearing the iciness in her voice, I'm not so sure. "My lady-in-waiting may look me in the eye, from time to time. And I need to see your eyes to know if I can trust you."

I raise my eyes to her, slowly, and as I do, she blows a puff of air that makes the lace thing over her eyes billow out. I imagine even her breath is sweet. When she stands, I see that she is wearing a short, tight-fitting garment over her breasts, with a silky cape that descends over her hips. Open to view in a small window is the smooth white skin surrounding her perfectly round navel. Her navel! I've never seen another woman's navel before, except for my own, and that only rarely, as doing so also affords me a look at my horrible, deep scars.

"I'm sorry," I say, my eyes falling to the floor. I can't do it. I'm afraid my looking would turn into gawking like mad.

She motions to a servant, who brings her a cloth napkin and retreats to the corner of the room. She dabs her mouth daintily, and all the while I can't help thinking that her napkin, this piece of cloth she wipes her mouth with, is finer and more delicate than anything I've ever even touched. "You're not the first person who has had trouble, but no mind. Your eyes… They are unusual. They do work, don't they? Can you see quite well?"

I nod. "Well, they hurt some in the daylight," I mumble.

"That is no mind." She continues, "What I need is someone who can draw me my bath every day and dress me. Who can take care of my needs. Who can dine with me when I choose and carry on a conversation and be at least somewhat interesting. Obviously that rules out most of the people on this godforsaken island." She laughs, a bitter but still delicate sound, and I feel her eyes running over me. "I'm still not convinced *you* are. Interesting, that is. But you'll have to do."

I swallow. I have no idea what I'd converse with her about. It's doubtful she'd want me to go into detail about how to clean a craphouse.

"You'll begin training right away. Of course, next season, your sixteenth Soft Season, you will be given Kirba's position in the formation. Space twelve. I've not made much of a study of the formation, but it's quite a valuable piece of real estate, or so I hear," she says.

Space twelve! Space twelve! I'd always assumed that once I reached adulthood, I'd be cast into the outer ring of the formation. Space twelve is very nearly at the center. I am sure I am salivating. "But…what will become of Kirba?" I repeat, softer this time.

She laughs. "I am offering you the world, and you are inquiring about a scrap of seaweed?"

I swallow. "No, Your Majesty. I just—"

"Kirba is not your concern, but she will be placed in the formation according to her new duties, since you must know. Kirba has always been like a mother to me, and I will not neglect her." She pauses. "One thing, though. Since you will not look me in the eye, I need to ask. Are you trustworthy?"

I open my mouth to answer in the affirmative, but she stops me. "What I mean is, you will be living in a new world now. In the castle. But of course you will travel out for various tasks, and of course for formation. You must never tell anyone outside what goes on within these walls, do you understand?"

"Yes, Your Majesty," I say, breathless. That, of course, goes without saying. My cheeks are already burning from the exhilaration. I can't help feeling that no matter how many tides I have left in this world, when it all ends I will look back and remember today sweetly, as the day that my life—my real life, as someone with purpose—began.

Four

Fading Star

I'm led down a never-ending, arched hallway, glimmering with mother-of-pearl everywhere. It's so bright I almost have to shield my eyes. As much as I had heard and dreamed, I had no idea it was this amazing inside. I don't think anyone on the outside could imagine this.

Burbur, the head of castle housekeeping, scurries about the floor quietly, fussing busily over who-knows-what. I've stood close to her in the formation—she is number four—and she is always dressed very smartly in a plain, but always clean, white tunic. She's about five Hard Seasons older than me, and her face is always pinched as if she's smelling something bad. I'd always envied her, but now, things are different. I wonder why the princess didn't pick Burbur as her lady-in-waiting. After all, she's more refined than I am, and she has both hands.

She leads me upstairs, past at least a dozen other rooms. Each one is blocked off by a red curtain, and there is a square tub outside each door. I wonder what the tubs are for. She takes me into a room that she calls my quarters. My *own* quarters! It's about the size of the craphouse, but size is the only thing they have in common. There's a mat in one corner and a large circular stone tub in another. Orange curtains swirl in the breeze, carrying the scent of the sea and the screech of seagulls. I walk over to the tub. There's a strange white foam billowing in there, and when I inhale, there's something I've never smelled before. Something beautiful.

"Lavender," Burbur says with a rare smile. "We have very little left in our stores. But the princess said you'd need it. And I have to agree."

"Oh," I say. "Does it…"

She laughs sourly. "Burn off your skin? Ridiculous. I am sure there are many rumors that you have heard on the outside that you will find to be untrue."

I blush, inhaling again and again until my nostrils burn and I feel giddy. There's a pile of green cloth so thick and dry near the tub that I have to fight the urge to bury my face in it. I whirl around, trembling, wanting to scream my thanks from the top of the tower, when I suddenly come face-to-face with it.

With me.

I take a step closer.

"It's called a mirror," Burbur says, but I already know what it is. I know it from a story I've read. *Mirror, mirror on the wall, who is the fairest of them all?*

"Oh?" I murmur, feigning ignorance as I step so close

that my breath creates a circle of fog at my lips. My cracked, bloody lips.

"Everything you need is on the dressing table. Your new garment is hanging on the door. I'll leave you now," Burbur says, and disappears as if she can't stand to be with my stench a moment longer.

For the first time, I am completely alone, in a room of splendor and beauty. And yet all I can look at is the ugliest thing here. My reflection. It's fascinating and shocking at once, more vivid than anything I could see in the tide pools. My eyes look like two empty pits, black walls with those two round pink eyes at the bottom, like festering sores. My shoulders jut away from my neck at an awkward, upward angle, and there are deep holes in my collarbones. I look like a skeleton. Except for the scars. Strangely, the scars make me look alive.

I pull my tunic off my shoulders and let it slip to the ground so that I am naked. I can't remember a time I was naked, since we are never alone. My breasts are shocking to me, high and white, and would probably be something to be proud of if not for the red lashes crisscrossing them. For the first time in a long while I can see, under my breasts, the worst of the scars. There are two deep red slits between my ribs on either side, windows to my rib cage, two hideous smiles that seem to grow wider every time I inhale.

And the hair. Goodness, the hair. High tide isn't for a long time yet, but I'd need a hundred tides to fix the wild, miserable mess above my eyebrows. It's crisp and brackish and black like a dried piece of seaweed, matted with sand. There is a hairbrush on the table, a comb, some barrettes and ribbons like those Star wears… All useless. There are other things in jars, a small hand mirror and a few shells and stones arranged there…for decoration, I guess. It's the first time I've ever seen anything for decoration. King Wallow thinks that's useless. It wastes time. For commoners, anyway.

I wrap my hand around a sharp piece of coral. What I need is to start over. To hack it all off. I bring it to the back of my neck, pull a tangled piece taut and am just starting to saw away when I hear, "Oh, no, you don't!"

I whirl around. Princess Star is staring at me from the doorway. Her eyes widen when she runs her eyes over my scars, as if she's seen something terrible, as if I'm so much more hideous undressed than she'd possibly imagined. "Those lines on your body," she gasps.

"Scribbler scars," I mumble. Instinctively I avert my eyes, then drop to the floor, searching desperately for my tunic, cheeks flaring.

She stands there, confused. "Scars?"

I nod, grabbing for the fabric. Surely she knows about the accident that nearly took my life. It was shortly after that I was forbidden to play with her. My father never said as much, but I knew the scars made me too hideous to be in the company of someone so ethereal.

She rushes forward and tears the coral out of my hand. "I will not have my lady-in-waiting looking like someone's bottom," she says. She kicks the tunic away from my grasp and motions to the tub. "Get in."

Using my hand to shield my skeletal frame from her, I scramble into the tub. The water is warm, but any sense of pleasure I would have gotten from my first real bath ever is gone because *she* is here. Without warning, she pulls out a very menacing weapon, two horrific blades that move together in an awful, shrieking sound. "What are you—"

"Quiet," she says, bringing the blades close to my head.

I can't help it. I scream and duck my head under my arms. When I look up again, she's standing with the blades in one hand and a knotted ball of my hair in the other. "These are scissors," she says. "I do not think we will be able to salvage all of your hair, but we should be able to salvage most."

"Oh." She continues snipping away, and soon little tangles of my hair blow about on the breeze wafting in from the large picture window. Then she reaches over, grabs my head and dunks me under. I come up, sputtering. "What—"

The next thing I know she is pouring some nice-smelling green stuff onto my hair. She starts to rub it in. This is all so surreal. The princess is washing me. I thought she had servants to do that. I thought she had servants who washed her servants. "Very simple," she mutters, working it in. I feel her picking through my hair with the comb. She groans. "Just stay still. It'll all come out. Eventually. Goodness. Have you *ever* combed your hair?"

"I've used my fingers. I do not have a comb."

"I do think most of the beach is in here." She reaches over. More green stuff. It smells sweet, like the lavender, but different. Maybe another flower. My dad told me that there once were hundreds of kinds of flowers. I have a drawing of one of them in my book. She starts to comb again. My scalp screams. I think soon I *will* be bald, despite her best efforts. "I think you will be pleasing to look at once you get this under control. Even with those—*scars*." She says the word as if it's foreign to her, and I suppose it is.

I snort lavender-scented water out my nose, doubtful, wondering if that's a requirement for the job. What if I disappoint her?

She combs for a few moments in silence while a thousand thoughts jumble in my mind. I stare at the wall ahead of me, at the shadows of our heads. Hers is smooth and perfect; mine still sticks out in all angles. Beyond that, for the first time, I see that there is an intricately engraved panel on the wall, and there are letters above it. A N R Y, I think it says, but the letters are very faint.

She catches me looking. "Nobody knows what those things mean. They're all over the castle. I think they had the silly notion of naming all the rooms, when reading and writing were of importance. Can you imagine, naming a room as you would a person? Absurd! Do you remember?"

"Remember?"

"When you and I were just babies and used to play together here," she says, which shocks me. So she does know that I was the one who used to play with her. Perhaps that is why she is being so nice to me. "You do remember, don't you?"

"Not very well," I admit. I remember chasing down a long corridor after Star's braided head, her giggles echoing upon the stone walls, but I don't remember anything else about the castle. I think I lost a lot of old memories. It's almost as if my life began when the scribblers tore off my hand.

She sighs. "Oh, that is right. You are younger than me by

more than two entire seasons, so I often had to explain things
to you. Well, we used to run up and down here and pretend
we knew what all the words said. The three of us pretended
it was our own language, and only we could speak it. You
and I thought they were the names of the people who once
lived in the rooms. But Tiam said it was a secret code that
would lead us to treasure."

I can't help but laugh. That sounds like him.

"He made us swear together that one day the three of us
would crack the code and find the treasure." She smiles a
little wistfully. "It's silly. But even after we stopped playing together...after your—" her eyes trail down toward my
stump, which thankfully I've buried under the suds "—after
we could no longer play together...I kept trying to find the
treasure. There *is* treasure here, you know."

I believe she is right; this whole beautiful building is the
most wonderful treasure I've ever seen. And yet, she must be
very brave to venture out in this castle alone. One of the oldest
legends about the castle is that it is haunted by the ghosts of
the dead. There are so many dead, it must be quite crowded
with them. "Have you ever seen one of the ghosts?"

She laughs. "Oh, there are plenty of ghosts within these
walls."

"So it is true?" I ask, inspecting the walls. While the bed in
the corner looks comfortable and welcoming, if staying here
means being visited by spirits, I'd much prefer the cramped
sleeping compartment.

"I've never seen one. But I know how the servants talk.
They come up with their own legends. You don't remem-

ber the Dark Girl?" She shakes her head. "Oh, of course you don't. You were probably too little. But when I was a child, all the servants talked about was the Dark Girl. They saw her all the time—hair black as night, with the palest, most translucent skin, roaming the castle hallways at night. They'd see her one moment, and the next moment, she'd be gone. They were all so terrified! Their stories made me terrified, which was one of the reasons I played with you. I wasn't so scared when you were around."

"The Dark Girl?" I repeat. It sounds dreadful.

"Don't worry, though. Nobody has seen her in ages. And I certainly *never* have." She sits back on her haunches and picks up a strand of my hair. "I'm sure that if you go walking the castle at night, they might think she has returned. Your hair is so very odd. It reminds me of…someone.…"

"Who?" I ask. Someone from a dream, obviously. No one at all has hair the color of night, as I do. Most have silken white-blond hair that reflects the sun.

She blinks. "No mind. It is a beautiful color. I am jealous."

Of me? And all this time, I'd been jealous of Star's reddish hair, like the color of the sunrise. The tops of my knees are sticking out of the water, and goose bumps begin to poke out on them. "Why are you…"

"No, I don't normally wash my servants' hair, if that's what you're thinking." She straightens, sticks her chin out. "And don't think I'll ever do it for you again.… It's just…I want us to be friendly."

"Friendly?" I choke out. *Friendly* is not something we islanders do. We keep our distance. We're wary. We do not trust.

She smiles. "Yes." She looks around, and her face turns serious. I feel something on my head trickling over my forehead and edging toward the corner of my eye, making it twitch. "There was something I could not tell you out there. Something you are not to share with anyone."

At that moment, the horn in the tower blares. From here, it's such a horrible and jarring roar that my eardrums rattle. The two tower guards manage the task of sounding the horn. It's the horn that signals low tide. It means that the tide has reversed and is now coming in, and our completely safe time is over. Usually it means there is still plenty of time remaining before formation, but one never can tell. During Hard Season or a storm, the tides come in with much more fierceness, so one always needs to be on guard once the horn blares. But instead of worrying about that, all I can do is stare at Star, knowing somehow that her next words will be ones which I will regret hearing.

"I don't need a governess," she says, rocking back on her knees. I know that my hair can't possibly be fixed yet as it would take a hundred tides and a miracle to make it like Star's, but Star sighs and begins to absently play with her long red braid. "Kirba was always checking to make sure I ate up, and washed up, and kept my posture and said 'please' and 'thank you.' Those things are important to my father, because a royal needs to behave with grace and dignity. But I dare say I'm easily the most graceful and dignified being on this island. Her work is done."

White foam drips into my eye and down my nose. I try to blink it away, but a moment later it begins to burn worse than jellyfish stings. I yelp.

She reaches for a cloth and carelessly places it in my hand. I swab desperately at my eye. How can something that smells so sweet hurt so terribly? "I don't even really need someone to dress and converse with me."

The stinging subsides. I open my mouth. "I thought you said..."

"Yes, I know what I said. That's what I want the others to think. But I need to trust someone, Coe, and Tiam recommends you. And he says you are an expert at melting into the scenery, at living among the people unnoticed and learning things that may be of use to me."

"Tiam said that?" I say, shocked. Why would he tell such an outrageous lie? He knows how little I listen to the gossip, how I avoid everyone on the island as much as possible. "You want me to be...like...a spy? For what?"

Her eyes turn cold. "Just as there have always been people who work in the royal family's service, there have always been people among us who would like to do us harm."

I stare at her, unsure what she means.

"Some people forget the Wallows' gift to them so many tides ago. Of course this has happened before. Many times before. And we have to weed these people out and bring them to justice before they...poison the thinking of others."

I lie there silently, imagining her lying in her tower day after day, fearing for her life. But if her life is in danger, I don't know it. People respect the king. He has kept us safe.

"In the coming tides, you are going to be more important to me than you realize. But I must know I can place my trust in you."

Me? My mouth must be hanging open, because somehow I've swallowed lavender. It doesn't taste as beautiful as it smells; in fact, it tastes rotten. "But, Your Majesty, I know nothing..." I begin, but then I realize what Tiam was doing. He wanted me to have this job for some reason. And I can't let him down.

"Tiam says you're a clever person."

I shiver. The water suddenly feels icy against my skin.

"I am always your willing servant," I say dutifully, because I don't know what else to say. I wonder how many tides will pass before I'm exposed as a fraud. "And you can trust me."

"Oh. And your dressmaking skills are required at once. I haven't had a new dress in ages!" she says.

My stomach drops even lower. "My— Excuse me?"

She stands and wipes her hands on a cloth. "All done," she says. "I told you it could be saved. There's still sand in it, so dunk yourself a few times. Stay in there awhile and let the lavender soak into your skin.... I would get Burbur to bring you more water, but our reserves are low today. It hasn't rained in so long."

She wrinkles her nose, and I think she must be able to see my stump beneath the water, but then I realize that nothing can be seen beneath the surface. It's an oily, dingy brown.

My scalp burns. I bring my hand to my head. The hair feels smooth, and when I look down, it falls over my shoulders quite nicely. Though it's totally the wrong color, I imagine it shining in the sun like Star's, adorned with pearl barrettes and ribbons, imagine everybody in the formation gazing at me with envy instead of disgust. I imagine Tiam unable to control his feelings for me and sweeping me into his arms right there, for all to see, the way the prince does to the princess in *Sleeping Beauty*. And then I shake my head and wonder when I'll grow up and stop dreaming of things that don't matter and can't possibly happen.

She drops the comb beside the tub and then disappears through the doorway.

It's comfortable in there, alone, almost too comfortable. I spend only another few moments in the tub. Not that I care about the dirty water; it still smells heavenly. But high tide is coming, and I'm afraid of falling asleep. Or of getting lost in this huge castle and not finding my way out in time. People have missed formation before and drowned, usually after small, careless mistakes. I don't intend to be one of them, not now, when I'll be inheriting space twelve.

After I towel off my body and hair, I slip into the new garment. It smells sweet, like lavender, too, crisp and new. It's prettier than the simple tunic that Burbur wears—this one is white and flowing and comes just above the knee, which is rather risqué and not at all practical. I look at the ribbons and barrettes and, not having any clue how to use them, decide to just leave my hair straight. I hope the princess won't object to that. Standing there in front of the mirror, with my hair beginning to dry and puff out in soft waves on my shoulders, I feel a tingling sensation in my limbs. I look presentable, if not a little pretty.

"Gathering!" someone is shouting down the hall. I hear a squeaking noise, coming closer. It's Burbur. She pokes her head behind the curtain. Just when I expect her to say something pleasant about my appearance, she barks, "Gathering!"

I turn to her. "Gathering?"

She has a large metal thing on wheels, and it's filled with square tubs like the ones I saw outside the rooms when I was being led to my quarters. "Yes. Before high tide. This room will be underwater in a bit. Put whatever you don't want to lose in the tub outside your room, and I'll take it to the stores in my cart."

"The stores? In the tower?"

She seems annoyed. "No, underground. There are watertight compartments there. Surely you know that I am the manager of those stores? I daresay it's the most important job in the kingdom." She straightens, proud.

Of course I knew this; this is why Burbur is space four. There is no more important job than managing the watertight compartments under the castle. Once, the compartments held boxes and boxes of food and supplies for the survivors of the floods, but now they are virtually empty of useful things, and so the ones that are still watertight are used for storage of necessities we need to keep dry, like firewood. It's also quite the dangerous job, because of the ghosts and bloodthirsty demons and other vicious creatures that dwell in the hellish never-regions below the castle stores. Many earlier stores managers' lives have been claimed. I've always had questions upon questions about the mysterious stores, and being this close to Burbur, I itch to ask her them. What are the stores like? Had she ever seen any frightening creatures? Is it true that some of the compartments were flooded through carelessness tides ago? But looking at her, I clamp my mouth shut. She's flitting around like an insect, too busy for conversation.

She walks into my room and begins piling things into a bin for me. The towels, the ribbons, the jars, the pieces of coral and shells for decoration. "Don't worry, you'll get it all back. I try to have things arranged soon after the rooms drain."

"Oh!" I say, marveling at her efficiency. What a difficult task. It makes me wonder even more about the unspeakable dangers of the stores. To think that we have to scramble about on the platform for the last bit of space while the compartments keep safe the ribbons and other worthless trinkets. "There is very little dry room in the stores now, I guess?" I venture.

She grunts, but I can't tell if it's a yes, or a no, or a mind-your-own-business. She hefts the bin out of the room, and as she leaves, affixes the curtain over a hook attached to the ceiling. I take another glance at myself in the mirror, and this time, a slow smile pulls up the corners of my mouth. *Space Twelve.* Then I head off toward the platform.

Five

The Dead Land

I step out into the glare of the setting sun, shielding my eyes, and immediately a cold wave rushes up to greet me. I splash through it, onto dry sand. My skin feels strange, unprotected by the layers of grime that once covered it. The sun is sinking in the sky but still high, and again, no clouds or chance of rain. A drought may be coming. It's such sweet irony to think that we may all die of thirst, surrounded by all this water.

Trying to keep the short white dress from mushrooming out and showing everything I've got underneath, I climb up to the platform, feeling all the while as if I'm forgetting something. My bag. I know Tiam will have kept it safe for me, but it almost feels as if I've lost another limb. For the past five thousand tides, I'd never let that bag out of my sight. I'd done everything the same...formation, craphouse, bath, food, sleep, craphouse, formation, craphouse, bath, food, sleep... Now my entire world has turned upside down. Everything about today feels odd. Despite the blistering heat, there are goose bumps on my shoulders.

When I make it to the space that will be mine only until my sixteenth Soft Season, Fern is sitting cross-legged on space number one. She squints in the sun as she looks at me.

"Oh, Coe, what have they done to you?" she says, jumping up.

I grimace. "Is it good or bad?"

She picks up a lock of my hair and lets it fall. "So shiny. So pretty."

"You think?"

"Definitely." She sticks out her bottom lip. "I want to grow up. I can't stand being the only baby in the world."

"You're number one, though," I point out. "That's the best space there is."

She frowns. "They're making *me* clean the craphouse now."

"Oh!" I say. I hadn't thought of that. "I'm so sorry."

She shrugs. "That's okay. I like having a job."

Fern rifles through her bag and produces her wand, which she presses to the skin of my arm. "Your wish is granted."

Dear, dear Fern. There is so much hope in her. How else would she be able to find a bright side to something so terrible? I wonder how long it will take before she sours of it, before it breaks her. I can't bear the thought of Fern, the one pure example of what we could have been, broken. I want all of her wishes to come true.

More people are arriving now, and I'm distracted from our conversation because so many people seem to be staring at me, wondering what imposter is standing in space two.

Blushing, I look across the way toward space twelve, which will be my new space in a matter of tides. It's a good space, not at the center but very nearly. Much better than I'd ever dreamed I'd receive once I came of age. My eyes scan upward to Kirba, who is glaring back at me. Wherever she is going when she leaves her position, she's not happy about it. I look away, shameful. Even though it's not really my fault, it feels as if it is.

The sun is nearly gone before I see Tiam crawl up onto the platform. He's carrying both bags and his spear over his shoulders, hefting them as if it's no work at all and striding toward me. He'd always walked confidently, but now he seems even more regal. I pretend to be interested in something behind him, even though the only thing I've been able to think about since I left the tub has been his reaction. *Tiam is very sensible. He won't notice something so trivial. If he does, he probably won't say a thing,* I tell myself, preparing for the heartbreak. *After all, my skin is still ruddy and blistered, my eyes still pink, my hair still black. I'm still weird, different. A bath can't change that.*

When he is standing in his space, he drops my bag beside me. "Thank you," I say.

"Anytime," he says, reaching his hands over his head and yawning with the most luxurious stretch. You'd think he'd just been napping instead of catching the food for the evening meal. "Did everything go all right?"

I nod. "Thank you for recommending me."

He shrugs innocently. "I have no idea what you're talking about. What happened to your bracelet?"

For a moment I don't know what bracelet he is referring

to, but then I remember that bit of plastic with RUN on it. It's gone. I can't remember where I lost it. "I don't know."

There's a long break in the conversation, and just when I'm sure he isn't going to say anything more, he smiles. "Did anyone ever tell you, Coe Kettlefish, that you are positively stunning?"

"Stunning?" I ask. No one has called me that before. "You mean...frightening?"

He laughs. "I mean beautiful."

Beautiful! No matter how hard the waves pound against the sides of the platform, even if I get carried out to sea today and the scribblers make me their evening meal, I know I won't be able to stop grinning like an absolute fool. I do my best to try to control it, but a few seconds later I always find the edges of my mouth creeping up again. The last thing I want to do, in formation, when everyone can see me, is look like a lovesick idiot.

But this time I don't try to press closer to Fern to avoid him. This time, when his body presses against mine, I press back, wanting to feel every inch of his skin against me. I pretend I'm doing it innocently, and at first I think he doesn't notice, but then I feel him leaning in toward me, and his breath is warm on my shoulders. He inhales deeply, taking in my scent. If I turn, our lips would touch. I imagine the feeling of his lips, warm, soft, saying my name over and over again. The thought sends a wave of tingles over my bare arms, down my back, everywhere.

I'm jarred from this euphoria when someone suddenly screams.

The whispers begin. I sneak a look at Tiam, but now he's facing the other way, standing on his toes, trying to see what has happened. He is one of the tallest on the island, so he has a better chance of finding out than anyone else in the center of the platform. That's the one negative thing about the center. Even though we are safest, we are always the last to know when bad things happen.

It's Hard Season. And things are like this during Hard Season. We expect it.

I grab Fern's hand, and she presses against my thighs. "Tell me one of your stories," she says.

"Okay," I say, relieved to have something to take my mind off the havoc around us. I try to think of one from the book I've never told before. "Once upon a time, there was a cook named Gretel, and her master never did give her enough to eat. One day, he was having a guest over for dinner, which is the evening meal, so he ordered her to make two roast fowl for the—" I stop and answer the inevitable question on her lips. "Fowl are birds. Like seagulls. Anyway, she makes these two birds for dinner, but as the night wears on and the guest doesn't arrive, she ends up eating them herself."

I hear someone whisper, "On the west side! At least twenty!" and I clutch Fern's hand tighter. Someone jabs me in the back, and I stumble forward. Clutching tight to Fern, I steady myself.

Fern, thankfully, is absorbed in the story. "Did she get in trouble?"

"You'll see. Unaware that the feast has been eaten, her master goes outside to sharpen his knife to cut the fowl, and while he does, his visitor arrives at the door. Clever Gretel says to him, 'Shh, go back as quickly as you came! If my master catches you, you'll be in a terrible fix. He invited you to dinner so he can cut off your ears. Listen, you can hear him sharpening his knife.'"

Fern's jaw drops open. "But that was a lie."

The new moon climbs ever so slowly into its perch in the sky, a silent witness to our panic. People are muttering under their breaths, final prayers in the darkness. Voices rise, and I know what this means. The crush will begin. Bodies push against one another, closer together, into the center. Elbows and hands come at us. We stand at the very edge of our spots, at the exact center of the platform, so near to one another that we can barely breathe. But that is not enough. I suck in my stomach, tilt my chin upward, toward the star-filled, peaceful night sky, and draw in the cool air. Our spots are being usurped, and we may be squeezed to death in the ensuing panic. I bring Fern in front of me and drape my body over her as a shield, as she presses into my thighs. A breeze blows a spray of salt against my bare arms, making me shiver. It is too close.

Tiam wastes no time moving behind me, acting like a barricade between me and the horde. He pushes back against them, groaning. "Get back!" he shouts, and I can feel every muscle of his back against mine.

People are whispering along with the crashing waves, but I bow my head low to Fern's ear and try to remember where I'd left off. I try to keep my voice calm, but it's shaking as I finish the story: "You're right. And then while the guest hurried away, Gretel ran screaming to her master, 'Alas, you invited a fine guest. He stole the fowl!' The master rushed after the thief, knife in hand, crying, 'Stop! Let me have just one!' and the guest thought he meant an ear, so he ran faster than ever, until he reached home and bolted the door." By this time, Fern's eyes are wide. She's still waiting for more, so I add, "The end."

Fern grins. "She was pretty clever."

"So are you. That's the name of the story. *Clever Gretel.*"

"I like that one," she says.

It feels like an eternity before our bodies are no longer crushed together. Before the tide finally begins to go out. By then, the moon has risen to its height in the sky. Another tide survived.

I turn to Tiam, who was just conversing with Ana, behind him. "What happened?"

His face is stone. "There was a large wave on the west side. Ana says we lost twenty. Maybe more."

"Oh!" I gasp softly. I begin to ask who, but Tiam is talking with someone else.

I exhale a few times, but I can't stop myself from shaking. Never has a tide been that terrible. Never had I felt so close to being crushed like that. I'm about to step out of my circle when Tiam suddenly turns back to me. "What are you up to now?"

I whirl around and blush, speechless. Truthfully, I'm not sure how to answer the question. Star never told me what I should do. I suppose I am expected for training. Or maybe I'm supposed to be roaming about among the rest of the commoners, eavesdropping. But my legs are wobbling so much that I can barely stand. "I—I don't know," I answer.

"I wanted to see if you'd come scavenging again with me. I want to try the *east* side this time," he says with a small smile. I know that he sees me shaking, and that smile is for my benefit, to make me feel at ease. "No scribblers on the east side."

"But...it's dark," I say.

"Full moon," he says, pointing skyward.

"Oh," I say, feeling dumb. I wonder if backpedaling will make it too obvious that I'm dying to accept his invitation. After all that's happened in the last formation, I'm still shaking. I don't want to be alone. Out of everyone on the island, no one can comfort a person as well as Tiam. It scares me to think that right now, I *need* him. "Well, I guess I could go for a little bit."

"Hey, good," he says with a grin.

He climbs down the rope and is waiting for me as I descend the ladder. I have to press my knees together so he can't see up my dress, even though it's dark and he isn't the type to look. The second I jump from the last step, I realize he's holding out a hand to help me. Clumsily, I fall into it, then into him, and we both stumble backward a little before he catches me. Once again, his face ends up inches from mine. I look away first, wanting to bury my head in the sand.

"Thank you for protecting us today," I say once we are farther away. "In formation. I was afraid this time we were done for."

He nods. I know he doesn't think he did anything special. It's just what he does.

"Who…who did we lose?" I ask, my voice still shaking.

"Mostly scavengers, a couple fishermen, too. They're counting the survivors right now. If that's right, that leaves only about 470 of us."

I try to breathe normally, but it's as if a heavy hand is holding me underwater.

He notices, because he says, "Coe. You know as king, I'll try to think of something. I will. I won't be like Wallow and just sit there—"

"Is that what you—what people—think about him?"

He looks at me, an odd expression on his face. "Of course."

"But Wallow is good," I protest, although my voice is weak, faltering. "He has kept us safe."

"*You* have kept you safe. He's useless," he mutters. "But you didn't hear that from me."

There is a wall I've built around myself. Of certainties. Things like the rule of the Wallows. Of Buck Kettlefish. Of a heaven after death. These things, knowing they were there for me when everything else fell away, comforted me. Everything else didn't matter. Everyone else, I avoided, just as they avoided me. But gradually, that wall has been eroding, much like the platform, and now, as I stare at Tiam, I feel more exposed than ever. "Is that what people say? But the Wallows saved us, so long ago…."

"That was some Wallow a million tides ago. Everyone here says that *this* Wallow is a do-nothing nobody. If he weren't already dying, someone would probably try to kill him."

I gasp. The wall is crumbling, almost as if he's pulling

it down with his bare hands. I shudder, feeling my ankles weaken. "But who's saying that?"

"Everyone." He studies me. "When Buck was here, things were different. He respected the king's rule. And people respected him. So he kept the peace. But lately, the unrest has been growing. And everyone—"

"Everyone? But in assembly—"

"People don't talk about it in assembly. They know the royals have their spies. But there are whisperings. And everyone—"

"Including you?"

He looks away. "I understand where they're coming from. Your father knew he had to keep the peace because there was no alternative. But I think even he knew that Wallow was weak, that he doesn't look out for us."

I shake my head. "But you need to stop it. I can't believe this. The princess said the same thing to me, but I didn't believe it. Because it can't happen! Chaos will reign, and we'll—"

"I *will* stop it. When I become king, I will take care of them. I won't be like Wallow." He must see how flustered I am, how my world is crumbling, because he pats the top of my head. "Coe. Calm. Everything will be all right."

The pat is something my father would have done, and yet when Tiam does it, it sends shivers right down to my toenails. I am glad it's dark to hide the flush in my cheeks. "How can you say that? Twenty people—"

"I have ideas. Trust me."

I stare at him, doubtful. We do not trust. But, oh, how I

want to. When I look into those eyes, I almost believe that we'll be safe and live happily ever after, like in one of my fairy tales.

"What are you revealing to me this time?" I say when we've walked a few moments in awkward silence.

He cocks his head. "Huh?"

"We've never gone scavenging together before, until this morning. The last time we went it was because you were dying to tell someone that you were going to be king. So what's up now?"

He smiles. "All right. Great. If I'm going to be king, I think I've got to stop being such an easy person to figure out."

"Well, smartest person on the island, and all that."

"Oh, right." He laughs, such a mesmerizing laugh that I barely notice when he changes the subject. "So, how was your visit to the castle, really, genius?"

I know there's something he wants to tell me, something he's having a hard time with. And a big part of me is frightened of what it could be. Part of me just wants to go on talking with him, laughing, like two friends, forever. So I say, "Interesting. Frightening. I'm not supposed to talk about it outside, though."

"I know, but I've been there, too. So you can tell me."

He doesn't have to twist my arm. "It was *amazing*," I gush, words bubbling forth like floodwaters. "Just incredible. I never imagined it would look like that. Not in a million tides. I can't believe that I—that we—are going to be living there."

He laughs. "You act like it was your first visit to the palace."

"I told you, I was too young to remember being there before. And guess what? I have my own room, with my own *bed*. Can you believe that? But I'm a little scared about the ghosts," I admit.

"Ghosts? That's a bunch of bunk."

"Well, I don't want to wake up to find the Dark Girl standing over me."

"Dark Girl?" He laughs. "I remember that legend. Haven't heard it in a while, though. She probably found a nicer place to haunt."

We walk on for a few more strides, when I say, "Why did Star think I could sew her dresses for her?"

He shrugs. "Why, can't you?"

"Of course not!" I say. I'm sure I don't have to show him my stump to get him to understand why. "I mean, I can do just a few stitches to piece my clothes together, but not *real* sewing. I don't think anybody on this island can sew anymore."

He smiles. "Oh. I may have told her that. My mistake."

"And she also thinks I know everything about the island's people. That I can be this spy for her. She's going to throw me off the balcony when she finds out you lied." I sigh.

"No, she won't," he says. Then he turns to me. "Look, I really didn't need to convince her of anything. *She* asked me about you first. After I got done talking to the king, she took me aside and asked me what I knew about you, and if you were, as she put it, *a good sort*."

"She did? Really?"

"And so I told her you were the worst sort of ocean scum

there is, and that even Mutter would make a better lady-in-waiting."

I narrow my eyes at him until he laughs.

"Come on, Coe. Really. I told her that you were a perfect choice. So what if I embellished some things? The truth is, she had her eye on you from the start. Just do your best."

Easy for Tiam to say. He's always excelled at things on his first try. He could probably do any or all of the jobs on the island, so he doesn't understand a person like me, who is fit for none of them. I bet he could even sew. "Maybe she won't need any dresses for a while, and I can practice," I offer weakly, feeling every inch of my lost hand. "But spying… Why did you lie about that?"

He doesn't answer, just looks at me in a kind, sincere way. In my dreams, there's desire in the way he looks at me. But in real life, it's much more sterile. The look says, *Because you are pathetic and helpless and wouldn't last a second on the outer edge of the formation.*

"Oh," I say. I suppose I should be happy that he even cares. It's more than most would do. Toward the horizon, the castle is straight ahead of us, in the distance, glowing pink in the moonlight. "Star's very…interesting."

"I know," he mutters, rolling his eyes. "She's always been a little dramatic. Don't you remember when we'd play together? She'd always pretend to hurt herself whenever she was losing a game. We never finished anything."

I give him a blank look.

"Okay, okay. You don't remember," he says with a laugh. Then his face turns serious. "I promised Wallow that I would look after his daughter when he is gone. That's what his largest concern is."

I can tell from the wrinkle above his brow there's something more, something he's not telling me. "Okay…" I prompt. That's when I see a bunch of builders rushing down shore with a good-sized piece of driftwood. They dance excitedly around it before hauling it off toward the platform. "Look at that. That's a good find."

"I wish…" He stops, and his face turns even darker. "Coe, that's what I wanted to talk to you about. I wanted to let you know that they're starting to build the new ship today."

"Sure," I say. I'd expected they'd start any day now. After all, my father has been gone for a season and a half. And they should keep building ships, in case he doesn't come back. "That's all right."

He runs a hand through his long hair so that it spreads over his shoulders, something he only does when he's anxious, which is rare. Then he reaches into his bag and pulls something out. It's a blue I know well, and it's more tattered than the last time I saw it, as if it had a fight with a bunch of scribblers. I gasp.

"It's his, isn't it?" he asks.

I nod. My father never went anywhere without that blue kerchief. He'd tie it around his neck and use it to wipe the sweat from his forehead. Or he'd pull it over his head to keep the hair out of his eyes. "Where did they find it?"

"It washed ashore today." He takes my hand and gently pools the fabric into it. It, like everything, is damp. "I thought you should have it."

"Oh. Thanks," I say calmly, even though the world's crashing around me. And to think only a heartbeat ago I'd been having stupid, stupid daydreams that Tiam had asked me to go off with him because I was special to him. When, really, all he wanted to tell me was that everyone who ever cared about me is dead.

"It might not be his, anyway," he offers, but I know he's just saying it to make me feel better. Material is hard to come by these days, and another scrap of material that faded sky-blue would probably be impossible to find.

"It's his," I answer.

"He may just have lost it. He may still be—"

"You know he isn't," I say. My limbs feel numb. My one hand, holding the fabric, doesn't even feel like part of my body. I don't think my heart is beating anymore. "Everyone who goes out on Explores never comes back. You know that."

He says, "But everyone *isn't* Buck Kettlefish."

I know he's trying to comfort me, but the words bounce off me as if I'm wearing a shell. I just stand there, dumb, as if I'm in a nightmare. Unable to do anything.

"You know," he says gently, "I never really put too much faith in the Explores until your dad left on his. Because even if an explorer did find a way out, did find civilization somewhere else in the world, there was nothing to get that person to come back to save the rest of us." He looks up at the sky. "But when your dad went on his Explore, I had this feeling. Like *finally, something's going to happen*. And that piece of material doesn't change my mind. Don't let it change yours."

I back away, grinding my teeth together so violently my

jaw aches. Then without another word, I head away from him, down the shore. I know that what I need to do is stop myself from caring about Tiam. Just stay as far away as possible. Because if it hurts this much to lose a person you love, I don't think I can live through it twice.

Six
Deliberate Disguises

We get our best sleep before the low tide horn, but I don't sleep. When the sun rises, I'm still sitting alone at the base of the platform, popping the blisters and picking the brown scabs on my stump raw while watching the outlines of the fishermen in the distance as they throw their lines into the tossing waves. I've spent most of my life trying to press my stump against my ribs, keep it out of sight and sun with hopes it'll be less noticeable. But right now I don't care how visible it is.

I reach into my bag and pull out a small, ancient box. I am not sure what was once kept inside. There were words written on top long ago, but now they are gone. I slide it open and tap the smooth brown shell a few times. A claw pops out. "Hi, Clam, it's me," I whisper, sticking bits of kelp and fish beside him. "Sorry I neglected you."

The hermit crab attacks a bit with its claws and then disappears. I think I have more in common with Clam than anyone on the island. "I know," I say to it, looking down at my silly white dress, "I may look different, but I'm still the same. I don't like coming out of my shell any more than you do."

Clam was my dad's pet. He gave it to me before he left. As a companion. He knew I didn't talk to anyone else. Only him. He wanted me to have someone to tell my troubles to. Someone to trust.

"He's a good little fellow," he'd said, *popping him into the back of my bag.* *"He won't let you down."*

"Dad, do you have to go? Why does it have to be you?"

"It has to be me. I made a promise to our king. And I can't put this off any longer. And…look at me."

I looked into his soft blue eyes. I knew what he was going to say.

"I want to keep you safe. And I can no longer stay here, on this island, and keep you safe. Do you understand?"

And he turned around and pushed the raft into the churning waves.

I remember wanting desperately for him to say he would be back, even if he knew it was a lie. But he didn't. It was as if he knew he'd never see me again. As if he knew he would fail. But he'd made a promise to the king. He never lied, and he never broke promises.

Xilia and Mutter are arguing a little ways off. Something about scribblers on the platform again. I realize Mutter has a spear with a dead scribbler attached to it. He's poking it at her, taunting her. "It's coming after you, Xil!" Mutter hisses, as Xilia spits and throws handfuls of sand at him.

I shiver and look at the crab. Clam is a good listener, sure, but a sad substitute for my father. In a million tides, I'd never understand why he thought sending himself off to certain death would keep me safe. Surely I'd be safer with him here.

I suppose that my mother didn't love my father and just used him to have me. He certainly never spoke of her, and whenever I asked, he'd quickly change the subject. But as long as I can remember, Buck was always there for me, always smiling. He was the one who taught me to read, filled my mind with history of ages past. Here, love doesn't exist, and we don't talk about it. I think some people on the island don't even know what it is anymore. But though we never said it, I know: my father and I loved each other.

Once, he told me about the solar system, about all the planets, and how they rely on the sun. How nothing in this solar system could exist without the sun. When he left on the Explore, I felt so weak I couldn't help wondering if he was my sun. If every day without him, I'd wither more and more. Yesterday, when I'd gotten my new job, I'd almost felt as if there was another source of energy giving me strength. I almost felt as if I could make it. But now, as I sit slumped against the concrete barrier, I feel weaker than ever. My sun has gone out.

I'm not sure how long I sit there, staring at the horizon, willing my father to come back, to take that blue kerchief from my hand, pat my head and say, "Ah! Thanks for finding it." Eventually I put Clam back into my bag and stand, swallowing the knot in my throat. He's gone. Tiam will soon be my king, and then he will become almost as distant to me as my father. I'm alone. Completely alone. I wonder how many chips need to be made in my shell before I succumb to the madness like Mutter and Xilia.

Outside our sleeping compartment, a line begins to form. My stomach rumbles, and suddenly I remember. It's time for the morning meal. I haven't eaten anything since the last morning meal. We always have fish, probably bluefish, with fine, translucent bones that stick in between my teeth and catch in the back of my throat. Very rarely, we'll have corvina, my namesake, but it's a rare delicacy, and there's no room to be choosy here. If I don't line up in a hurry, there may not be enough for me. Even if there are twenty fewer people in line today, because some of the casualties were fishermen. Not having enough food is something new. There always used to be enough to eat, I think, because my father was a fisherman, and he would sooner die himself than see others starve when it was his responsibility. Now, though, the fishermen rarely pull in enough for all of us.

I walk to the end of the line, behind Xilia. I wonder what things she's seen, what terrible losses have brought her to her state of madness. Somehow, I feel closer to her, as if I understand her. But then Xilia turns to me and scowls, her mouth opening into a cave so that I can see each rotten brown stub of tooth. "What are you doing here?" she demands. "You're a royal servant now. They take their meals in the castle."

"They do?" I ask. I'd never noticed.

"Of course. The king doesn't want the royal servants to associate with rabble like us," she says.

"That's not true," I protest. "What about the formation?"

"They have no choice about that," she says. "Now scoot

before us commoners get after you for being greedy and going after two meals."

"But that's not what..." By now the others in the line are looking at me, their eyes frightening slits. I always knew I disgusted them, but I've never seen such hateful looks in their eyes. I back away. "Okay, sorry," I mumble, and hurry toward the castle.

Before I make it even ten steps, someone tugs on my sleeve. I whirl. It's Finn. His face is pleasant, the first welcoming face I've seen in a while, and I guess it's just what I need right now because I find myself leaning into him. "Don't be alarmed. They're just on edge because of what happened during the last formation, and because we haven't been bringing in much food lately."

"Oh," I say. "I know. It's okay."

He smiles. "I wanted to congratulate you on your new position."

"Thank you."

"And it's obviously hard to turn down an offer like that. I did want to..." He seems reluctant, but as if there's something he needs to say. "I heard that the king's men dragged you off like a criminal."

"Well, yes. It was kind of unexpected, but—"

"It wasn't right, Coe. If I'd been there, I'd have done something."

"Oh, no. I wouldn't have wanted you to. They didn't hurt me."

"Still, it was wrong. And some of us think it was too much. How dare they?"

"Some of you?" It suddenly dawns on me what he's saying, but it seems impossible for them to get so worked up over me. "No, it really was no big deal. Tiam was there. He could tell you what—"

"I saw you speaking with Tiam. Be careful with him, okay?"

"With him?" I shake my head. "We've always been... It's like—" I bite my tongue. I really don't know what it's like, and I feel myself blushing because of what I want it to be.

He nods. "Well, that's good. He's not a very serious person, is he? He has a rather silly side. One that I think will get him in trouble."

I nearly burst out laughing. Tiam isn't going to get in trouble.... He's going to be king. And he's the closest thing to a friend that most people on this island have. He's no threat. Yes, he's different, but... Suddenly I realize something. *Different* people are the ones who seem to suffer most in this world. My father. Me. And now Tiam. "But why? You mean because of how he acts in formation? He was just trying to get Fern to calm down."

"That may be so, but his conduct is less than appropriate, considering people are losing their lives," he says. "It has a lot of people upset."

I stare at him. A lot of people? Surely he's mistaken. Tiam is well liked, as Buck was. He and only he would be able to restore the peace we need in this kingdom. Without him, there is no hope for us. "You're wrong. It's just a bit of fun," I whisper. "Everyone must know that."

"Does fun have a place here?"

"Yes, it does!" I say. "I hate this. I hate tide after tide of gloom. Tiam makes us forget—"

"But not in the formation," he says, his eyes boring into me. "Not when people are fighting for—and losing—their lives. I know it's good to blow off steam. But blatant disregard—"

"He doesn't mean that," I say.

"Maybe he doesn't, but it comes off that way. Consider it. And consider your place with the princess. She obviously chose you for a reason. Do you see what I mean?"

I shake my head, but as I study his face, it begins to fall into place. If people don't like the royals, and I'm in the princess's favor, where does that leave me? And if they hate Wallow so much, if Tiam becomes king, will they accept him, if it's under Wallow's direction? "I understand," I say. "But I'm not on anyone's side. I'm just doing my job."

Finn nods. "But like I told you, it doesn't matter what you think. What you show...that matters. Do you see?"

"Yes," I answer, swallowing the knot in my throat. "I saw in the assembly that you were nominated. To take over when the king dies."

"I thought you guys were spying out there!" He laughs, then hangs his head. "I suppose. If that's what the people want, then I will not go against it."

"What if the king wants something else? What if he has plans to be carried out before he dies? This is the Wallows' kingdom, and we wouldn't be here without their generosity. Is there no allegiance to their rule at all? Do we just throw it away?"

"I understand how you feel, Coe. That is the way Buck

felt, too. Do whatever can be done to preserve the peace. But that was when most of the world believed in the goodness of the Wallows. They believed that Star was a sign from the gods that things would get better. But things have only gotten worse. And now, most of the world thinks his leadership, and his ideas, whatever they may be, are damaging to us. Whether I take his place, I think, is up to the people of this world. That is the best way to preserve the peace, don't you think?"

I nod.

There are a thousand goose bumps springing up on my arms, and he must notice them, because he says, "I'm sorry. Hey. Do you remember when we were younger? When that giant sea turtle shell washed up on shore?"

Yes, of course I remember. I was about ten, and he was maybe thirteen. Back then, he and Tiam were even friends. But eventually Tiam, though younger, started besting him in races along the shore, in pulling in fish, well, in everything. I think that was why they grew apart. Finn couldn't stand a younger kid doing things better than he could. Anyway, one day, a turtle shell washed up on shore. It was huge. We took it to the royals, thinking they'd want it, but it smelled, so they let the commoners have it. The commoners spent twenty tides trying to determine what to do with it. Ana wanted to use it as a pot for soup, other people wanted to make it into a bathtub and let everyone use it on rotation. "Oh, yeah. That night. We all convinced Mutter it would make a good boat."

He smiles. "And he believed it. And it sank like a rock the second he launched it."

I laugh, remembering him thrashing about in the ocean, shrieking like a seagull for his "boat." We never found it again, after that. "He had one foot in, ready to cast off, and it just disappeared. He was so sure it was going to float!"

He nods. "Now, *that* was a bit of fun. But things were different then."

Things *were* different. He doesn't have to tell me how. Back then, we still had shreds of hope. But fun does seem out of place when there is no hope left.

He says goodbye, and still warmed by the memory of us as kids, I turn toward the castle.

At the castle entrance, two guards nod and pull open the enormous metal doors to let me pass. I'm less anxious than the first time I came this way, so I notice more. There are faded letters, like the ones in my room, written above the castle doors in big block print. W OW HO L.

WowHol? Then I make out an *I* to the right of the first *W*. WI OW. I think some letters are missing. Two *L*'s, probably, for WILLOW, the people who have always reigned. I wonder when in history they began substituting an *A* for the *I* and started going by Wallow. I guess it probably happened gradually, as everything does, once they stopped learning to read and write. The HO L must have once been HOTEL. The Willow Hotel was mentioned in the diary I have, though the Kettlefish ancestor who wrote about it used a lot of antiquated phrases that didn't make sense. I'm not really even sure what a hotel is. I suppose it is another word for palace.

As I walk down the vast foyer, I notice there are faded letters above the arched doorways to every room, but I don't stop to read them. One has the letters DININ over it. The smell of cooked fish wafts out to meet me, and my mouth starts to water. There are tables and chairs inside, and some people are eating. A moment later I realize the letters must have once spelled out DINING.

I follow an incredible aroma toward a banquet table. I've never smelled anything that has made my mouth water so much. Cordon, the cook, who is permanently blue-tinged, bulgy and hairless, like a jellyfish, is doling out heaping spoonfuls of some sort of fish chowder from an enormous pot. The pot is so huge I think that everyone on the island could eat and go back for seconds and thirds. He doesn't look at me, just places a bowl in front of me, and I go and find a seat alone, in a corner. It feels weird to eat at a table instead of sitting in the sand, balancing my bowl between my knees.

Even though it burns my tongue, I practically pour the chowder down my throat, it's so good. I am not sure what Cordon has done, but this has a taste I've never experienced before. Every meal outside tastes the same, like fish and salt. When I'm done, my belly growls, wanting more. I wipe my chin and realize it's wet, then look down and notice my stupid white garment has an orange stain down the front. Perfect.

"You'd best change before the princess sees you looking like that," a voice says.

It's Burbur. She has her cart with her and is placing little shell-and-seaweed sculptures at the center of each table. Ridiculous decorations. Considering all the ridiculous decorations I've already seen in my short time in the castle, that poor woman probably never rests.

"Change?" I ask. I was thinking I would find some water and try to wash it out. After all, I've only been wearing it a day. I'd worn my old tunic a thousand-plus tides without changing.

"Of course. You'll wear a fresh garment after every formation. I've hung yours in your room."

"But that isn't—"

"It's the king's orders. Besides, pressed together with the commoners, our garments tend to get dingy and smelly." She presses her lips together. "Now, go on, hurry. If the princess sees you, she will be upset."

Muttering to myself about how unnecessary it all is, I jump to my feet and scurry up the formal staircase, trying to find my way back to my room. At the door, I pull back the curtain to find that all the little trinkets are back in place on the damp vanity. Other than a few wet spots on the stone floor, there's nothing to indicate the room was underwater a short time ago. As promised, a new gauzy white garment is hanging near the doorway. It's probably just my mind playing tricks on me, but it looks even shorter than the other one. I quickly change into it and realize I'm right—this one hits only my midthigh. I think of Star's bare navel and wonder if this is the way it's supposed to fit.

As I'm turning in front of the mirror, trying to stretch the material to at least graze my knees but getting nowhere, a form appears in the door. I know from the flash of pink that it is the princess. She's wearing a scowl. "I must have forgotten to mention. After every high tide you must, immediately, come up to the tower to see if there is anything you can do for me." She shakes her head. "Come at once. I require a bath."

I follow dutifully at her heels as she leads me to the winding staircase to the infamous tower. There is a bell at the base of the tower, small, shiny brass. Here, the hallway is nearly black except for the light streaming through a small window, open only a crack. I inspect the walls, and then I realize that the window is not closed off. It is not a window at all. It's simply a hole in the wall. There are markings surrounding it, and they remind me of my scars. Some are mere scratches, but others are deep, jagged slits, crisscrossing the wall, as if somebody had been digging away at it, trying to loosen the stones. Trying to make the tower fall?

"What is—" I begin, raising my finger to point, but she silences me with a loud shush. Her eyes linger on it for a moment, and she shudders, then hastens her pace up the stairs.

All of us commoners have seen this tower every day of our lives, but I know I am one of only two or three who will have actually had the luxury of going inside, so my heartbeat echoes in my ears as I climb. It's dark here. We climb a dozen stairs, then a dozen more, and just when I think the passageway will never end, a cheerful light glows ahead. It illuminates the stone walls of the tower so that a white line of salt is visible; below this line the stone is worn and gray, dotted with a rainbow of mold, and above it, it's polished and black. This must be where the tide reaches. I marvel at it, noting that we still climb twenty or thirty more steps before we reach an enormous black door, blocked by two royal guards. Star waves them away from the entrance, then steps aside and motions for me to open the door. When I do, I expect to see a small, simple room, slightly bigger than my own. But the room is so vast, I inhale sharply. "Tread lightly," she instructs. "We don't want the tower to be any more unstable than it already is."

"Yes," I answer. Everything certainly *feels* stable, but then again, it's a still day. I imagine what it is like to be here when the wind is blowing hard, which is often during the evenings of Hard Season.

"These are my quarters. The king's are through that door," she continues, pointing to an ornate stone archway. "You are not to enter there or disturb him in the least. Just conduct your business quietly and be gone. Understood?"

I nod.

"You may come up to my quarters only after ringing the bell three times," she says. "Three is your personal signal."

"Bell?"

She sighs. "Down at the entrance to the tower. If I need you, I will ring the bell thrice. If it is clear for you to climb the stairs, I will ring you back once. If it is not, I will ring twice. It is necessary because we cannot have more than five people up in the tower at one time. There is my father and myself, and of course our two guards. When the medic is treating my father, you will not be allowed to come up."

"I understand. But what if there is an emergency?"

She shakes her head. "The tower is very old, as you might note. In the past, people have tried to raze it, which accounts for the markings you saw in the stairwell."

"Who would do such a thing?"

"I've told you about the danger the royal family is in. Which is why I have guards outside the door at all times, even while I sleep. Like I said, more than five people and we fear the tower may crumble from the weight. Of course, we've never tested the notion, but then again, we do not have a death wish, now, do we?"

She smiles and, in one sweep, drops her robe and proceeds, naked, toward an enormous stone tub. Immediately I look away, but I catch the scent of lavender wafting from the suds as she sinks in. She instructs me on how to scrub her back and how to comb her hair gently as she lies there, so as not to disturb her daydreams. I fumble about nervously with my one hand and catch the comb twice in a knot in her hair, but she doesn't scold me. Then she says, "Coe, do you ever daydream?"

I clear my throat. All my daydreams involve Tiam, and they're so silly I'd never let anyone know about them. "Not really," I lie.

She sighs. "Shame. I thought we could trade daydreams in our talks." Then she clicks her tongue and settles herself deeper into the tub. "I will tell you my daydream anyway. Maybe it will inspire you. And then maybe you will be inclined to have your own."

I bite down so hard on my tongue I taste blood. "Okay."

"I dream that all the islanders who want to do us harm are gone. I dream that I have a hundred children, and they have hundreds of their own children. And we all live together, a peaceful royal race of humans, with no fear of danger." She smiles wistfully, then looks at me, a look of alarm on her face. "Of course our servants will be there, and they will be happy to serve us because they will know they are valued. That means you, Coe. You would be safe."

I nod lamely. Is she mad? It's only a daydream, so perhaps it's okay to think such fanciful thoughts. Surely she must realize that her children and children's children will have no dry land on which to stand.

"Are you surprised to hear that I want children?" she continues. "I do. Of course it is selfish for an islander to have children. The island is overpopulated. But a royal having a child…well, that is a gift. People need the royal family to inspire them, to lift them up." Her face turns dark. "It's unfortunate that a few islanders seem to think we're being greedy, when we are the ones who saved them. We allowed them to use our land, so many tides ago. The Wallows are benevolent, and yet the commoners seem to have forgotten that.

"Do you know how to make a child?" she continues, staring up at the ceiling as I wash her shoulders. "Of course you don't. I will tell you. A woman lies down with a man, and they press their bodies together until they become one. When they separate there will be a seed, which will grow into a child in the woman's belly." She strokes her taut navel. "Isn't that amazing?"

I nod, though in my knowledge, making a child is not amazing. It is fearsome and horrible, something we don't talk about. We do not become familiar, but that does not mean that people completely ignore their primal, animal urges. Men have taken by force. To do so is against the law, and both the woman and the man are considered to be at fault, and executed—the man for the violent act, and the woman for the seed she might carry. No, making a child is not a beautiful thing.

"You are close with Tiam?" she asks, startling me out of my thoughts. Bringing him up so closely after talking about how to make a child, it makes me blush. I'd thought about lying close to Tiam a million times, but the closest we've ever gotten is standing side by side in formation. My throat tightens when she brings up his name. I wonder if she is so special that she can read my daydreams, without my having to speak them.

"No. Not really. We stand next to each other in formation."

"Ah," she says, her brow wrinkling. "He spoke so…intimately of you. I was sure you were close."

Intimately? What could that mean? The flutter inside me disappears when I realize. He'd told her about my ability to spy and my cleverness and that I was an excellent seamstress. But those were all lies. The "intimacy" we share is nothing but a lie.

After telling me several more of her daydreams involving her blissful royal race, her skin has pruned. She steps from the tub and instructs me to dry each of her limbs with a new clean cloth. As I'm drying her, doing my best not to gawk at her unmarred, pale skin, my eyes catch on something, just on her ribs. Slashes. Two on each side of her belly, in perfect symmetry. Deep ones, almost exactly like my own.

I've never seen them on anyone else before. Well, certainly not on any of the men, who go around bare-chested. Until now, I'd thought I was the only one.

I want to ask her about them, but she rushes me to comb out her hair, and when I fail to affix the ribbons in quite the right way, shoos me away and does it herself. "You can sew, though, yes?" she asks, annoyed, staring at my useless stump.

"Um…" I don't want to say no because I don't want to lose this job; but there's no fabric around for sewing, so the best I've done was clumsily piece together two pieces of mismatched scraps. I've fumbled around so much I'm afraid I'm only inches from being cast back to the craphouse, so I say, "Oh. Yes."

"Good," she says, casting off the towel and strutting naked across the room. Again, my eyes catch on those scars. It amazes me that with all those fine fabrics she adorns herself with, she seems to like wearing nothing the best. I've always been ashamed of my scars, but clearly she does not feel the same way about hers. I quickly avert my eyes again, blushing. She pulls open a large door on a closet and retrieves something white and flimsy. "A servant started it before she stupidly lost track of time and was washed to sea. You can finish it. My wedding dress."

I blurt out, "Wedding?"

She smiles. "Ah, I know, there hasn't been one since well before you were born. I think the royal wedding of my father's parents was the last, and that was so many tides ago that I doubt anyone on the island can remember it. A wedding is a union of souls. A man and a woman. For eternity."

"No, I know what a wedding is," I say, but all the while my body is draining of its energy. A man. The new king.

Of course! Tiam is going to be king. Of course he would

have to wed Star. How could I be so dumb? That was what he was trying to tell me last evening, on the beach. He didn't just vow to Wallow to protect Star...he vowed to marry her.

Star tilts her head. "Oh. And how do you know that?" she asks, eyes narrowing. She's getting suspicious again.

"No. I mean..." Meaningless words and half syllables drift off my tongue as I no longer have the energy to speak. I knew it. Deep down, I always knew it. Tiam, Star. The two most perfect souls on the island. Of course they belong together. They've always belonged to one another. I was silly to deny that, to think that because the island was falling apart, everyone in the world would just fall apart with it.

She holds out the silky white pile of fabric to me, and I take it, though my hand is completely numb. Tiam is marrying a princess. And I will be putting together the wedding dress. Suddenly it is all clear to me. No matter what my position is on this island, it will always be the same: on the outside, looking in, constantly wishing I could be somewhere, or someone, else.

Seven
As the Wind Behaves

I spend the next several tides learning the trade as Princess Star's lady-in-waiting and coming to terms with the fact that in my new role, I will be constant witness to her life in the tower with King Tiam. Every time I see either of them, I think of them lying beside one another, pressing their bodies together so tight that they're breathing each other's breath. The thought makes nausea bubble in my throat.

Tiam tries to speak to me, but I can't face him. Since Tiam told me about my father, I've only spoken to him in formation, and very curtly—"Fine, thanks, and how are you?" It lends an entirely new kind of discomfort to the already arduous task of standing shoulder to shoulder; whereas before we'd talk intermittently, now, mostly, we stand in silence. Maybe Finn is right that I should be distancing myself from him. And why should I care about Tiam, anyway? After all, he didn't think enough of me to tell me about the marriage. Instead, I had to find out from her.

Every time I tend to Star, it's more daydreams about her life with Tiam. I'm constantly reminded of the sad truth that awaits me when he assumes the throne, so much so that I often wish I was Craphouse Keeper again, and occasionally I even want to jump from the balcony onto the stony shores below.

One morning, after a particularly excruciating bath where Star imagined what each of her and Tiam's children would look like, I walk out to the platform a little too early for formation. But being outside the castle, I can breathe again. I sit with my feet dangling over the edge of the platform, feeding Clam a bit of seaweed and watching the people lining up for the morning meal. Since we spend so much of our lives on the platform as it is, a person sitting atop it *before* formation is kind of odd. Most people dread going to the platform, detest it, run away from it when all the turmoil is over. That's probably why people notice me. I see Finn heading back toward the compartment from the beach, wrapping up a fishing line and carrying a few nice-sized bluefins over his shoulder. He looks up, shielding the sun from his eyes, and waves. Then he drops the fish off with Ana and starts to climb the rungs of the ladder to meet me.

"Hi, there, Coe," he says. "What are you up to, up here?"

"Oh, nothing," I say, pretending as best I can that all's right with the world. Not as if I can tell him about my Tiam troubles.

"You look sad. Everything all right with the new job?"

I guess I'm not doing a very good job at masking my sorrow. "Yes, it's fine. I've just been thinking about what you said about the royal family. And Tiam."

He's quiet for a moment. "I didn't mean to be so negative about Tiam. I know you are friends. I'm sorry."

"I always thought everyone liked Tiam," I say.

"It's not that people don't like him," he says softly. "But this season, he's been a little, shall we say, difficult to deal with. He's just learning the trade as a fisherman, and yet everywhere I go, he's there, trying to prove himself. If we pull in twenty fish, he'll pull in forty. If we tell him something can't be done, he'll still try it, because he has this air that he's better than everyone else."

I don't say anything. That does sound like Tiam.

"And recently he's been dragged to the castle in the night, just like you were. We all thought he would get in trouble for his antics in formation, but instead, nothing happened. And when you were dragged to the castle in much the same way, only to be made the princess's head servant…" He bites on the edge of his thumbnail. "Well, I think the king is up to something with Tiam."

"Like what?"

He tries to look me in the eye, but I falter, instead staring at the tower. "You know, don't you? Tiam is going to marry Star. They're going to try to make him king."

Hearing the words outright makes my body quiver. I think of him and Star together in the tower, making perfect babies and having the life I'd only dreamed of. My eyes begin to blur with tears, but I squeeze them back. "Yes," I finally say.

I cringe. Why did I say that? Tiam has done nothing but protect me. The moment the word is out, I want to swallow it back.

"You like that idea? You approve of it?" he asks.

"He's a good person."

"He is. Nobody denies that. But not all good people should be king."

"Is that what everyone thinks? That Tiam should step aside and let you be king?"

"Most definitely. It has nothing to do with Tiam. Unrest has been brewing for a while. Right now, the people hate Wallow. They hate the old regime and want to make a clean sweep, and that means anything that the king wants, they don't. Tiam should realize this and concede," he says. "But he won't."

I look at him. "You asked him?"

He nods. "It appears he will not go down without a fight."

I gasp. I'd known for so long about Tiam being king, but he's also been an agreeable person. Someone who would do what he could to preserve the peace. "Did you really talk to him? Tiam is reasonable, Finn. He would listen to you. And if the people really did want someone—"

"Coe. I told you. We're past that now. He's not budging on this."

"So...what does this mean?" Finn is grinding his jaw, telling me exactly what it means. "Finn. You can't fight him. If you go against the king's wishes and fight him, there will be chaos. The whole island will—"

"I am not sure chaos can be prevented, unless Tiam backs down," he says. "Which is why I wanted to talk to you. If Tiam does not bow out quietly, it can only get worse. I know you two are close. Can you convince him?"

Me? I think of how hopeful he'd been, talking about becoming king. "I've never been able to convince Tiam of anything."

He nods solemnly.

I bring my hand to my chest. I can't breathe. "Please, Finn. You know my dad wanted to preserve peace at all costs. You know he never would go against the king, even if he didn't agree with him, because if we don't have peace—"

"That was then. The Wallow on the throne now would love us all to die. He'd probably feed us to that spoiled princess of his." He pauses. "Coe, be careful. I see the way that Mutter and some of the others look at you, and...you've always had enemies because you're the weakest and the smallest. It's already so easy for them to hurt you, but if they think you're in allegiance with the royal family..."

I know this. I shiver.

He reaches into his bag, pulling out a little piece of fishing line. He starts to twist it every which way, then hands it to me. It's in the shape of a perfect heart. "Do you know what that is?" he asks me, his voice soft and awkward.

"Yes," I say. "It's fishing wire."

He gives me a look. "No, I mean, the shape?"

I wonder what he means. I do know the shape, if only vaguely. Kimmie, the first girl who wrote in the journal I carried, was fond of putting them everywhere. What surprises me is that he knows. Maybe there is more to him than I thought. "Of course. It's a heart."

He nods. "My mother had a pendant with that shape on it. I never knew what it was. It was actually your father who told me." He clears his throat. "It's a symbol of love. Do you know what love is, Coe?"

I stare at the little wire heart. "Yes. It's caring for someone more than you care for yourself. But…that's dangerous." *Unless you're royalty,* I think bitterly.

He takes my hand in his, and I can feel the calluses, the wear from his long days tending the nets and lines. When I look at him, his eyes are serious. "Not always," he says. "I happen to believe that the sea can swallow us all it wants… but what really would signal the end of civilization is losing the ability to love. Your father knew that better than anyone. When we stop caring about each other, that's the end."

"Most of us already have," I say.

"Not me. Coe, I made a promise to your father to watch out for you."

Buck told me he had made assurances, and often I'd see him talking to Tiam and Finn, as if they were his own sons. I imagine the three of them standing around a fire, sealing the pledge with handshakes.

I'm startled from my imagination when I hear his voice: "Coe. If I were king, I'd want you to be my queen."

I think about Tiam and how I've always wanted to hear those words, but from him. But he never wanted me, only Star. Ethereal, perfect Star. The pain of that is like a dagger in my chest. I find myself moving closer to Finn, as if there's some unstoppable force pulling me toward him. Maybe I just want to be wanted, and it doesn't matter by whom. "Why?" I murmur.

"Because I want to take care of you," he whispers, pressing

the wire heart into my palm, which is moist with sweat. My pulse quickens. He knows these words are what I—what all of us—have been craving. He knows he is offering me something that is just as precious as dry land.

Then there is a noise below, on the rungs. People have begun to climb for formation. I stand spear-straight, and he does the same, then whispers, "Think about it."

I move away from him silently, and am halfway to my spot when I open my curled hand and find the wire heart in my palm. I touch it with my finger, telling myself, *I can do this. I can live. I can be okay without Tiam.*

I whisper those words over and over again until I think I finally believe them. By then, everyone is standing in their place and high tide is close.

But it can't be. It can't be, I realize, as my maniacal chanting slows to a stop. And I'm left with a giant hole, as if something is missing. Something so basic but so necessary, like the air I breathe. And then the realization comes crashing down on me like the waves. I can't live, and I can't be okay. Ever, as long as I live in this world.

Tiam.

Fern grabs my hand and finds the heart there, but she doesn't ask what it is. "Where is he?" she squeaks instead, moving her head side to side. More than a head taller than her, I have a better vantage point, but already the bodies have closed in around us, pressing together so that the smell of lavender is drowned out by the stench of sweat and seawater. But that's not the reason I'm having trouble breathing. The reason is the one gaping hole to my left, one that has never been there before, as wide as the ocean. Despite us all pressing together, I feel alone. Open to attack. Clutching the heart, I try to think of Finn, but instead all I feel is the cold damp air on my left side, where Tiam should be.

Shortly after, the whispers begin. Did he become the latest scribbler victim? Did he fall asleep somewhere and miss formation? There are only so many places on the island one can hide, and nobody has seen him for most of a tide.

Today the ocean is calmer than usual. When it bears down on us and reaches the edges of the formation, Mutter whoops. "Number three is gone. Let's all move to the right one space."

I glare at him, and at that moment the horn blares above us. We all look up, and from our position just the tops of three heads are visible. From the sparkling jeweled crowns, I know the king and princess. And beside them is the blond hair and tanned forehead I'd know anywhere.

Something in my throat tastes sour. I know I should be happy he's safe, but seeing Tiam and the princess, together, I feel lonelier than ever.

Everyone looks up silently, shielding their eyes from the sun with their hands. I exhale slowly as the princess calls down to us. "I know it will come as a shock to all of you, but my father is dying." She pauses dramatically and waits for the gasps, but either they're muffled by the wind or, more likely, everybody already knows. Star knows little of how fast news can travel down here.

"And what will we do?" someone calls up to them.

"I will be marrying Tiam, a commoner like yourself, at the evening of the next full moon. The king has given us his blessing, and most importantly, he has given Tiam rule over Tides." She pauses. "He is reaching his sixteenth Hard Season, and so, he will be your king."

This news, though clearly not a surprise, sends shock waves through the platform. It's almost like high tide striking all over again.

"He's not our ruler!" Mutter shouts. Vixby pumps his fist angrily in the air. Someone shouts, "No!"

Everyone is staring up at the balcony. So I feel heat rise in my cheeks when I search among the angry faces and see Finn, his eyes on mine. His face is strangely calm, as if to say, *I told you nobody would accept this.*

The horn blares again, which is our signal to bow before them. I look around, but I already know what is going to happen. Nobody even attempts to bow. Not a single person. Well, Mutter does, but it's with a mocking flourish. The horn blares again, but voices rise in protest to meet it. Tiam's face is stone, as if he expects it, but I'm frozen, unable to believe that this is happening. That this is what the rest of our world has been reduced to. I want so badly to show him that I'm not like them, that I accept him, but Finn is looking at me, and I can hear his voice. *You have enemies.*

Suddenly, rocks bounce off the edge of the tower with a thud, and sand showers down on me, stinging my skin. People are throwing sand and whatever they can get their hands on. The tower is too tall for them to do any damage, but nevertheless, the royal family retreats without another word. The last thing I see is a flash of pink cape, disappearing beyond the balcony.

I'm completely dazed as I trudge out of formation with a few others, who are still muttering with their heads down. "I'm not letting him tell me what I can and can't do," Vixby mutters to the men beside him. They crowd together, whispering, until I can't tell what they're saying. I've never before cared to be a part of the crowd, to know the secrets they share.

Now, I realize, I'm too afraid to know.

As I'm lying on my mat in my quarters the following evening after formation, I keep thinking about Finn's words. *If I were king, I'd want you to be my queen,* he'd said. I think of my father. I've been spending many sleepless moments wondering what my father would tell me to do in this situation, and I still don't know. I know that he liked Tiam, and that he liked Finn, too. I know that he taught me to respect authority. But I also know he'd want me not to be stupid, to do whatever it took to keep myself alive.

And that is why I couldn't bow. And why, if it means saving myself, I'll have to vacate my new position. As much as Tiam wanted it for me, because he thought it would make me safer, even he can't save me now. He has enough to deal with on his own. I have to save myself.

While I'm thinking, a commotion brews in the open window. Men are shouting, and their voices drift up to me. For the first time, I peer outside to see a crowd of a dozen or more people fumbling in the moonlight at the water's edge. Someone is lying there, in the center of the huddle, but I can only see the sweaty backs of the fishermen glistening in the light and a pair of ruts in the sand, heel marks of the person's feet. Someone screams something about a "fishing accident." I cringe. Another scribbler victim.

Far above me, I can just about make out the tower balcony. Someone up there—it sounds like the king—shouts, "Bring him to the doors. At once!"

To the doors? I wonder. *Whatever for?* Our medics can't perform miracles; they can bandage a cut or tie up a sprain, but we have no medicines, no means to perform complex operations. Usually when a person has been stricken by a scribbler, the wound is severe, and they are tossed into the waves so that the scribblers can finish their meal. Curiously, I watch as four of the heftiest fishermen reach down and bring the victim up to their shoulders, so that his bloodied face and stomach greet the moon. There is a huge gash just under his collarbone.

The fish chowder I'd eaten earlier gurgles in the back of my throat.

Tiam.

No.

Unaware of how I end up there, I find myself breathless and trembling at the top of the staircase, watching the doors swinging open and the fishermen carrying him inside. They stand at the entrance, their bodies glistening with sweat in the orange torchlight, gazing at the hall just the way I did the first time I was brought here. "Drop him," one of the guards says.

And they do drop him, as if he's a thing instead of a human. As if he's something without a soul. Without hope. He's not conscious, and when they carelessly throw him to the floor, his head flops to the side, his mouth falls slack and a trickle of blood escapes. I feel tears on my hand, and my hot breath burns my palm; it's fastened over my mouth because I know otherwise I will scream. Everything left in this world that's worth something is lying in broken pieces on that floor.

I rush down the steps. Halfway down the stairs, I become aware of the severity of his wound. The gash is so deep that the white of his collarbone is visible among the torn sinews of muscle. I'm about to run to him when the king's voice booms behind me. "Guards, escort those commoners out at once."

Turning, I see the king, his face ashen and swollen, eyes yellow with sickness. He is at the top of the staircase behind me, his pink robe swishing along the marble floor. The logical part of my brain urges me to fasten myself against the wall and let him pass, but another part, far stronger, is teeming over, ready to explode. It's the part that knows time is of the essence, and the king is moving at too leisurely a pace to help him. "He needs medical attention at once!" I yell at him.

King Wallow raises his head toward me sluggishly, a peculiar expression on his face. I clench my teeth. My direction was supposed to get him to act in haste, and yet now he's standing still, staring at me. I want to grab him, get him to move, to act, but as his gaze hardens on me, I cringe. A shiver overtakes my body and a trickle of sweat runs down my rib cage. When he nods at a guard, I know I've said too much already.

The guard steps forward, turns his spear to the flat end and raises it over his head, and it whistles down over me. I feel crushing pain in my skull as I'm falling head over heels down the remaining steps of the staircase, coming to rest in something sticky, wet and warm. The last thing I remember is thinking, *Please, please, please, don't let it be Tiam's blood.*

Eight

The Valley of Dying Stars

It feels like a hundred tides later when I wake up with a start. I'm on the mat in my quarters, and the ropes holding it in place squeak as I throw my legs over and rush to the window. About two steps later my skull feels as if it is being crushed between two stones, and I fall forward, against the window ledge. The ocean crashes somewhere in the distance. I peer over the ledge, but everything is just a blur. Blinking furiously to get my eyes to work, I finally make out a line of blue in the distance. The tide has not yet come in. I exhale. I'm safe.

There is a sloppy bandage over my eyes, and when I bring my hand up to touch my forehead, my fingertips are coated in blood. My garment splattered with it. My face and neck feel tight from where it has dried on my skin. Dizzy, I crawl to the mirror to inspect the damage, and suddenly, one image hits me and sends me reeling back against the wall, sobbing.

Tiam.

Tiam. Gone.

I can't put the words together in my mind. All my life he's been beside me in formation. And I'd always thought that he'd get a prime spot in the formation while I was cast out to the dangerous edge. I always assumed he'd outlive me. I think of that horrible wound, his body covered in blood, his limbs tight and lifeless, and wonder what they did with his body once the last of his life was drained. Did they throw him out into the ocean as carelessly as they'd dropped him on the ground? Will no one else mourn him?

I think back to that morning, when he told me about being king. He was so hopeful and excited. *I think I can help us. I think I can do good.* The words keep ringing in my ears because after my father, Tiam was the last person. The last person on the island capable of making a difference. The rest of us just exist, flailing helplessly on the shore like fish struggling for air, waiting for the waves to come and wash us off the map.

Across the room, I finally focus enough to see my reflection in the mirror as I huddle pathetically on the ground. My hair is hanging in mangy black ropes over my face, which is ruddy with dried blood, except for two pale streaks under my eyes that my tears have washed clean. A horn blares above me, deafening, signaling the end of low tide, but I don't even flinch.

I don't even care.

I'm done.

Let the tide take my last breath. Let the scribblers get the rest of me.

"You've come to," a voice says from the hall. I know it's Burbur. "Good."

Nothing is good about this. I don't answer, don't even turn to look at her. I just lie there, pressing my face against the cold wall below the window, wishing my heart were broken enough to stop beating.

Guilt tangles my thoughts. I think back to him standing at the balcony, looking so regal. I was too afraid to bow to him. He deserved my allegiance. He deserved my respect. And I was too afraid to show it.

"Now, don't pout. Why in the world you would speak to the king without first being spoken to is beyond me," she continues. I hear water pouring into the tub. "Come, now. Brought you some fresh water to bathe in. No lavender, of course, but good and clean. Come, now."

I don't move. I hope she'll think I'm dead and just leave me alone.

A moment of silence passes, so I think it worked. I wait another moment, and then another, then lift my head up and turn toward the door. She's still standing there, though, holding a pile of fresh towels. She reaches down and pulls off my garment. I'm too weak to fight, so she manages to shove me into the warm water easily. My bloody skin instantly turns the water brown, but it still relaxes my muscles, comforts me. She dunks me, and I wish I could stay under forever, but when I come out, she's whispering, "That's a good girl," in a way that makes me start to weep all over again.

"Tiam," I whimper. "Tiam."

"Shh," she says, lathering up my hair. "Let's get you all clean, and then you can go to see him."

I choke on some soap. "See him?"

"He only wants to see you." She makes a "tsk" noise with her tongue. "Which seems odd to me considering he is betrothed to the princess."

"You mean, he's alive?"

"Yes. For now. He's in the room across the way," she answers. "The medics have been wanting to treat him, but he says no. He wants only you. Did nobody tell you this?"

I shake my head and dunk myself under the water again, then jump to my feet, hastily swab off and throw on the new garment that Burbur has hung at the door. My body is still wet, so it clings to me, but I barely notice. I wring it out, rake my hand through my hair and quickly cross the hallway. Before I get there, I can already hear the moaning. Why, if he's in that much pain, does he want to see *me?*

I creep into the room. His face is strangely serene, his eyes closed. In the torchlight, it appears as if he's just catching the last few moments of his evening sleep. There is a blanket over him, and underneath, his chest rises and falls in spasms with every breath. But there is something odd there, something where that hideous wound had been earlier. Whatever it is, it's tenting the blanket up over his body.

Suddenly he moans again, making me jump. Arching his back, he exhales, his breath coming out in spurts, face twisting with pain. I move closer, calculating every footfall on the floor so as not to make a noise that will wake him. When my thighs are pressing against the side of the bed, I slowly reach down to lift the blanket.

Lightning fast, his hand whips out from under the blanket and grabs my wrist. His eyes dart open. I stifle the yelp in my mouth as his face softens. "Coe," he breathes, his voice weak and gravelly. "It's only you."

When I'd heard he only wanted to see me, some small, pathetic hope ignited in me, but *it's only you* makes me wonder if he's disappointed. Of course he is. Burbur is wrong. He wanted Star, not me.

"Yes, it's me. How are you? Do you need anything?" I ask, coming closer. His eyes are unfocused, and they seem to be staring at the space below my shoulders. I look down and notice that in my haste to dress, the white tunic is sticking perfectly to the curves of my body. The dark outlines of my nipples are visible. I wrap my arms over my breasts and blush as I sit beside him.

He quickly looks away, focusing on the wall ahead of him. "Coe, I'm sorry. I should have told you about Star." His voice is only a whisper.

I shake my head. I think about him, standing on the balcony a tide ago, perfect and healthy and ready to rule. I didn't bow to him. And now look at him. "I'm the one who should be sorry."

"I need…" he whispers, grabbing for my hand. "I need you to keep them away from me. The medics."

"What? Tiam, the medics will help you," I say. "That's what they're for."

He shakes his head. "You don't understand. Everyone wants me dead."

"The king will protect you. He will make sure that—"

"The king couldn't even protect himself. I made a mistake. I mean, who was I kidding, thinking I could just…" He labors to swallow. "I thought that people were rebelling against the king because they wanted someone else. Someone who understood them. But they don't."

"They want Finn. I—"

"No. They don't want a ruler. They don't want *anyone*." He motions me closer. "I don't think I'm going to live through this, so I want you to know. My plan was to get us, all of us, out of here…."

Get us out? He's delirious, babbling nonsensical things. I shiver. "Tiam, you're hurt. You've just had a bad fishing accident, and you're not thinking straight. Right? It was just an accident. You need someone to care for you."

"No. I just wish I could have made a difference. For you. For Star. For everyone. That's what I wanted." He pulls back the blanket, and I gasp. Under his shoulder is a terrible wound, black with blood, and in the center, poking just above the surface of his skin, is a pale bluish spike. What I'd thought was his bone earlier is actually the jagged edge of a scribbler's nose. "Look what I got for my sixteenth Hard Season."

It's Tiam's first day of manhood. I can't believe I hadn't realized it before. These things are never celebrated here, but it's so sad to see him like this on his first day as an adult that I immediately begin to cry.

"They want to tear down the castle and use it to make the

platform higher." He sighs. "I thought… I knew some people were… But…" His body begins to convulse as he is racked with a fit of coughs. I look for a glass of water, but there is nothing in the room besides the small bed. He catches his breath. "And if they do that, if they destroy the castle, all hope of us surviving will be gone. I tried to tell them. I need time. I need to figure out what it all means. And when I do, I can…"

I swallow. "It wasn't an accident, was it? You fought with them? With Finn?" When he doesn't answer, I say, "Tiam, why? Why are you so desperate to be king? If you had just let them—"

"I *can't* let them," he says, his eyes blazing. "Coe, that's why you need to do it now. Don't make the mistake I made. Don't trust them. If I'm not here, you need to talk to Star."

"Stop, Tiam. You're going to be fine."

He shushes me with a finger. "I can't trust anyone. Even the medics." He coughs again. "You need to go with Star. And don't let them know. They'll kill you for it."

"For what?" I whisper in horror. He's out of his mind, talking crazy. Does he really think I'd go with Star, that she'd *get us out?* Out where? There's nowhere for us to go! Seeing Tiam reduced to a blithering lunatic, like Xilia or Mutter, it might as well be the end of the world.

Suddenly, it dawns on me, something my father had told me. This is the end. Before civilization, before people made tribes and tribes evolved into larger communities, it was every man against each other. We built and built and became more sophisticated, using the resources we had. And then when we began to lose those resources, we started to slide down the slope we'd climbed. Now we're almost at rock bottom, exactly where we were when we began. Every man for himself. My dad taught me that. It was the reason he cared, the reason he tried to help people. Because when that's the case, when everyone is fighting for that last bit of space in the formation… That's it. It's over.

"Look," he whispers, "don't let the medics near me."

"No, of course I won't," I say. There is a shuffling in the hallway, then more footfalls. Far down the darkened hallway, Burbur is shouting for Gathering. Formation is soon. Formation! "Can you move? Can I help you to formation?"

He shakes his head. "I can't."

A sickly feeling falls over me. Tiam is the last person I ever thought would give up. I always imagined him fighting long after every other person on the island succumbed. He can't be giving up this easily. "Listen to me. You are going to live through this. The Tiam I know wouldn't let a little pain stop him."

He swallows again. "Pain's not that bad. It's…just…" He lifts his other arm. For the first time I notice a thick, rusting shackle around his wrist.

"Someone chained you to the bed?" I whisper in disbelief, every part of my body tightening.

He grins a little nervously. "Yeah, so, I could use a little help. Do you think you could find something to…"

The grin warms me, but at the same time it's a weight pressing against my chest. He's still the old Tiam, still willing to fight. But he can't do this without me.

Without another word, I walk out into the hallway, unsure

as to what I'm looking for. More people shuffle by, making
their way to the formation, but I scan the walls, then hurry
into my room. The piece of jagged coral scrapes my palm as
I hastily grab it, but I toss it down. It's no match for a metal
chain. Nothing on the dresser is right for the job.

I rush into the hallway and check the tubs that have been
filled for Gathering. Nothing but shell trinkets and towels.
Burbur is coming through, emptying them. She says, "You'd
better get up to formation."

"I can't leave Tiam. He's chained to the bed. Do you have
a key? Or something I can use to break it?"

She quickly finishes loading items to her cart and mutters, "If he's chained there, someone must have wanted him
to stay there."

"But he'll die."

She doesn't answer. Instead she continues to wheel the cart
down the corridor, and I hear it squeaking long after she is out
of view. Glancing at the wall, I notice that several of the stones
are crumbling. Using my finger, I pry at the edges of one,
trying to loosen it from the wall. I spend what seems like forever digging at the mortar, until my fingernails are bleeding
and sore, and still the stone stays put. It doesn't even wiggle.

Aborting that plan, I look up and down the corridor, finding nothing else of use. What I need is something heavy and
metal, like a hammer. There is only one hammer I know of,
but the builders kept a close eye on it, and I'd heard it had
been lost several seasons ago. I'd used it only once, to repair
the door to the craphouse.

That's when it occurs to me. My shovel!

I hurry back to my room, looking for my sack, and when I reach it, I remember that I surrendered the shovel when I gave up my job as Craphouse Keeper.

"I'm going out to formation for something," I call to Tiam. "I promise I will be back."

He mumbles something, and though I can't hear, I know what he is saying. *I'll handle it. Don't worry about me.* As if that's even possible. I propel myself down the now-deserted hallway and toward the grand staircase, then plunge down the stairs two at a time, only taking notice of the bloodstain—mine? Tiam's?—on the marble floor by the entrance when I see what is creeping toward it.

Black water, swirling with foam. A wave crashes, somewhere very near, almost as if it's on the other side of the wall. The tide is coming in. Soon, very soon, much of the castle will be underwater.

I push open the door, and a wave trickles up to meet me. Out of the castle's torchlight, I can barely see anything. In the dark skies above, seagulls circle overhead, squawking in warning. Once my eyes adjust to the moonlight, I slosh through the wet sand and ankle-deep water, willing myself to go faster as I cross to the area where the water has not yet come. I race up the shore, toward the craphouse, but the second I throw the door open, I curse myself for my stupidity.

The shovel needs to be taken into formation during every high tide. Otherwise, it would have been lost ages ago.

Slamming the door behind me, I race across the dry sand, my lungs burning in the heat. As I scale the platform, the scavengers begin to whisper when they take notice of me.

Soon the fishermen are talking as I push my way through the mass of bodies. Then the palace servants. Eventually the entire formation is abuzz. "Cutting it a little close, aren't we?" someone, I think Ana, says to me.

Ignoring her, I stalk over to Fern, scanning the space around her feet. "Oh, Coe! I was so worried!" she exclaims.

"Fern. I need the shovel, quick!" I demand, wrenching the bag from her hands.

She begins to chew on her fingernail. "Oh. The shovel?"

"Yes, where is it?" I ask, pulling open the tie on her sack. But I can already feel from the outside that there is nothing in there that even remotely resembles a shovel. "No time for games, Fern. Where is it?"

She is wringing her hands. "I—" She leans forward and whispers, "Please don't tell Ana."

"What?" I demand.

"I accidentally dropped it into the hole. In the craphouse," she admits, a small sheepish look on her face. "Please, don't tell!"

I don't have time to answer. I shove through rows of people, the way I came, fielding all sorts of curious looks. The sun is beginning to lighten the horizon as I come to the edge of the platform. Mutter gives me an oily smile and says, "Looks like we'll have another free space in the formation. They're dropping like flies, fellas!"

A few of the other fishermen laugh. Finn grabs my hand. "What are you doing?" he whispers to me when he notices where I'm headed. "You can't leave!"

"I have to," I say, snatching my hand away.

He makes a move to grab for me, but I'm already scrambling down the ladder as quickly as I can. I skip the last five rungs, springing toward the craphouse faster than I've ever moved. I hear some of the people of the formation cackle as I rush away, louder than the waves crashing only inches from the castle doors. They'd all be happy to see me die, to be one of the many who succumbs for stupid reasons. I pull open the rusted latch of the craphouse door and focus on the task at hand.

I quickly reach behind the seat and pull out the line and hook I've tucked there. I've been Craphouse Keeper for over a thousand tides, and as adept as I was at the job, having only one hand meant that I'd often lose my grip on the shovel. After the fifth or so time, I'd snagged a fishing line and hook from my father and made my own device to retrieve it. I'm a horrible fisherman, but I am pretty good at retrieving shovels from crap. This time, though, it's so dark, with not enough morning sunlight streaming through the cracks in the shed to be useful to me. Squinting, I throw down the line and bob it up and down in the dark, gooey surface, until the hook plunks against something hard and metal. The sweat leaks into my eyes as I try to loop the hook around the handle… once…twice…three times. Usually the third time is a charm, but the pressure is dizzying. *Don't panic, Coe. Don't… Yes!*

With a yank I catch the handle of the shovel and pull it up into my hand. It's coated in scum and slides through my fingers, but I fasten my hand tight around it and turn toward the door. Then I step backward, surprised.

Finn is standing in the doorway, his form taking up every

inch of the free space there. "What are you trying to do?" he asks.

"Go back to formation," I tell him firmly, moving forward, hoping he'll clear a space for me to pass through.

He doesn't. "Look at you," he says, studying my blood-spattered tunic. "Are you hurt? Let me help you."

I shake my head. "Please," I whisper, trying to push past him.

His eyes narrow. "This is for Tiam, isn't it? What did I tell you about siding with him? The others won't like it."

"I'm not on anyone's side," I snap, unable to meet his eyes as a wave crashes through the doorway, pouring into the hole in the ground. "It's like you said, Finn. The end of civilization has come, and we're at each other's throats. But at least *I* haven't lost the ability to care about my fellow man."

"He's just like Wallow, Coe. He's been in Wallow's pocket for too many tides. He came to the beach last night trying to convince everyone that if he was king, he'd save us all. But we can't afford to believe him or Wallow anymore. They'd let us all die. We have to say 'no more.' Think of what your father would say."

I shake my head. "My father would not let a person die like that."

"Coe, listen. You can't help him." He puts his hands solidly on my shoulders. "He's as good as dead."

I look over his shoulder and realize that curiously, his scribbler-nose spear isn't fastened to his back. He must notice my suspicion because he immediately drops his gaze from mine. "It was you who did it?"

He doesn't answer. "Don't be stupid, Coe. I want to… just…" He moves forward suddenly, closing the space between us, and his breath is hot and urgent on my face when he says, "Please, Coe, understand. It needed to happen. To preserve the peace."

"My father never would have let you do that!" I shout, and this time I'm more sure of it than ever. I've never been this close to a man before, even when we're in formation, and his hot skin pressing against mine burns like a torch. He tightens his grip on me, pushing me to the ground, and when we tumble to the wet sand, his full weight bears on me, crushing my chest. Another wave comes through and suddenly we're both choking and gasping underwater. "Stop!" I shout with my last bit of breath, suddenly feeling the handle of the shovel in my hand. I raise it and smash it down over him, striking him in the ear and shoulder. His eyes immediately flash wide, and fear rips through me.

"You stupid Bait!" he whimpers, falling to his knees as his hands reach up to the side of his head. In the darkness I see the black blood coursing over his bare shoulder. I scream as he reaches for me, then squeeze around him and stumble into the bright sunlight. "I tried to help you!" he rages, and by now several people in the formation are jumping and craning their necks, staring at the crazy girl with a death wish with morbid fascination. I'm outside, in the cool air, and yet I can't breathe. As I race down toward the ocean, where the door to the castle once stood, my heart rattles in my chest. From here I can see it is almost completely submerged; a wave pummels against the facade, covering the WI OW letters above the door.

I gulp air as if these are my last breaths. Maybe they are. I can't swim more than a few strokes. But I can't think about that. I will learn. Trial by fire. Though I have no plan of attack, I don't slow until I reach the edge of the water, and only then it's just a second's hesitation. There is no choice. I have to do it, even if I drown, even if the scribblers get me. I already know that if I don't, for the rest of my life I'll wish I was dead. I dive in, headfirst, and paddle against the fierce current toward the door.

Immediately the reason why nobody goes in the ocean anymore hits me full force. It's like being in a dream where the one thing you want is just out of reach. Every stroke I take toward the door seems to pull me in the opposite direction. The door is there, its gilded hardware glowing eerily in the murky blackness. Fingers of seaweed caress it, but no matter how hard I push myself, it's impossible. Stupid, stupid lame hand. Finally, I rise toward the surface, take one breath, and as a wave smashes me against the side of the palace, I hear it, very near. Hissing.

My heart stops, even though my body keeps moving. Diving underwater, I use the shovel to edge open the door and slip inside. I swim up ten or fifteen steps before I reach the surface. *Thank goodness. Thank goodness he's not already underwater,* I think as I rush down the hall to his room. When I get there, he's now sitting straight in bed, intently watching rivulets of water trickling along the floor. A surprised relief dawns on his face when I hold out the shovel, as if he never expected to see me again.

He clears the sheet from his wrist. I lift the shovel over my head with my good hand, but the salt is still stinging my eyes, so that I see double, and I'm so exhausted from the fight with Finn and the swim I can't stand straight. "I'll just—"

He gives me a nervous smile and holds out a hand. "Please. Allow me." I hand him the shovel. With a grunt he brings the shovel down twice, and a link breaks loose. Massaging his wrist, he swings his legs over the edge of the bed, and I help stand him up.

In the hallway, his face fills with the same dread I'm feeling. The water is inching up over the top stair, readying to meet us down the hallway. "There were scribblers," I say.

"We can't go that way," he says. We turn toward the other end of the hallway. "We have to go to the tower."

As we limp together toward the winding entrance, I think about how fragile the tower is. "But what about our weight? We'll make the tower too heavy."

"It's our only chance. Besides, the water level doesn't reach the top of the tower. We won't go all the way up. We'll stay outside the door. They'll never know we're there," he huffs as we climb.

Maybe it's just my imagination, maybe I'm so dizzy from all the excitement, but I could swear the tower begins to shift as we take the stairs two at a time. I try to tread gently, but it doesn't help. I look at Tiam, but his eyes are intent on the steps and his face is twisted in pain; he's hunched over slightly, grasping his side. The swaying seems to stop a bit once we've made our way about three-quarters up the tower, where the waterline is etched on the wall. Tiam sinks down on the step above it, his breath raspy and uneven.

"We'll be safe here," I say, shivering in the damp sea air, trying to convince myself.

I hear the wind whistle outside. It's a windy day. And standing here, still, it's very obvious. The tower *is* moving. Swallowing the bile gurgling in the back of my throat, I push against the side of the wall to stop myself from being sick.

"That's...interesting," he says, studying the walls as if he's looking for ghosts as the tower sways again.

"Let's just hope no one up there notices," I say, pointing at the ceiling.

He tries to adjust himself on the step but grimaces. What he needs is rest and not to be moved for days and weeks. This must be excruciating for him. "I can't believe you did that, Coe. I thought I was done for."

I shrug. "Why wouldn't I? You know you would have done it for me."

He doesn't say anything for a long time. The moment he opens his mouth to speak, a door above us swings open. I bite my tongue as the shadow of the princess appears on the step. *She will understand,* I think. *Tiam is soon to be her husband. She will let us stay.*

But all those hopes disappear when I see the terror in her eyes. "What are you two doing here?" she shrieks. "Get!"

I say, "The water's too high. Tiam is hurt. We can't...."

She bites her lip, contemplating for a moment until a loud gust of wind slams against the outside of the tower, echoing through the narrow staircase. The tower lurches with it. "But the tower is swaying!" She shoos us vigorously with her hands. Bewildered, we just stand and stare at her. Surely she's not serious. "You'll kill us all! Please, go! Find somewhere else!"

"But—" I start.

"Guard!" she shouts into her room. She disappears, and a few moments later, one of the guards approaches us with his spear.

He jabs it at Tiam's chin. "Move out to formation."

Formation? "But the water—"

Tiam knows better than to argue. He takes my hand and pulls me quickly down the stairs. Down to our doom. There is nowhere to go.

"But what do we do?" I whisper, my voice hoarse. "There's no way out there. And the scribblers…"

When we arrive at the base of the tower staircase and splash into ankle-deep water, his expression is bleak. He's surveying the walls, the markings above the doors, biting his lip, as if waiting for the elusive answer to appear.

He has no answer.

"I can't believe she did that to us!" I shout as the water swells over my shins. There is no escape. We're going to die.

"It's not her fault. The tower is swaying. And she doesn't know," he says calmly. "She has no idea how bad it is down here."

I bite my tongue, feeling stupid. How can he defend her like that? "You have to talk to her. You need to get her to come to her senses. Otherwise we're—"

"Do you know what these markings on the walls mean?" he asks suddenly. "You do, don't you?"

I stop. We're not playing treasure hunt now. Annoyed, I say, "Yes. But we don't…"

"Tell me."

I sigh. "Some are just markings that tell what the room is for. Like outside the room where they serve the food, it says DINING. Others, I can't understand." I think back to the letters on the engraved panel across from my bathtub. "They might be…"

And then it hits me. The panel beside my bathtub. The letters.

I grab his wrist. "Come with me."

We race down the hallway, just as the tide rises high enough for the ocean to begin pouring through every window on the east side of the second floor. It smashes against the inside walls, swirling with foam. Waves boom around us, and black water immediately swirls up to our thighs…our waists…

I pull Tiam into my quarters and grab the shovel from him. *Oh, please, let me be right about this,* I repeat to myself as I begin to pry away at the engraved panel on the wall. The water surges up to my chest. In another few breaths it will rise over our heads, and it will be too late. All I am really doing is making dents in the metal and scratches in the stone wall. Without asking questions, Tiam scuttles beside me, pulls the shovel from my hand and starts to work. The shovel makes a clanging noise, and with a final creak he bends the metal panel back. Stale air puffs forward. There is a dark hole there, maybe two of my feet wide, leading down into the unknown.

We don't have time to celebrate. Celebration would be premature, anyway. I have no idea where we're going, or if this will work. Maybe this is just another way to die. "Go, go!" Tiam urges behind me as I climb to the edge of the tub and take a deep breath. I pray it's not my last as I stuff my bag into the chute and dive headfirst into the narrow passage.

Nine

In Our Dry Cellar

I pass in and out of consciousness in the dark, as if I'm in some horrible nightmare. It seems like an eternity later when I wake to a scrape-scrape-scraping sound very nearby. I'm in complete blackness, lying in something wet and sticky that I would think was blood if it weren't bone-chillingly cold. I shiver as a spark flies in front of my face, and as I'm blinking twice to convince myself it was just my imagination, it happens again. Suddenly there is fire, burning bright above me, and beyond that, Tiam's face glowing orange.

"Can you find something to light?" he asks.

I look around and luckily, the first thing I see in the small pool of light is something that looks like a torch, attached to the wall. I've seen these in my fairy-tale book—it's called a candle. I lift it out of its metal bracket and bring it down. He drops the small piece of paper in his hands onto the end of it, instantly casting the enormous room in light. We both look around in stunned silence. The room seems to stretch on into the darkness, and the part of it I can see is about as large as our sleeping compartment. It's piled to the ceiling with giant boxes. The walls are made of crumbling blocks, and there are what look like thick black pipes, staged at perfect intervals, attached to them, stretching from the ceiling to a metal spigot. "What is this place?" Tiam asks. "Is this the royal stores?"

I nod. Well, that is what it was most recently. This is the place that meant so much to the people who came before us. This is the place that held mountains and mountains of food, for those who'd come to survive the floods. But that was a long time ago. The rumor now is that the rooms are empty of useful things, that everything that remains no longer has a purpose in our world.

"How did you know that passage was there?" He's grimacing, and it's only then I realize he's pressing his back against the wall. There's a metal grate there, bulging, and I can hear the sound of something scraping against it.

"Is that… Is that where we came through?"

"Yeah. And there were scribblers and an ocean of water ready to follow us down here. It's a good thing we got down here before the ocean rose any higher, or I'd never have been able to get the grate back into place."

"Oh!" I run over to him and crouch next to him, pressing my back against it. This is clearly going nowhere fast. Flustered, my words tumble out. "I really wasn't thinking much when I… I mean, I couldn't see any other way."

"Calm, Coe," he whispers. "It was a good idea. You saved our lives. How did you know this passage was here?"

"Oh. In here." I hook my bag with my foot and draw it

to me, then fumble around in it and pull out the damp hard-bound book. To Tiam's questioning look, I say, "It's a book. A diary, actually."

"What is a diary?"

"People used to use them to tell the stories of their own lives. Centuries of Kettlefishes have written in it. My father gave it to me. He taught me how to read with it."

He inspects it, amazed. "And it told you there was a hole in the wall up there?"

"Well. Sort of." I open the book to a page. I have a good deal of it memorized, though much of it doesn't make sense to me. I read aloud: *"Yesterday I threw my dirty clothes down a laundry chute to the basement and they were delivered up to me three hours later, clean and folded, but this morning someone came to seal up the chute."*

"You did what?" He's utterly bewildered.

"Not *me*. She did."

"Who is she?"

"The person who wrote this. Kimmie. One of my ancestors." I show him the words, but he just shrugs, as it's nothing but nonsense to him. "Do you want me to start from the beginning?"

The sound of scraping on the grate behind us seems to intensify, and a muffled hiss follows. The scribblers sound angry. "It's not like we have anywhere else to go," he says.

So I read him this entry:

June 20, 2046
This is the diary of Kimmie K. I am 13 and live in Otter Lake, Pennsylvania, for now. My mother says the floods are

due to reach us soon and that we must go to a hotel far in the mountains to wait it out. She says it will be an adventure, and I am very excited. After dad died and mom had to sell our car, I thought we were kaput, but I think our luck is changing because she, my sister Fee and I were one of only three hundred families chosen. My mom says that over a million people put their names in. She said even a blind squirrel finds a nut once in a while! I'll write more when I get to the hotel! XO

I look up for a second, and he's gazing at me with confusion. "You mean, that thing is from way back when the floods started?"

"Yes. I guess. I know a lot of it makes no sense, but—"

"You've had it all this time? How come you never read it to me?"

I just stare at him, mouth open. Surely he must know I would have spent tide upon tide reading to him, anytime he wished, if I had thought he'd been this interested. I motion to the book. "Can I continue?"

"Yeah," he says, so I keep reading:

June 30, 2046

We are here now, at the hotel. It's not the first hotel I've stayed in but it's probably the biggest and strangest. It's really creepy. Agnes Willow, the old lady who owns it, is what my mom calls a Doomsday Prepper. Her husband was a U.S. senator, but since he died, she's spent her entire fortune preparing for the end of the world. She wanted to make something that looked like a part of the mountain, so part of it is carved right

into it, and there are supposedly rooms upon rooms, with secret spy passages and cool things like that! The whole place is
surrounded by trees, so it's really dark inside. All the floors are
cold stone that echo when you walk on them, and most of the
walls are, too. It's like a fairy-tale castle. When I was growing
up, the newspapers used to say she was out of her mind. Now
they say she's genius.

I can't imagine this hotel, on this mountaintop, being even
partially underwater! But that is what they say might happen.
They don't think it will be for long, but I saw them bringing
in truckloads of supplies through the back entrance when I was
snooping yesterday. There are a lot of military vehicles, too, always coming up the mountain.

Mom says we will be completely safe up here, but today on
my walk outside I saw that they're building a giant tower! I've
heard Crazy Agnes built this place dozens of years ago, and
yet she still isn't finished—she keeps adding more and more to
it, new wings, more floors. But they're working really fast on
this tower. This morning it was just a hole in the corridor, but
now it's climbing up into the trees. It makes you wonder....

The room I share with mom and baby Fee is really small.
It's just a bed and a dresser and a TV that only gets local chan-
nels and a window. All times during the day and night I hear
this weird, loud rumbling noise, like the mountain is alive and
buzzing underneath me. It's hard to think that it might get
worse. Yesterday I threw my dirty clothes down a laundry chute
to the basement and they were delivered up to me three hours
later, clean and folded, but this morning someone came to seal
up the chute. My mom isn't even sure the electricity will hold

out, so she has been pocketing candles wherever she can and hiding them under her bed!

Mom is nervous. She doesn't say it, but I can tell from the way her hands shake all the time. I worry about poor baby Fee. She is so tiny and helpless. I have to take care of her if anything happens to mom. She is my little sister, and it is my job to protect her.

Other than that, there's a cute boy across the hall, and I think his name is Jack, but when he said hi to me I was too shy to even smile at him. I am such a dorkus!

I stop reading when I realize I'm blushing for this poor girl, or maybe because her shyness and awkwardness around boys show that she is so obviously one of my relations. I doubt she ever imagined a million tides ago that I would be reading her personal yearnings to another boy in the same palace where she had lived and died. I flip to another page and read:

August 1, 2046
The electricity flickered and went out again today, but this time it may be for good. At least until the flooding subsides, which may not be for several months! Or maybe even a year!

I keep wondering how long everything else will hold out. Right now we are in the middle of a heat wave. It's 110 degrees in the shade up here, and it's never been this hot. Mom says it has something to do with the floods. But in the winter, who knows how cold it will get. Will we have heat? Will we have enough food? It's hard to imagine we won't have all those things I've come to take for granted. Today I watched mom feed-

ing baby Fee her bottle and realized we are all so like her. Totally dependent upon others for food, shelter, everything. We are
not survivors. I wouldn't even know how to start a fire unless
someone gave me the flame. If I had to catch and cook my own
food, I'd starve. If I had to clothe myself, I'd be screwed because
I don't know how to sew. Without a 24-Hour Mini-Mart or
a mall, most everybody I know is screwed. But the irony of it
is, we created this. We went on to learn things that were "more
important," but we forgot the most important things of all. We
called it progress, but maybe while we were busy building machines that could make it so much easier to access information
like the average daily diet of the Northern Cuckoo, we were
also building our own coffins.

I know, I've been thinking about it way too much. But can
you tell I'm scared?

He doesn't say anything, so I turn the page and read some
more.

August 20, 2046
Today Jack and I went exploring outside, since he says it'll be
any day now when we can't even go out at all.

Jack showed me a giant steel door in the side of the mountain. He said that was where all the military vehicles went. He
said that he'd come here before, and there were dozens of guards
outside. But now, the door is closed, and the guards are gone.
He says that Washington, D.C., is gone, and he thinks that
the president of the United States took refuge in the mountain.

Washington, D.C., is gone. I can't believe those words, even *as I write them. They're just words. I didn't ask Jack because I didn't want to hear it, but I know what else that means. That most of the East Coast must be gone, too. Probably Otter Creek, too, my school, and my home. And all my neighbors… They were not as lucky as we were. I hope they got out in time. I hope they're safe. But I heard an old man say the casualties are too numerous to estimate, so I know the odds are not good.*

Jack and I walked down a little path through the thickest part of the woods and came to something huge and mountainous, like a giant anthill, a hundred feet high. Jack said that he'd heard people talking at lunch, and this rich old man who owns a concrete company was having truckloads and truckloads of the stuff delivered every day for a year. That was the rumbling noise I've been hearing. He's building his own mountain of concrete, a mountain on top of a mountain, and he plans to put his house at the very top.

I laughed and said he's crazy, but Jack just shrugged.

Then Jack told me we should take off our sandals and run barefoot through the grass, so I did, even though it felt pretty silly. He said I need to remember that feeling. He said he isn't sure that what they're saying about the floods receding is true. He says they may just be trying to keep panic from setting in, but that he wishes he was in the mountain, too. It really started to freak me out, and I guess it was obvious on my face because that was when he kissed me.…

I stop. I can't get my mouth to form the words anymore. Tiam nods, oblivious to the blood rushing to my face. "So we're in that place… The place she calls a hotel. And this was a…a laundry chute. And now we're in…the basement?"

"I guess."

"The platform… That was the mountain on top of the mountain. So maybe the sleeping compartment and the craphouse were just buildings near the hotel, at one point. So what happened to that girl? You know her whole life story?"

"Not really. She didn't write in it all that much," I lie, trembling as I think of her last entry.

"Read more."

"I don't really feel like it. It's kind of dark here, and…well, my eyes are tired."

"Fair enough," he says, and inwardly I breathe a sigh of relief. The fact was that she and Jack had had something that she called a "romance," like something right out of my fairy-tale book. All those thoughts about Tiam that I am too scared to even have, she'd had the same feelings about Jack and written about them in here. Back then, people had those feelings freely, and it was a wonderful thing. I almost feel that if I'd been alive when she'd been, we would have been so alike. And while I can think of few things more embarrassing than having to read those out loud to Tiam, the real reason I don't want to… The reason my eyes well up every time, and I have trouble breathing…is that eventually, she went mad, waiting for the water to recede. Her cheerful, bubbly handwriting gradually diminished into almost inhuman scratches. The last dated entry was when she was only seventeen, and it was just a jumble of letters that didn't make sense to me. The last entry, about a quarter of the way through the book, was undated:

WE ARE NEVER GETTING OUT OF HERE

I think she killed herself. The thought makes me shudder. People kill themselves all the time here, and I barely blink an eye, so I'm not sure why the thought of this girl ending her life makes me weak. Maybe because she was so hopeful, so filled with dreams of the future, dreams she shared with me almost as if she'd whispered them in my ear each night. She was so alive. So unlike us. The people of Tides are just hopeless, rotting skeletons, waiting for death. When I think of her, of how she once was, I almost think we deserve death. We've come this far, we might as well take the next small step.

After a moment of silence, Tiam finally speaks. "What is on your mind?" he asks.

I want to tell him about the girl in the book, about how it kills me that nobody on the island notices it but me because I have the written evidence and can see how far we've fallen. I want to tell him how scared it makes me to think that we don't have souls anymore, we don't have any of the good in us that makes living worthwhile. I want to tell him how I feel so alone, and ask him to hold me. But he'd look at me as if I have three heads if I did that. So instead I ask, "Do you think we can find a way out of here?"

"I'm not sure I *want* out of here," he says. "Do you realize that everyone on the island now thinks we're dead?"

"Is that supposed to be a happy thought?"

"Well, yeah. Since that's how they want me."

I shudder at the thought of my exchange in the craphouse with Finn. "I don't think I'm much better off."

"Well, then, I'm in good company." He laughs a little and

ends up coughing and grasping at his side. He looks down at his injury and grimaces. The rough black edge of the scribbler nose is protruding from below his collarbone. "Wait. What do you mean?"

"Finn," I say softly. "He was the one who hurt you, right? When I was getting the shovel, he tried to— I don't know what he was trying to do. But he frightened me. I hit him with the shovel."

His eyes flash to mine. "You did?"

"I didn't know what else to do!" I say, defensive, still feeling guilty. "I think I hurt him bad."

He smiles wanly. "Well, he probably had it coming." He is silent for a moment, staring at his wound. "What do you think a...a squirrel...is? You know...she said, 'even a blind squirrel finds a nut once in a while.'"

I shrug. "Maybe some kind of animal. I know nuts used to be food. It's in the book. One of the writers had a thing for pistachio nuts."

"Thought so. They used to talk so funny. And grass. What do you think that is?" When I shrug again, he starts to lean back, then, very offhandedly, but still loud enough to make my ears burn bright red, he says, "What is a kiss?"

"What?" I ask. It's the only word I can get out. But his face is serious. He's never read my fairy-tale book before. And he, like me, has never seen a kiss performed. Nobody kisses anymore, just like nobody hugs or shows any affection. That's what happens, I guess, in a world where everything is dead. "Oh," I say quickly, looking away so he won't see my eyes flickering. "I don't know," I say, quickly changing the subject. "What are all these crates, do you think?"

"I have no idea. The stores are supposed to be empty, of anything useful, at least. We should check it out."

The thought makes me squirm. "There are supposed to be ghosts and demons down here," I say, shivering. I don't want to turn around and end up face-to-face with any Dark Girl.

"Right. Ghosts," he says, doubtful. I should have known Tiam wouldn't be afraid of a little thing like that. He motions to the chute grate. "Think you can hold this on your own?"

"Probably not. What are you…"

"On the count of three, I'll pull away. Just for a second. One…two…and three. Good. You've got it. You okay?"

Before I realize what he has planned, he's already moved away from the wall. He gets behind a massive crate with the words C BATTERIES HEAVY DUTY on it, and grunting, begins to edge it over toward me. Finally he slides it beside me, and as I inch slowly away from the grate, he quickly inches it into place. I wait for the room to begin filling with water, but it never does.

Success.

"Okay, let's check it out," he says, and in the silence after that sentence, just before I agree with him, I swear I can hear a soft swishing sound coming from the crates that are half drenched in darkness. Tiam freezes, and his eyes widen and scan circles around the room. It's not my imagination.

He heard it, too. Whispering.

Ten

Those Who Have Crossed

Tiam straightens. "I don't think I want to know what that was," he mutters.

Ghosts. Demons. Instinctively, I move closer to him. "Is there someone else down here?"

He doesn't answer. Instead he holds the candle out ahead of us, sweeping it slowly in a half circle around him to light the dusty floor ahead of us. Nothing but piles of crates, neatly aligned, all perfectly untouched. I can read the words on some of them: PLASTIC DINNERWARE. PLASTIC TABLE-CLOTHS. TABLE SUGAR. But I can't say I know what any of those things are. He holds the light still, and immediately I see what is wrong. There's a large hole in the TABLE SUGAR box, as big as the head of my shovel, as if someone kicked it in. No, gnawed it away.

Something moves inside the box. Two tiny orbs of red glowing at us. Two devilish eyes. A demon! I swallow as it squeezes its head out of the crate. Its head is easily bigger than my own. It licks its paws—or are they claws?—and begins to make that same whispering noise, but this time it's wetter and gurgling, and that's when I see a row of jagged white teeth. It opens its mouth wider, baring them fully, then draws back on its hind feet, black hair on its back bristling, and leaps forward.

Within a second it is on Tiam, and he topples backward under the thing's weight. It's almost as long as Tiam, with a white, coiled tail that thrashes wildly in the air as it attacks. Tiam lets out a groan, and I hear the sickly sound of bones cracking as Tiam wraps his hands around the creature's neck. Tiam's arm muscles strain as he tries to push it off him. The candle falls to the ground and rolls out of reach, throwing fire in all directions before going out. In the darkness I can feel the thing's warm oily fur at my ankles, the whiplike tail thrashing my knees. Frantic, I bring the edge of my shovel down again and again on its back until my skin is coated in blood and chunks of mottled fur and my arm feels as if it's no longer attached to my body. The thing makes a grunting noise, and all is quiet.

Finally I exhale. "Tiam?" I ask in the darkness.

"Here," comes his voice, muffled. I hear some scratching on the floor and pray it's him and not that creature. After a moment I hear the scraping of the flint again. Thank goodness. I locate the candle and soon the light is back. Now there are two small round punctures under his collarbone, and blood is trickling down over his chest and pooling over the scribbler nose. He grimaces. "On second thought, I *don't* think I want to stay down here."

"Is anything broken?"

He tries to move his shoulder, which is slanted awkwardly. Then he groans and kicks the mass of fur at his feet. "Probably. What is this thing?"

"I don't know. Do you think there are any more of them?" I ask, shivering as I survey the area.

"Yeah. Definitely. So let's find a way out of here." He claps his hands together. "Here's the plan—we get out, find the princess and figure out what we're going to do from there."

Of course, he thinks of Star at a moment like this. Star, who is so alluring that men like Tiam are easily able to overlook the fact that *she almost got us killed*. I'm glad it's dark and he can't see the jealous scowl on my face. He motions for me to follow close behind him, and I do, feeling guilty as I watch him limp into the unknown like an old man. But I guess I don't feel guilty enough to offer to lead the way. That thing makes a scribbler look like Clam, my pet crab. My heart is beating so fast it might escape my chest.

The room just keeps going and going. The walls are lined with crates at least five high and ten deep, hundreds and hundreds of them. Most are covered with cobwebs and perfect, smooth layers of dust, so it's difficult to see what they contain. A few have giant gashes gnawed in them, and Tiam obviously sees the holes because he makes sure we don't tread near them. As we inch forward, I see dozens of tracks in the ground.... Big, clawlike prints. Not a single human footprint.

"It doesn't look like anybody—any human, at least—has been here in a long time," I whisper.

"Yeah, you're right," he answers without turning back to glance at me. "Look."

We come to an enormous wall, and directly ahead of us is a small metal door. An exit. I catch my breath as I'm exhaling in relief. What if it doesn't open? What if—

I grab Tiam's hand as he's placing it on the rusted handle. "Maybe nobody's been here in so long because it's flooded out there."

"What?"

I hold out my book. "Cass. She was baby Fee's great-granddaughter. Somehow she got possession of the book and started writing in it. It was her job to man the stores. Well, the East Stores. She said there were dozens of rooms. She even made a map of them in here, somewhere. But she said that there was a horrible accident, one of the doors had been left open, and there was a leak. Several passageways got flooded out. She said that several people drowned, and the other stores managers were never seen again."

He turns to me, his eyes fastened on the book. "Show me the map."

I shrug and flip to the correct page. I know it won't do any good. We have no idea what storeroom we're in. And I don't think it's complete. Several pages have been ripped from the center of the book. He studies it, asking me what different markings say here and there, and turning the open book in his hand. Then he closes the book and hands it to me with a sigh.

"We should still try this way," he says, putting his hand on the door again. He motions for me to stand back, and then slowly tries to turn the lever. He pulls and pushes with all his might, but nothing happens. He shakes his head. "It won't budge. I think it's rusted shut."

"Because it's flooded out there."

"Maybe. I think we need to go back the way we came."

I cringe at the suggestion. "But how can we?"

He doesn't answer me. His jaw tenses as he turns back to study the vast cave of a room. We slowly make our way back to the chute and he takes the shovel from me and lays it against the nearby wall.

"Go stand against that crate," he says, motioning to something that is quite far off, almost out of the light of the candle. "But stay in the light. Just in case."

"What are you going to do?" I ask, though I already know. I just can't believe he's going to do it.

Slowly, he inches the crate away. As he's pushing, he catches sight of my face. "Don't worry. The tide should have receded by now. There'll be some water, so...just stand back again."

He's leaving one thing out. The scribblers.

I hold my breath as the water pours through. It only reaches as high as my ankles before the puddle begins to stretch out across the room. Immediately the hissing echoes through the chamber. The water glistens in the firelight, and the black bodies writhe together, screeching. I count...four...seven of them, all jabbing their spear noses at whatever they can. They're royally pissed off. This time, though, we have the advantage. Tiam takes the shovel and uses the sharp edge to sever their heads, one at a time. He does it with a little grin. Revenge.

When the hissing quiets, we take turns peering up the narrow chute, toward the daylight, about twenty or thirty of my feet above. I have a feeling climbing up is going to be a lot more difficult than going down, but I don't want to stay in a room with those nasty creatures another moment. Then, even louder than if they were in the same room as us, I can hear voices, coming from above. The walls of the chute amplify the sound somehow.

"Told you, she's not here. Probably got washed out to sea." I'm almost positive the voice is Kirba's.

"She could be with the princess. After all, she's her new *lady*." That voice is Burbur.

"Oh, no. The princess would never allow her up there during high tide. Never," Kirba answers. "Stupid girl."

"Stupid *girls,* the both of them," Burbur agrees.

"They think I'm dead," I whisper, but there is only silence in return. I turn to Tiam, and that's when I see him staring down at the scribbler nose protruding from his collarbone, contemplating it.

"Are we going up?" I ask.

"Um. Yeah." He ducks and pokes his head up the chute. When he returns, for the first time, all color is gone from his face. "Um. No."

"What?"

He clears his throat. "I'm so much bigger than you. And I think it will get caught in the chute."

"Don't be stupid. It didn't catch on the way down."

"That was a miracle. Please. Just…do it real quick."

"What?"

"Snap the end off."

"Me? Why me?" My voice is an octave higher. I start to put a hand on it, then recoil. The scribbler nose is half an inch thick; it's not as if it'd snap like a fish bone. It'll take work. When I imagine attempting it, the only outcome I can foresee is Tiam bleeding to death in my arms. Because of me. No way. I'd rather be stabbed with a scribbler nose myself. "No. I'll do something wrong. Do it yourself."

He frowns and bends his arm so that it's touching his shoulder. He tries to wrap his fingers around it, but I see the problem. He can just get his fingers around the tip but can't fully turn his wrist to snap it off. "Can't really grab it with this arm," he says, and then shakes his other arm limply at his side. "And this arm is broken, I think. So?"

"Okay." I swallow once, twice. My throat hurts. I put my fingers on the edge of the scribbler nose. It's sticky with blood. I clench my teeth, count to three and try to snap it between my fingers, but it's too rigid. It goes nowhere. He holds his breath, features tight. Each time I try again, his face gets more and more contorted until finally he opens his mouth in a silent scream, then bites down on his hand.

When he removes his hand and whimpers, I say, "Told you I'd do something wrong."

He gives up and wraps a piece of fabric around his chest as a bandage. "No. You did it right. But it's not working."

"Oh, really?" I grumble. "From the look on your face, I thought it was going perfectly. What do we do? Do you think you can make it up?"

"I don't know. I'll try." He takes a deep breath. Then another. "In a little bit."

More time passes. I watch him in silence. It looks as if he's planning for something, for the battle of his life. His breaths start to come quick and even. He clenches and releases his fists. There's a new coat of sweat on his forehead, and his eyes are focused very intently on some imaginary spot in the darkness. After waiting as long as I can stand, I can't keep myself still anymore. I scramble to the chute and poke my head inside. There's no way of knowing how long it will take us to shimmy our way up the narrow passage, especially considering that neither of us have use of both of our arms. We might not make it up at all before the next tide comes, and then what? Finally, I say, "What are we waiting for?"

He swallows. "I...I can't do it. I can't go up there." He looks away from me, and there's something new on his face. Shame. "I get kind of...sick in closed spaces."

"Sick?"

"Dizzy. Like the walls are closing in on me."

"What? Why?" I say, clearly shocked. This is Tiam we're talking about. Tiam, the bravest person I know. Tiam, who laughs in the face of scribblers and ghosts and taunts the vicious ocean.

"Long story. And with this thing in my shoulder..." He looks at it disgustedly, his voice weakening until he clears his throat. "So just go on up without me. I'll be fine."

It may be a long story, but it's a story I'd give anything to hear. What on this earth could have possibly made him afraid of closed spaces? I think back to him sleeping under the stars every night, instead of in the cramped compartment, with its wall-to-wall people. I'd always thought it was because he loved the outdoors. "Don't be stupid. You can't stay here forever. I'm not leaving you."

"I'm *not* going up that way." It seems he's as sure of that as he is that the sky is blue.

"But you went down—"

"Not the same thing. Just go."

"Okay, okay. I'll come back for you."

"Don't worry about me. Just get to the princess. Tell her there isn't much time. She'll know what to do."

I just stare at him. Clearly he mistook all of her beauty for brains, because I don't think there's anyone in the world who knows *less*. She's blissfully ignorant to most everything the rest of the world has to deal with. Finally, I nod and say, "Just… take the shovel. In case you meet any more of those things."

He isn't looking at me, so I just lay it by his side. It's totally ludicrous. He'll die down here, just because of this fear. But I have my own fears, so how can I argue? As I slide my head and rib cage into the chute, then push with my legs off the ground so that I'm standing erect inside it, I start to think he's not really all that stupid. I'm tiny, but this could make anyone sick. The slick metal sides of the chute are only two inches at the most away from my body on all sides. It would be an even tighter fit for Tiam. I begin to wonder how we ever made it down here in the first place.

I look up. Only twenty feet. Thirty at the most. I can do this.

I press my arms and feet against the sides of the chute and push my way up, making it mere inches. But my toes can no longer touch the bottom of the chute, so I know I am making progress. I wiggle up some more, and then some more, until I'm certain I must be almost there. Maybe it's the sweat seeping into my eyes, but when I look up, the exit seems to have crawled farther away.

I can do this, I chant to myself, wiggling my arms, then my hips, then my knees, feeling like a butterfly emerging from a never-ending cocoon. Then I think of Tiam sitting there alone, Tiam the brave, who is afraid of *this,* and I slide back down, erasing almost all my progress before I regain my grip on the sides. Maybe I *can't* do this. Cursing, I start again. This time, I quiet my doubts by thinking of a plan. A plan to save Tiam. After all, I put him down there, so it's up to me to get him out. I can figure out the map. Maybe I can check with Burbur, snoop around the stores, see if there's another exit. That's the least I can do. I have to.

Before long, I escape, gasping, into the cool sea air that's wafting into my room. It's heavenly. I lie there for a moment, staring at the ceiling and breathing all the air my lungs can hold, until I hear voices in the corridor. Quickly, I hurry to the wall and bend the metal panel back into place.

"Oh, dear!" a voice gasps in the hallway. Something shatters. Standing outside my room is Burbur, surrounded by the pieces of some pink shell decorations that used to adorn my room, looking as if she's seen a ghost.

I stumble over to my mat and collapse on it, panting, without a word to her.

"Oh, my goodness, I thought the Dark Girl was back," she says, fanning her face. "Everyone thinks you're dead."

Lying there, the full extent of my exhaustion hits. Maybe I am dead. "I was…" I can't very well tell her I was in the stores. That's her domain, one she'd protect to the death. "I was with the princess."

I expect that she'll begin sweeping about the room, laying the little trinkets in their correct places. I expect the scent of lavender to fill the air, and another gauzy white garment to be hanging in the doorway. Instead, when I open my eyes, I realize the room is quite bare. It's past the tide; she should be arranging everything by now. "Burbur!" I call with all the energy I can muster.

She appears in the doorway, and I realize she is holding her own bag. It looks larger than I've ever remembered her carrying into formation, almost too heavy to carry. She's blushing. "Yes?"

"Are you…" But I know what she is doing. Goodness knows what things I'd find in her bag, if I dared wrestle it away from her. "Do you no longer work in service of the king?"

She coughs. "Excuse me?"

"Where are my things? The things you store and bring back when the tide goes out?"

She swallows. There is sweat on her forehead. She shakes her head. "You've… You don't seem to understand, do you?"

"Understand what?" I study her for a long time. She can't seem to keep herself from fidgeting from one foot to the other. She clutches her bag to her chest and keeps surveying the hallway behind her. Something is clearly amiss.

"The king is dying. Tiam is dead. A new ruler will assume the throne." She gives me a condescending look. "You can't expect everything to stay the same once that happens."

"Of course not. But…the watertight compartments under the castle are still watertight, yes?"

She straightens. "Yes."

"Can I visit them with you?"

"Of course not," she answers with finality. "That is not allowed."

"By order of the king? The king who is dying?" I ask, which makes the color drain from her face.

Quickly, she says, "You'll not ask questions about those compartments, if you know what's good for you. I must leave." She hefts that large bag over her shoulder and scurries away. When the sound of her footsteps disappears down the hallway, I walk over to the panel, scrape up a corner and peel it back only an inch or so from the wall. I put my mouth up to the opening and call down, in a voice just above a whisper, "I made it. I'm going to find a way for you to get out."

A voice floats up. "No. Find the princess. She will know what to do."

"But—"

"Coe. And as far as everyone knows, I'm dead. Okay? And you were in the tower tending to the princess. The last thing we need is people getting suspicious of you because you weren't in formation. Do you understand?"

"Right," I huff. I bend the metal grate back into position so that it is flush against the wall, grab my pack and throw it on my back, then head down the stairs. If he wants to find his bride, he can come up and do that himself. But right now, some things are more important. Right now, even if he has too much pride to ask me, I'm going to find a way to save *him*.

Eleven

The Idea and the Reality

It occurs to me on the last step of the staircase that there are dozens of doors and corridors on the first floor, and I have very little idea which one leads to the lower level of the castle. Despite the fact that there are fewer than five hundred people on the island, Burbur is constantly flitting from room to room, so I doubt I could slip away unseen, even if I did know where to go. It's already hopeless, and I haven't even gotten to the maze of rooms in the basement. As I'm trying to decide which way to turn, a bell begins ringing. I almost don't hear it, I'm too wrapped up in saving Tiam. But then it gets more urgent, and I realize it's a pattern of three short rings, over and over and over again. My signal. From the princess.

Groaning, I run back up the stairs and ring my response. She rings again, telling me to proceed. I brace myself for her anger. I know I've neglected my duties. By the time I make it up to the landing, I can already hear her voice. It's not directed at me. She's speaking to her guards. "If he is, have someone retrieve the body. They can at least do that, for my beloved."

When I come around, she's curled up in a ball at the top of the steps. She turns to me. "They're saying he's dead. Is it true?"

For a moment I think she must be talking about her father, but then I remember Tiam. I don't answer; after all, she refused to let us into the tower. If he were dead, it would be all her doing. Instead, I help her to her bed and pull the covers over her.

"How am I supposed to go on without him?" she sobs. "I'll never find my way alone."

It all sounds so melodramatic, considering she's the one who nearly killed him. "He would have been alive, had you let us into the tower."

She shakes her head miserably. "We *all* would have been dead. The tower is far too unstable. But I suppose that's not important anymore. It's only a matter of time before the commoners destroy the tower and everything in it." She begins to sob again, her body convulsing. "I don't want to die."

"Then you need to help me, Princess."

She buries her face in a pillow. "Why? I am lucky to still have my guards, as they are the only things keeping me alive. None of the servants come anymore when we ring the bell. Not even you. I knew I shouldn't have trusted you. I suppose you're in league with them. If I go with you, you'll slit my throat."

"I am here to *help* you," I argue with her. "I promised Tiam

I would help you, and I don't break promises. You have to trust me, or you *will* die."

She turns and props herself up on her arm, studying my face. "And what will you have me do?"

"First, you can't trust anyone. You're right about that. They attacked Tiam to prevent him from assuming the throne."

She sighs. "Stupid commoners. You know, Coe, they have a lot to learn. We royals are far from helpless. We're superior in many ways."

There she goes again, with her superiority speech. But she's staring right at me, so I fight back the urge to roll my eyes.

"And Tiam was stupid. He wanted to save the world. He wanted to take them all. And look how they repaid him for that kindness." She sighs. "Dead."

I lean into her and whisper, "Tiam is not dead."

"But you and I will be smart about this. We'll—" Suddenly she stops. She sits up, and her blue eyes bore into me. "What do you mean?"

"I don't have time to explain. He needs your help. Is there a way I can get access to the stores?"

She narrows her eyes. "How can he not be dead? You are tricking me. What do you want to steal from the royal stores now?"

"I thought there was nothing down there of worth?" I challenge.

She throws up her hands. "How do I know what is down there! Royals don't go there." She clasps her hands together. "It is true? My beloved is alive?"

I nod.

"Oh!" She covers her mouth with her hand, and when she removes it, she's smiling from ear to ear. She rushes to a mirror and inspects herself. "Oh, my goodness, I have never been so happy! Where is he?"

"Down in the stores. That's where we went when you forced us from the tower, Princess," I say, unable to keep the irritation out of my voice. "He's trapped there and in danger, and the only way I can get him out is by getting access to the stores. Once he's free, the three of us can decide what to do about Finn and the others. But you have to stay here, with your guards. You're safest here."

She studies me for a long time, then says, "If he is alive, you need to bring him to me at once. We're running out of time. My father..." She looks around and then shakes her head. "No matter." She reaches underneath her bed and pulls out an old key with a red cord tied around it. "This is the key to the door. Go to the third hallway on the right when you get to the bottom of the stairs. It's the second door on the left. It sticks, or so I've heard. But, Coe, you must remember to bring the key back to me. It's my only one, and we'll need it."

"I will," I say, wrapping the cord of the key around my wrist. "So you've *never* been down there?"

"Of course not! That moldy old place! That's not fit for royalty."

There's no sense in asking her if she knows where I might find the old laundry room, then. I stand up to leave and am almost at the doorway when she says, "You were not excused." Then she just sighs and waves me off.

I hurry down the stairs and follow her directions to the

basement doorway. Surprisingly, it's not watertight. It's a metal door, rimmed with rust, and there are decaying metal bars crisscrossing a giant semicircular window near the top. The door handle is rough from decay as I turn the key in the lock and pull it open. It opens to a completely black staircase. I grab a torch off the wall and take the first step. I know mold, and I know filth, but the deepest, most rotten stench greets my nostrils before I'm halfway down the stairs. Crusty barnacles and green slime coat the stone walls.

"Hey, you!" A voice startles me. I whirl around to see one of the palace guards at the top of the stairs, his spear pointed in my direction. "What are you doing down there?"

"I…" I begin, thinking quickly. "I'm the princess's lady-in-waiting."

The scowl doesn't leave his face. That's not enough of an excuse to satisfy him.

"She is looking to make a gift of some items in the stores. To the commoners. As a peace offering," I explain, my hand tightening around the key hard enough to leave marks on my palm.

"I should still check with Burbur. She's the only one who is allowed down there," he says. "Me, my father and my grandfather have all been royal guards. There's nothing much of worth down there anymore."

I hold out the key. "But the princess would like me to see. See, I have her personal key here."

Just when I think my story is getting me nowhere, he nods and looks over his shoulder. "Forgive me. The commoners have been getting rowdy. They killed a guard today."

I suck in a breath. "They did?"

He tightens his grip on his spear, and for the first time, I realize that he's afraid. "I believe it will take more than a gift to save her from them."

He says this with such iciness that I shiver. Seeing what was done to Tiam, I can only think that's just the beginning. I know he's right. "She would like to make amends," I say in a soft voice. "Preserve the peace."

His face is solemn. "Little good it will do now. Watch yourself. Dangerous things down there. Ghosts and demons in every corner."

I begin to turn away, but then I say, "I thought the basement was watertight?"

"Much isn't. There are two levels. The lower level is, but it is empty, and no one ever goes down there. You're on the top level. Many of the rooms are watertight, too. Your key will open them. Just…make sure you close any doors you open or else you'll flood them out."

"You wouldn't happen to know where the old laundry room is?"

"The old what?"

Of course not. I wouldn't know what it was if it weren't for my journal. "Forget it."

"If you are looking for something in particular, that map behind you may help," he says.

I turn around to behold the most confusing labyrinth I've ever imagined. It stretches from floor to ceiling, and about as wide as the princess's quarters.

My stomach tightens. How will I ever find Tiam in here?

The map is faded to practically nothing in areas and dark in others; it looks as if the lines have been traced over and over again as the tides have washed them away. Maybe there were once words there, but of course there are no more, just funny pictures scrawled everywhere. There is a big black X and a few rectangles laced together, which must be the stairs and the place I am standing. All the rooms nearby have big X's over them, as well. The nearest room without an X, which appears to be ten doors down, has the picture of what looks like a fat striped insect. Whatever could that be?

I pull out my book and try to superimpose the drawing that Cass did on top of some part of this new map, but nothing makes sense. It's hopeless. And Burbur isn't much of an artist, so—

Burbur. Of course she may soon come down here, and I can only imagine what she'll say if she sees me. There are two carts, much like the one Burbur wheels with her everywhere, against the wall behind me, and as I back away, I trip over a wheel, causing a clatter that echoes through the walls for what seems like tides. There are ruts in the stone floor for the carts, making it uneven and difficult to find footing. I move as quickly as I can without knowing where I am going, counting the doors as I go, until I arrive at the tenth one. Then I use the key and push it open.

This room is as large as our sleeping compartment and is piled high with crates. They stretch out, away from the dim firelight, dozens, if not hundreds of them. I think of walking the laundry room with Tiam and shiver at the thought of seeing another one of those horrible creatures. But the boxes all appear to be intact. Several are open. Closing the door behind me in case Burbur should come, I investigate closer, moving away scraps of packing material until I find what containers are inside. I read the words: *Local Raw Honey.*

Honey? The word itself sounds familiar, but I'm not sure what it is. The picture on the front is something that looks like…a big striped insect with wings. It's smiling at me—I've never seen an insect smile before. It's so fascinating I can't put it down. Does this can contain mashed-up insects? The things people used to enjoy eating!

But it's *food.* And food is not supposed to be here. Nothing of worth is supposed to be here. I wonder what is wrong with it. Whether it tastes vile. Maybe it's rotten. Obviously, it must be, or it wouldn't still be here.

Still, it's something. I fill my bag with as many cans as I can hold, then walk another few yards until I notice that my feet are no longer on solid stone. The floor below me is cold metal. I look down and see a round disc in the ground, a bit wider than a person's shoulders. There are two small openings on either side. What is it? A passage, I think. I think I can slide my finger in there and pry it up, but when I try to slip it into the groove, it's too big. If I had another hand, or my shovel, maybe I could make progress. I end up staring at it, dumbly, then kicking it in vain with my bare foot, sending fireworks of pain up to my knee. That's got to be an entrance to the lower level that the guard was talking about. And I have no way of getting in. I just hope Tiam's not down there.

I take another step when I remember something. I had seen the word *honey* once before.

Juggling the torch, I find a way to squeeze it under the crook of my deformed arm as I flip open my book to the map. Sure enough, there's an arrow pointing to one of the rooms that says *Honey*.

And if that is the case, according to the map Cass drew, there should be three more doors in the room, one on each wall. I can see one from where I stand, one that leads to *Flower Bulbs and Seeds*. Directly across from it, then, should be *Canned Vegetables*. I step a little farther in, fingers crossed, and peer around a stack of crates.

Sure enough, the light hits another door. I move closer, and as I'm about to place my key in the keyhole, I notice something etched, very faintly, in the center of the door, about chest level.

CAN VEG TA LES

They're marked! The doors are marked! What wonderful, wonderful letters. Finding Tiam might be possible, after all.

The celebration ends after studying Cass's map for another few moments. There are only about twenty rooms on her drawing, and not one is labeled Laundry Room. Considering that the writing over the map says East Stores, and from Burbur's drawing on the wall, there are probably well over a hundred rooms, it's safe to assume that Cass only drew a small portion of the area, only the rooms she managed. For all I know, there's likely West, South and North Stores, too. And then, if what the guard was saying is true, there's an entire subfloor below this one with even more rooms.

I consider going back up to my room, climbing down the chute and dragging Tiam up with me, but then I think of his face when he learned that was his only escape. It put my heart in a noose. He's never, ever looked remotely so vulnerable in all the tides I've known him. This isn't just a small fear—it's something big. I know nobody on the island would do the same, but maybe it's the desire to *not* be like them that propels me onward. I won't be reduced to someone who cares only for myself. I won't go back and tell him there is no other way. I will find another way.

I walk another few steps, toward a door that says SOUPS, and that's when I hear something. Something just slightly different than the sound of my bare feet swishing on the dusty stone floor. It sounds like...whispering.

Oh, no.

I whirl around quickly, waving the torch in front of me, but my arm knocks against a crate, and, shocked, I drop the torch. It clangs on the stone floor. The last thing I see are my bare feet before I'm consumed by complete blackness. The whispering seems louder than ever now, a lively song played to the ferocious drumbeat of my heart. It's so loud it's as if it's coming from all around me. Maybe it is. Maybe they're everywhere.

When I reach down again, though, the torch is gone. My arms fan out, cautiously, along the ground around me, but somehow it has just disappeared.

I am going to die here. I am going to be eaten by a horrible monster, or scared to death by a ghost or demon, and nobody will find me for a thousand tides. When someone does, it will be Burbur, and she will say, *Stupid girl.* And Tiam will die, too, because of me. We will both die, in the same basement, a hundred rooms separating us. *Together, apart.* That is the story of Tiam and me.

I think of me dying alone, in this moldy, metal room. And him alone, in that dusty room. Dying the same way, in places so different...

Suddenly it hits me. The floor. The floor of these rooms is stone. The floor where I left Tiam was dirt. Dust. Sand. The walls were altogether different, too. The walls here are stone. The walls in Tiam's room were metal. It's the subbasement. He's down on the lower level.

I've got to get down to the lower level. I have to figure out a way to pull open that metal disc in the ground. I need a spear, or...someone with smaller fingers and two strong hands.

Fern. I need Fern.

Shivering, I take baby step after baby step, trying to remember where everything once was, but I don't. I can't. Of course it's just in my head, but it seems as if everything is twisting around, and I find myself bumping into things everywhere, as if I'm in a giant maze where the walls keep moving. My hand catches splinters from the crates again and again and starts to sting as I find my way back... Or am I finding my way back? Maybe I'm just going deeper into the stores.

I finally touch upon something solid and cold metal. The door. I feel for the handle, pull it open. I inhale, relieved at the fresh air that greets me. I must be back at the main corridor of the stores, but it's transformed now, because the sun has set, and the only thing streaming down the staircase is moonlight. Swallowing hard, I make my way toward it, when I feel a cold, wet sensation that I hadn't felt before at my toes.

Cold, wet. It's the one feeling that everyone on this island dreads. Suddenly I feel as if I'm falling through space.

I have no idea what time it is. A wave crashes somewhere nearby. As the sound of rushing water echoes through the chamber, a thousand thoughts run through my mind. Had the siren indicating the end of low tide sounded? Could I have missed it? Could high tide be approaching already? Considering that I've been fumbling around here for what seems like forever, closed off from much of the rest of the island…
Yes, yes, yes.

No.

By the time I get to the opening, water is trickling down the staircase. It's already around my ankles. There's time, though, I tell myself, trying to calm my shaking limbs. There's time. I start to climb the stairs when I see the door at the top of the staircase. It's closed. Somebody closed it. Water is pouring through the rusted bars in the window at the very top. The water level on the first floor is already over my head. I reach up and push on the door, but it doesn't move. It's locked. Or stuck.

And where is my key? I fumble around for it but can't even remember where in my bag I put it. My mind is a frenzy of competing thoughts, none that makes sense. The water begins to surge faster through the open window now, its sheer force throwing me down the stairs. The back of my head slams against Burbur's map on the wall, but I'm too busy trying to keep my head above the swirling water to think about the pain. I push my hand flat against the stone ceiling, then my cheek, to take as much of the precious air as I can before the water swallows me completely.

Now *this* is where I die. That—and that, without my help, Tiam will soon follow me—are the last things I think about before everything goes black.

Twelve
Waking Alone

Drip, drip, drip.

While I sleep, I have the most vivid dream, one I've never had before. I'm in the fairy tale *The Little Mermaid*. The story is about a strange creature who is half human, half fish. In the dream, I am whole, and I am beautiful and strong. I swim about the island, immune to the attack of the scribblers. Either I am too fast for them or they don't want me. I swim everywhere, drawing water through my mouth, letting it course through my body, filling me, leaving me, pushing me forward. In my dream, the stump is gone; my arms are both perfect fins.

I surface. There I see Tiam. I try to wave at him, and I think he is waving at me, too. There's a beautiful smile on his face, and a thrill surges through me, knowing the smile is meant for me. But just then, Star embraces him, and they walk away together, hand in hand. And suddenly my perfect fins begin to tingle. I look down and see my body beginning to dissolve into the foam on the ocean's surface. I try to stop it, to swim away, but the faster I swim, the faster I melt away.

And then I wake to the drip, drip, drip.

The sound is the first thing I'm aware of when I gain consciousness. Next is the pain slicing through the back of my skull. It makes opening my eyes feel like lifting a weight bigger than myself.

When they finally do flicker open, I half expect to be in the ocean, the dream was so realistic. Frighteningly so. But the first thing I see are walls rising on either side of me, glistening wet. What is left of the water on the ground is making an exit through drains on the sides of the passage, with a deep *glug glug glug* sound. My neck is stiff, but I manage to turn it so that I'm gazing up at something familiar. Burbur's map. I'm still in the basement.

That isn't possible.

How can I still be here? Here and alive?

I must be dead. I shouldn't be here. This entire passage was underwater not long ago. There was no escape.

From head to toe, I'm soaked. My hair is matted in a web over my cheeks. I crawl to my knees and wring a bucket of seawater out of my tunic. I climb the slick staircase to the top, then yank on the door. Still locked.

What happened?

I locate my bag in the corner of the corridor. It, like everything else, is soaked. Soaked! Cursing, I reach through and pull out all of my belongings. All the things I needed to keep clean and dry. My mat is wet and crusted with sand, and my books—my beautiful books are sopping. I page through them and the ink is bleeding everywhere. How careless! After all these tides of survival, they meet their end with me. I curse some more, try in vain to shake the water from them, then carefully place them back inside the bag.

Then I reach inside and pull out Clam. His little box house is crumpled, but he's as happy as ever. He even pokes a claw at me, as if waving.

I turn to Burbur's drawing. All those big black X's marked over maybe only one-quarter of the rooms on the map. Maybe that was to say that all the material in them had been used up. If that's true, the other ones... Are they full? Full of only useless things? Is it possible the people before us would have packed the stores with a hundred rooms of worthless items?

Just then, something dawns on me.... Maybe...maybe the X-rooms are flooded out. Yes. That's probably it. The stores have been empty since before I was born.

I lift my bag, and the honey cans clink together.

Then, what were those honey cans doing there? What about them was so useless?

Rotten. The contents must be rotten.

This time, I easily find the key in the side pocket of my bag, just where I'd left it. Why had it been so difficult to find before? My muscles feel rubbery as I open the door and stumble onto the first-floor landing. Everything is wet and sparkling like crystal in the sun, making my eyes ache. There are no people present; they must all still be in formation. Water is trickling down the main staircase in the foyer, making it slippery. I climb the stairs carefully, enter my quarters and see that the laundry chute looks very much the same way I left it. I pull back the grate. "Tiam? Are you there?"

"Yeah."

"Is everything okay?"

"Yeah. Did you talk to Star? Is she okay?"

"No, I—" I say, flustered. "I mean, she's fine."

"What's wrong? You sound rattled."

"It was the weirdest thing. I'll tell you about it later," I say. "But now, I'm trying to find you. Through the main entrance to the stores. It didn't go so well this time, but I think I have an idea—"

"Don't worry about me. I'll find my own way out."

"There might not be another way out," I argue, sick of his pride. "I put you down there. I can't just leave you there. And you need to get out. We need you up here. Things may be falling apart. The guards... Burbur... They're acting very strange. Everyone's on edge. I think they killed a guard and—"

"A guard?" His voice is tight. "Was it really dangerous in formation? What's going on out there?"

"I..." I don't know how I can begin to explain what has happened, as I barely know myself. I should have been out in formation, to avoid making people wary. Now I've missed two formations. When I turn up alive, how can they not be suspicious? Even if I say I was up in the tower with the princess, that will be putting me on her side. And as Finn said, that's probably not the best side to be on. After all, look what happened to Tiam. I just repeat, "Everyone's restless."

"And you said the princess is okay? The king?"

I'm disappointed he would ask about her, but then again, what was I expecting? They are to be married. "I think the king is okay. And your princess is fine." I feel guilty the moment I say it, but I can't keep the bitterness out of my voice. That dream of him walking away from me, arm in arm with Star, feels so fresh, which is probably why my *your princess* drips with sarcasm.

"Coe," he begins with a deplorable tone that makes me squirm. "About Star. I wanted to—"

"Are you hungry? I'm throwing down a can of honey for you," I break in. The last thing I want is to hear him talk about his relationship with Star. I've had to sit through enough of her daydreams about him and her and their royal children to make me want to die a thousand times over. "I found a whole room full of cans in the royal stores," I explain. "The *empty* stores. Weird, huh?"

"Honey?"

"I think it might be mashed-up insects. It might be rotten, which is probably why nobody ever ate it. But I don't have anything else. Sorry."

"No, it's okay. Thanks. I'm starving."

"Look out below." I grab it out of my pack and drop it into the void. It rattles all the way down and lands with a loud clatter. "Have you seen any more of those things?"

"No. I'm good." There's a pause. "What the hell is this?"

"It's called honey." I say the foreign word slowly, so he can understand. "Can you open it?"

"Yeah. But what *is* it?" I'm about to explain that I really have no idea, when he says, "Wow. It's… Wow. It's…different. Good. Where did you get it? You said…there's a lot of it?"

It's good? Then why was it still there? Something pricks at my neck, but there's got to be a rational explanation. I think of my father, kissing the king's hand before setting off on his Explore. The king wanted the best for us. Buck Kettlefish believed that. There's got to be some reason for all of us to be nearly starving outside when perfectly good, edible food hides in the stores.

I open my mouth to ask Tiam what he thinks but I hear a shuffling upon the staircase. I flatten the thin metal of the grate flush against the opening in the wall as two guards rush by. I stand and peer into the hallway, wondering what they're after, when I hear them whispering. Two more guards join the commotion, gesturing to the tower and shrugging. Their faces are lined with worry.

I hear muffled fragments, but I don't need to hear the entire conversation to understand what is going on. The words *funeral* and *leaderless* are all I need.

I peel back the laundry grate once again and whisper, "Tiam. The king has just died."

Thirteen

No Nearer

A hush falls over the floor as two guards carry the king's body toward the exit. Appropriately, he's covered, face to toes, in his cheerful pink robe. I know the guards will take him out to the end of the island farthest from the castle and throw him in the ocean for the scribblers. They will strip him naked first, though, and the rest of them will fight over the best pieces to patch up their clothing. I'm sure for the foreseeable future a good number of Tides commoners will be piecing the garish pink Tiam had called "ridiculous" into their tunics.

I ring three times for the princess, but she doesn't answer, so I creep up the staircase and through the door. She is sitting at her vanity, looking blankly at herself in her mirror. "Didn't I tell you to ring first?" she asks softly. I notice her eyes are rimmed in red, just like mine. I begin to explain that I had, but she says, "You heard of the king?"

"Yes, Your Majesty. I'm sorry," I whisper.

A flash of grief registers on her face, but it disappears as she inspects me. "Why are you so filthy? You smell like fish." She shakes her head and makes a tsking noise. "You need to take better care of yourself if you are to take care of me! I suppose I am the only civilized person left on this godforsaken island. I have no idea why I allowed Tiam to talk me into this arrangement."

I look down at my clothes. My once-white tunic is now streaked brown. My knees and ankles are coated with grime. I look like my old self.

"Where is Tiam? Did you bring him with you as you said? Now that I am the highest-ranking royal in the land, I think we should be married at once."

"I think you should come with me, Princess," I say, though I'm not sure where I'd bring her. Where on this island could I hide her? She'd never willingly go down to the moldy, filthy stores.

"You need to finish my wedding dress," she says, sweeping across the room to her wardrobe. She pulls it out and lays it on her bed. "Oh, it is a mess. Just a mess. I hope you can make quick work of it. I expect it to be done right away."

Shock. She's in shock over the death of her beloved father. I think of Tiam's words. *The princess will know what to do.* I wonder what he would think if he knew she wanted me to sew a dress, instead of helping me find a way to save him. She doesn't notice me bristling at the suggestion because she is already ripping off her robe and wiggling herself into the unfinished white fabric. Once she gets it over her head, she stares at herself in the mirror, then gives me an icy look. "There are some pins on the dressing table. Come on."

"Star," I say gently. "You are not feeling well because of your father. I understand. But he is gone now, and you are not safe here. We need to—"

Tears form in her eyes. "I am not leaving the tower until this dress is done. And that's final, Coe."

To me, the dress is finished. It covers everything. The seams appear even. It's more beautiful than anything I've ever seen. The real problem is not what the dress looks like, but how I'm going to successfully produce the groom by tomorrow. But I've seen the way Star cares for Tiam. She didn't even want him in the tower. If I tell her I still haven't been able to find him, she'll tell me to work harder, that it's my concern, not hers. So, trying to think of the right arrangement of words that might coax her to follow me, I grab a small container of pins and hurry to her side.

She clutches a handful of material. "Pin this. Like this." I fumble with my one hand to gather it like she asks. She clicks her tongue and pushes my fingers away, annoyed. "No, like *this*. And be careful! You're filthy!" After a few more moments of tension, of me trying to make myself useful but getting batted away from her like a pesky insect, she crumples into a ball and begins to sob.

"I'm sorry, Your Majesty."

"Oh, you see," she says between sobs. "All these tides I imagined a grand wedding. Something the people of Tides would talk about for generations to come. But that's stupid, isn't it?"

I don't say a word. Of course it's stupid, but I don't think she wants me to agree with her. She wants me to argue, tell her that it's a great idea to have a wedding when the world is crumbling around us.

"But Tiam and I can have a small ceremony, right? Just a small one. Maybe just him and me. Right here, in the tower, where I was born and raised. That would still be nice. Right?" She looks around the room. "It would be a fitting way to begin my new life as a married woman."

I nod. I think if I were ever to be married, as impossible as that notion is, I would like that better.

"Everything is going away. Everything." She looks down at the dress, swishing the material miserably around her thighs. "I know a simple girl like you cannot understand, but Tiam is all I have left. I want to look perfect for him. Regal, something all the Wallow ancestors would be proud of. Do you think I will?"

I don't know why, considering she is so out of touch with reality, but part of my heart breaks for her. She is losing everything she's ever known. At least I never had anything to begin with. I nod and say, "Yes. I will make the most regal dress you have ever seen."

A hint of a grateful smile passes over her as she slides the delicate neckline of the dress below her armpits, then lets the entire thing fall in a puddle at her feet. Then she clears her throat. "There is a spool of white thread in the top drawer and a needle. Take it back to your room and bring it back to me when it's done."

I walk to the dresser and look down at it. It's obviously

thousands of tides old. It's made of some dark wood, stained and beaten in places, and the metal pulls on each drawer are shaped like little black flowers. There are three small drawers at the top, but I don't want to bother the princess further by asking which she meant, so I slide open the one on the right. I move things aside, but there is no thread there, no needle. I'm about to close it when I see a small lined piece of paper there. It looks like a map, a very old one. The paper is brown, with tattered edges, just like the pages of my book. I can just make out the letters B MT there before her voice rattles me. Something about those letters—

"Not that drawer! What are you doing? Snooping through my private things?"

I shut the drawer so hard that the mirror and perfumes in glass jars atop it shake violently. "No, I—" I open the next drawer and pull out the thread and needle. "I found them."

The dress is still lying on the floor. I reach down and pick it up.

"Please make quick work of it. And then we can be under way," she says, as I nod and pick up the dress, afraid to tell her that I'm not a miracle maker. She's so deluded, and with her father dead, I'm afraid any more bad news will only push her further out of reality. I'm five steps down the long staircase when she calls after me, "And take a bath! A long one! Please!"

When I'm back in my quarters, I notice that Burbur is nowhere in sight. Everything is quiet, shuddering, as if afraid of something. Even the waves have seemed to cease their unending noise. Little shell trinkets are strewn carelessly about the hallway. It no longer gleams with radiance in the late day sun. In my room, none of my things are arranged, no fresh garment is hanging in the doorway. There is water in the tub, but as I swirl my hand in it, I realize quickly that it is salt water. There are a few white jellyfish bobbing on the surface.

"Tiam?" I call into the opening over the tub. I'm eager to tell him the princess wants to marry him tomorrow. That in the midst of the chaos, she wants me to sew her dress. I'd like to hear what he has to say about that.

But there's no answer. I wait and then call again. Nothing. *Maybe he's just away exploring,* I think. After all, Tiam is not one to sit around and do nothing. I need to go back into the stores and find him.

I call to him again, still no answer. I think about my last conversation with him: *I'll find my own way out.* Maybe he did. Maybe he's far away from the opening, on his way back up to us. Or maybe one of those horrible creatures got him.

Formation will be soon. From the window, I can see the tides rising. I didn't hear the siren ending low tide. Perhaps whoever is responsible for that has given up on it, just like Burbur. I will need to go out there, to quell any suspicions. I also need to face Finn and ask him to forgive me. He probably hates me. When he finds out everything I've been doing to save Tiam, he'll be even angrier. But I couldn't let Tiam die. I can't. I try to think of what my father would do, what he would say to smooth things over, but I can't find his words. If he were here, it wouldn't have gotten to this point.

Before I know it, I'm lying on the bed, weeping next to the white heap of fabric that is Star's wedding dress and wishing my father were here with me. He would know what to do, and never would have made such a mess of things as I have.

Suddenly something moves in the hallway. A ghost?

I haven't slept. My head still aches, and my vision is blurred. I'm not thinking straight.

Then Star pokes her head in. I swallow. She's come to punish me for not finishing the dress.

Instead she says nothing, just sits there, breathing heavily. When my eyes adjust I see tears streaming down her own face. "Princess?"

She doesn't look at me, just lets out a muffled, "Huh?" She almost seems surprised to see me here.

"Is there something wrong?"

"Oh. Yes. Where is Tiam?"

"He's down in the stores. We'll need to go down there and meet him after the next tide. I'll have the dress finished by then. And then you can be *under way*," I say, using her term, although it sounds ridiculous to think of a marriage, something so beautiful, like a task to cross off one's list.

"Oh." She seems satisfied. And yet I can tell there is something she's holding back.

"Princess? Is there something else?"

And with that, the floodwaters pour forth. "I've never been in the tower without my father. He's always been there. His snoring would always comfort me. And now he is gone, and it feels so empty and quiet up there and I wonder if you might come up and stay with me."

"I—" I begin, hardly knowing how to answer. The only thing I know right away is that I would rather face the tide than spend the entire night comforting her. "I'd hardly call it suitable for a mere commoner like myself to share the royal quarters," I say.

She sighs. To my relief, she says, "You are right. What would people think?" She stands, and for a moment I think she will go back to her tower. Instead, she asks, "Might I stay with you here for a while?"

"Um…" Before I can say more she moves in and lies down beside me on the bed. I shuffle over, giving her most of the available space until I'm pressed against the wall.

"Goodness," she says, shifting uncomfortably. "These beds aren't suitable for royals at all, are they?"

Not as if I would know. "I'll have to go into formation soon," I remind her.

"Oh, that is all right," she answers, folding her hands daintily over her stomach. She sniffs. "Tell me one of your stories. It will improve my mood."

"Stories?" I'm not sure how she thinks I can tell stories, when I lack the creativity to daydream.

"Tiam told me that you tell lovely stories. He says you would tell them in the formation to pass the time. Is that true?"

I nod, a sick feeling building in my stomach that he'd spent the time sharing such things with her. Talking about me. *Oh, Coe tells lovely stories, but it's a shame she's so horribly strange-looking.* I wonder what else they've shared, two beautiful people, alone together. I wonder if he thinks about pressing his body next to hers, if that's what *he* daydreams about.

"Then, go ahead. Tell me one about a princess like myself, if you know any."

"All right." I begin to relate to her the story of *Sleeping Beauty*. It's one I've never told before, and I know it will require a lot of explanation, but I can't think of any others. I tell her of the beautiful princess who pricks her finger on the spindle of a spinning wheel and goes to sleep, only to be awakened a hundred years later by the kiss of her true love.

"True love?" she asks.

"Yes, long ago they believed that there was one man especially made for every woman. They called them soulmates. And sometimes a person would search their entire life to find their soulmate. And that would complete them."

"That is a silly concept. After all, nobody on this island has a soulmate."

"Well, it was a comforting thing for them, to believe they wouldn't live out all their days alone. It may not have been entirely true. But there were thousands and thousands of people then, more people than one could meet in a single lifetime, so it wasn't as though the notion could be tested."

"Perhaps it's only royal people, people of worth, who have soulmates," she continues on, ignoring me. Then, oblivious to the insult, she says, "It is rather sweet and comforting. I think Tiam…Tiam is my soulmate."

I swallow. "Is he?"

"Oh, yes. I've never felt about anyone the way I feel when he looks at me. It's hard to explain."

She doesn't need to explain. I understand that feeling perfectly.

"He is quite…handsome. Even filthy and ragged, he's handsome. And when he talks, his words vibrate in the deepest part of me. I could listen to him talk all day." She fingers a giant pearl on a string around her neck. It's perfectly round and white like the moon, and larger than any I'd ever come upon. Only one person on the island has the luck to find a pearl that large. The way she's stroking it, I can almost imagine the entire scene, him tying the breathtaking jewel around her neck as a promise of marriage. I try to blink the scene away, but the more I try, the more clear it becomes. Her voice is so fragile, almost childlike, when she whispers, "And he is all I have now. He is everything to me."

I flash back to the moment that Tiam fastened that gaudy red piece of stiff material around my own wrist. I'd been touched by that gesture, too. Now it just seems cheap. He gives me discarded junk that royals wouldn't find important. He gives her rare jewels of unequaled beauty. It's perfectly fitting, so I'm not sure why it hurts so much. "You are probably right, that he's your soulmate."

"And I do know what kissing is, too. The kiss of true love certainly is powerful. To awaken the princess after one hundred years and restore happiness to the kingdom!" She is silent for a moment, and suddenly her breathing quickens in a renewed spring of energy and inspiration. "Do you think that if Tiam and I are joined in marriage and kiss, it will reverse the tides? Do you think it can save us?"

I turn and stare at her. Her eyebrows are raised in question, her face not leaking a bit of irony. She was the sign from the gods that Tides would be safe, and yet safety still eludes us, so I suppose that's why I'm doubtful of her powers. "These stories are just stories. They're not real. I don't think that a kiss can—"

"It could, though. Don't you think? Inexplicable things happen all the time. I mean, sometimes I'll look out from the balcony at the brightest part of the day, and see the moon. During the day! And why is the sea filled with salt? Who put it there? How can seagulls fly, and yet no matter how fast I flap my arms, I cannot? I think about these things often, Coe."

I'm about to answer when suddenly thunder cracks the still, humid evening. A storm is coming.

Her body tenses next to me. "Do not take me for a fool. Do not think I don't know how you feel about Tiam. One only need look into your eyes to see how much you care for him."

I'm so shocked that I spring upright in the bed and blink twice at her to make sure I'm not dreaming this. Surely it is another nightmare. But it isn't; she is there, and in the darkness, I can see her eyes fastened on my own, narrowed in suspicion. "Princess, I don't—" I begin, grateful the storm clouds have rendered the room dark because I know my cheeks are burning. Is it true that the feelings I have for Tiam are written in my eyes for everyone to see?

"And you may think that he had feelings for you."

Well, at least she is wrong about one thing. I've never thought that. Not once. "I don't—"

"But he is mine. *He is everything to me.* I care for him deeply. This world dictates that we belong as one. Even if the king's rule is no longer valid, then nature's rule should persist. He *is* my soulmate. Do you see that?"

"Yes," I mutter.

"That is good." She lifts herself from the bed, scoops up the wedding dress and floats out of the room without another word, leaving me with that same image from my mermaid dream: Star and Tiam, two perfect halves of a whole, walking hand in hand, away from me.

Fourteen

Lost Violent Souls

I don't want to go back to formation. I've missed two of them now, and surely there has been talk. A guard was killed. The king is dead. I am very afraid this formation will be very different from the last one I'd attended.

As I step outside the castle, thunder rumbles. I remember Finn and cringe. He was the only one out here who'd made any attempt to protect me, and now… I'd hit him, hurt him, something I'd never done to anyone. He'd always been good to me. My father, who was an excellent judge of character, knew that. And what had I done?

Ana stops me. "Look who's back from the dead," she mutters. "We all *did* think you were dead. Finn said he'd tried to save you, but that you were crazy and wanted to die."

Maybe I am crazy, but I hadn't wanted to die. I'd only wanted to help Tiam, something that I'm afraid no one on this island understands. He'd once been their favorite, and now… it's likely Finn has poisoned their thinking, talking about how he'd insisted on becoming king. They all probably hate Tiam now. The thing I'd dreaded most was that I'd have to see them, sooner or later, and face their questions. That's the problem with this island. You can't avoid anybody. I start to walk toward my spot, shivering in the cold air. "I was tending to the princess," I mutter.

"There was a contest for Tiam's spot this morning. Almost had one for yours while we were at it."

I turn and stare at her. "Contest? What kind of contest?"

She shudders. "I wanted no part of it."

I start to walk away but brush against a fisherman, and my bag gets caught in his spear. It lifts off my shoulder and topples to the ground. The cans of honey are the first to spill out. It's not enough to hope no one will see; formation is just moments away, and the area is swarming with commoners. Soon, it's almost completely silent, except for the sound of the cans rolling on the concrete, clinking together. Everyone seems to stop moving and stare at them, and silence ensues.

Ana asks the question on everyone's lips. "Now, what are those?"

Quickly conjuring an excuse, I casually pick them up, then hand them to Ana. "They're from the princess. As a peace offering. Maybe you can put them in the next meal."

"Did she now?" She snorts and shakes her head as she inspects the cans. I have to agree with her; even though Star would never think to make a peace offering, this one will likely not buy her any favor. There's an ocean of misunderstanding between the princess and the people. How much peace can four measly cans of food bring? If it weren't for the royal guards, it's likely they would have already attempted to take over the tower. It's probably only a matter of time before they do it anyway, regardless of the risk.

Ana starts to walk away, then thinks better of it and takes the cans from me.

"Yes, isn't that nice?" I say, cheerfully as possible. "Honey."

"Honey?" Her eyes narrow. "But what are they? Where did they come from?" She is still turning them around in her hands. "I thought the stores were bare of food." Her lips pucker, and it's then I notice that more people are staring at us.

"There are many rooms in the stores," I explain. "And it's very dark down there. Things can be easily overlooked."

I place my things on my spot, noting with a bit of sadness Tiam's usual place. Today, for the first time ever, someone else will be standing beside me. I wonder who it could be. Who won the "contest," whatever that was. I look around, feeling as if I've been removed from this world for longer than a few tides. It's getting late, almost too late, and yet it seems as if a lot of people are missing. There's more than the usual amount of tension in the air. Usually people sit at their spots, hang their heads and wait. But today, people are darting their eyes about, suspicious, uneasy.

I whirl around to feel a pressure against my thighs as something throws all its weight against them. Fern. She sobs into my hip, clutching handfuls of my tunic. "Oh, Coe," she whimpers. "I thought you were dead. I missed you so much."

I kneel down to look at her. Her eyes are wide with fear. I can't believe I haven't given much thought to her, that I've left her in a situation that is clearly getting worse by the moment. "I'm so sorry."

"Please, don't leave me again," she moans into my tunic. This is more than her usual concern. A lot more. She's trembling so much she can barely get the words out.

"What is it? What happened?"

But she just stands there holding me tight, shaking. I rub her back, tracing my fingers along the bones of her trembling spine. Finally, she whispers, "The shovel."

"Oh!" I say. I reach into my bag, then remember I left it with Tiam. "I know where it is. I meant to give it back."

"Ana was mad. She said I couldn't have the next three meals."

"I am so sorry," I say. I stroke her hair. "I'll explain to Ana. We'll get you some food right after formation, okay?"

She nods, but her face doesn't brighten. There's something else.

"Is it about the contest, Fern?" I ask. "What was it? Who got Tiam's spot?"

Suddenly a voice whispers, "Hi, Coe," behind me.

When I turn, Finn is standing there, holding his spear and baring his teeth in a thin smile. He's wearing King Wallow's pink robe around his shoulders. It's in perfect condition, as if he'd stripped it from him not long after the last breath left the king's mouth. There's a huge, bloody scar stretching from his ear to the tip of his jaw. I gasp. I hadn't known I'd caused that much damage.

He notices my looking at the robe. "Do you like it?" he asks, stretching the cape in front of him as we both settle into the formation. I can imagine him, untying it from the king's neck and pulling it from his body before his blood went cold. What's amazing to me is that the others would let him. That they hadn't insisted he'd share, as we do nearly everything.

"It looks just as ridiculous on you as it did on him," I say, to which he laughs. Encouraged by that, I whisper, "I'm sorry I hurt you, but you shouldn't have grabbed me. You scared me."

"Yeah," he mutters. Then his voice softens. "Coe, I was trying to help you."

"But what you did to Tiam is…unforgivable."

His voice is harsh. "You think so? He gave us no choice."

"How can you think that?" I seethe under my breath, though I know other people can hear. We're pressed together so close, I am sure that people on the other edge of the formation know what we're talking about. In fact, never before have I felt all their eyes burning into us so deeply. They're all very interested. My voice is quieter still the next time I speak. "You just needed to talk it out."

"With his spear drawn?" Finn says, to my surprise. I'm about to argue this point, and he must anticipate it, because he says, "A dozen other men were there, too. They saw what happened. You didn't."

"I…" I begin, but he's effectively silenced any argument I could have made. Tiam had his spear drawn? Whatever for? Maybe he was afraid for himself. After all, all of those men had been heckling him from the platform. "He wouldn't do that if he didn't feel threatened."

As close as I press myself toward Fern, it's not nearly enough to stop me from rubbing against Finn. He taunts me again and again with his body, moving closer to me every time I move away. An attack from all directions: Finn on one side, Fern on the other, her fingernails digging into my thighs, the ocean all around, closing in. How much longer can I take this?

By the time the tide gets closest, I'm halfway in Fern's spot, and Finn is taking up his own, as well as most of mine. When the water climbs up the sides of the platform and the waves begin to pound loudly against it, I cringe and try to concentrate on the sky. But there is no moon. Instead, heavy clouds blanket the heavens. And then it begins to rain. Not a heavy, pounding rain, but a thin drizzle that's enough to make steam rise from the hot ground. Soaked, I shudder and feel Fern trembling beside me. She doesn't ask me for a story, and I'm glad of that; my jaw is clenched so tightly to stop my teeth from rattling that my mouth couldn't form the words.

Tiam would always stand at the very center of his circle; he would take advantage over no one. I was smaller and more feeble (not to mention willing), so he could easily have taken some of my space. But he never did. Finn, however, towers over me, and I feel his skin against mine, hot and damp with sweat and rain. Several times I elbow him in the hips, not as much by accident as I pretend it is.

I think about what he'd said only a few tides ago. *If I were king, I'd want you to be my queen.* That seems so long ago. I don't look at him. I know it's better to ignore him. Ignore him and hope we can eventually bury whatever is brewing between us.

When it is all over, the clouds have parted to welcome the bright stars, but Fern is still trembling. Our bodies are sticky and soaked. Someone on the other end of the formation screams as if they're being murdered, and she grabs me tighter. Burbur is talking with Ana, who is motioning to me. Burbur seems to be shrinking away, her eyes wide with innocence. Something about honey. The word *honey,* once foreign to us all, is now the hottest topic of conversation since the scribblers learned to bury themselves in the sand. People are obviously comfortable with the word now, because I hear it whispered all around me. And they're all looking at me as they say it. When Burbur finishes the conversation, she turns to me and her wide-eyed innocence dissolves to hatred. *What did you do?* she mouths.

And I know. I know my mistake will cost me dearly. The honey will never be seen as a peace offering. Instead, it's the first shot in this war.

Finn, who'd been talking with a bunch of men, turns to me, his garish pink robe flapping in the breeze. He says, "Honey?"

Oh, I'd do anything to have him, have them, unhear that word. To strike it from their knowledge. I turn to leave, but he catches my arm.

"Coe, where'd you get it?"

I shrug. "From the princess. She was trying to make peace."

He snorts. "But you know it shouldn't have been there. Something tells me that we'll need to go down and see what else is in the *empty* stores."

I shake my head. I just want to go away, but there is no escape.

He puts his hand on my shoulder. "Coe, get away from the

castle," he warns. "Go anywhere. But don't go there. There's going to be trouble, and I want you to stay out of it." He holds in a breath and slowly exhales. "You may hate me, but I still made a promise I'd look out for you."

I shake my head. "What are you going to do?" But I already know. I can tell the way the rest of the men are sizing up the giant stone building ahead of us. They are going to attack the castle.

"Coe, I—"

Desperate, I push up against him. "You can't hurt the princess. Her guards—"

I stop when I notice the way he's looking at me, his jaw clenched. He plucks my wrist off of his chest with his calloused hand, very gently despite the menacing look on his face. He can't believe I'm still thinking about the princess, that selfish, spoiled brat. Of all the words he could use to convey his disappointment, he chooses complete silence, which is probably the most effective response of all. He simply turns and walks to the edge of the platform, leaving me to wallow in my guilt.

Fern is sitting on her circle, waving her magic wand in the air with one hand and clutching her tummy with the other. She's hungry. "Come with me," I say, grabbing her by the hand and rushing toward the ladder.

She looks confused, but follows anyway. When we reach the entrance to the castle, Fern's eyes widen. "I can't go in there. I have to clean the craphouse. And where's the shovel? Ana will be so mad."

"Fern, don't worry. I will look out for you." We hurry up

to the castle doors. I have never known a time between tides when two guards weren't stationed outside the doors. But they're not there now. We pass right on through. The hallway is empty.

"What are we doing here?" Fern asks as we climb the stairs.

"We have to get the princess."

I'm halfway up the staircase when one of the guards, who I'm sure used to be in the service of the princess only a tide before, appears on the landing above. He catches sight of me and immediately turns and runs in the other direction. "Finn!" I hear him shout.

Oh, no. "Change in plans," I whisper, taking her by the wrist and leading her back down the stairs. The princess will just have to use some of her royal superiority to fend for herself, for now. We creep down the deserted hallway toward the stores. "Let's go find Tiam."

"But he's dead," Fern says as I find the key in my bag. My hand is slick with sweat as I reach for the door and realize that it's already open. Somebody is already down here. Perhaps it is Burbur, but now, it could be anybody.

"Quiet. Hurry," I whisper, ushering her down the staircase. In the distance, I see firelight bobbing in the darkness. Someone is in the corridor to the right. I steer Fern to the left, toward the honey room. It's nighttime, and even the moon seems to be hiding, anticipating the terror to come. The dark presses against us until I know how Tiam must feel in closed spaces. Everything in my bag is damp as I rifle around, looking for my flint.

"It's so dark here!" Fern's voice is high and fragile.

"Do you have anything to make a light?"

"Uh-huh." Fern's platinum head bobs as if it's on a fishing line. She reaches into her own bag, a little too slowly for my liking, and pulls out her flint.

There's a bit of moonlight streaming through a high window in the wall, farther down the corridor. That's what we'll have to go by. My eyes have adjusted a bit more, and it's not as bad. "Come on," I say, tugging on her sleeve.

"Aren't you going to light that?" she asks.

"Not yet." It's not safe yet. But I don't tell her that. She's worried enough as it is.

The dripping noise sounds like footsteps sweeping down the staircase behind us, so every few steps I look over my shoulder only to see nothing. We make it to the honey room, and I quickly open the door, then slam it shut when we're inside. In the dark.

"It's so dark in here! I can't see anything!" Fern squeals, grabbing my hand tighter. "Where are we?"

In here, it's impossible to tell. We're not ten paces away from the entrance to the lower level that I'd spotted earlier, but it might as well be a million miles. I tear a piece of cloth from my tunic and strike the flint against the wall furiously, finally igniting the fabric after five or six tries. Then I find a torch on the wall. Immediately, a halo of gold light stretches out into the dark chamber, illuminating the metal disc in the floor.

"What is this?" Fern asks, taking a can and inspecting it. "Is this some kind of weapon?"

"It's food. I know you're hungry. I will give you some in

a little bit," I say, pocketing a can for later. I can't remember when the last time was that I ate, and there's no telling how long we might be looking for Tiam. Or what kind of food might be available where we're going.

She shakes a can near her ear, suspicious. "Where did it come from?"

"It's been here since the floods began. Hurry," I say, thinking of those terrible creatures. It may have been my imagination, but I'm almost certain I heard them here, as well. I lead Fern to the entrance to the subbasement, the small raised disc in the floor. I wasn't sure before, but now I can see her tiny little fingers will be perfect for this job. "Can you open this?" I ask her. "Just put your fingers in there and see if there's a release? Or if you can pull the cover up?"

She squats and surveys the thing. "Sure." Moments later she's dug up the metal cover and I help her heft it the rest of the way and slide it to the side. "Easy," she says, smiling broadly.

There's a strange smell coming from down below, not so much moldy as earthy and decaying. It's familiar. I think it's the same smell I'd noticed in the old laundry room. And the laundry room was chilly, too. This air that rushes up to greet us is colder, and the steady dripping of water is louder now. Dripping...in a watertight compartment. That is what the guard had said; that the subbasement was watertight. Something tells me it's not so watertight anymore.

I shine the torch down and see two small rungs of a ladder, nearly rusted through and coated with greenish slime and barnacles, and then...nothing. I reach my arm in and swing the light around. Just blackness, from all directions. Beyond those two steps could be a bottomless pit, for all we know. Still, I know this is where Tiam is. I hand Fern the torch and lower myself down slowly. Before I'm halfway down, I know something went wrong here once. I slide into dank water, stagnant and ice-cold, up to my waist.

I stand there for a moment, shivering, wiggling some slimy substance between my toes. Something grazes my calf. A weed. A piece of underwater plant life, that's all. I hope. I wait, cringing, but feel nothing.

"What's going on?" Fern cries down. "I hear noises at the door up here."

"Come on down," I say. "Quickly. Pull the cover shut if you can."

"I can," she breathes heavily, working hard. I hear the metal screeching against the stone as she pulls the cover over the opening, locking us in here. I try to shake the feeling that it's forever as I pull her waifish body from the ladder and set her down. Everything beneath her armpits disappears into the black water. Her eyes bulge out perfectly round, and her lips curl. "Oh! It's water. It's so cold!"

"It's not so bad once you get used to it," I lie. It's icy. I can no longer feel my toes, my ankles. I wonder how long this water has been down here. I wonder how it came to be down here, whose mistake it was. We're in the center of a narrow corridor. I hold the torch up high and squint down each way, but the path disappears into darkness only a few yards ahead. I try to determine where above us my quarters are in relation to our position, then motion down the corridor. "Let's go this way."

"Ohhhkay," Fern says, as if she'd rather not, but follows behind me anyway, shivering. "Tiam is down *here?* Why?"

"Yes," I say. "Long story."

My foot rams into hard metal, and I yelp before realizing there's another cart down here, like the one Burbur wheels through the halls. It's just a rusting, rotting skeleton, leaning badly over to one side as if it's come here to die and doesn't want to be disturbed.

The passage begins to slope downward, and the ceiling does with it. I look up ahead, where the entire passage delves underwater. Not passable. Maybe I'm wrong. Maybe it's the other way. I turn and motion for her to do the same. "On second thought...let's go this way."

Fern's teeth chatter as she nods, her eyebrows raised suspiciously.

We come to a door on the left side. There's a raised metal panel in the center, with a patchwork of a dozen or so circles punched into the frame. It's a pattern I've seen before. The door to the laundry room was like this. We're getting close. I raise the torch to illuminate a plaque on the wall that says BOILER. It's a word I don't know. But it's not LAUNDRY, so we move on.

This corridor begins to slope downward, too. I turn to Fern as we walk. Her teeth chatter in rhythm, and her eyes have now taken on the shape and luster of the full moon. The water is now nearly to her shoulders.

Suddenly, she rocks to the side and catches her breath. "Coe…" she begins, but stops.

I turn to her. Her mouth is frozen in an O. "Yes?"

"Something…" she begins in a whisper, but her teeth are chattering too hard to form the words. Finally she spits it out, the thing I'd had an inkling of all along. *"Something is under the water!"*

I shake my head. "It's just seaweed," I say, trying to keep the doubt out of my voice.

She doesn't move except to shake her head vigorously in disagreement. The rest of her body is stiff. "It's a scribbler!"

"Don't be silly. How would it get down here? And what would it—"

I stop suddenly when I hear it. It's a sound that seems to come from everywhere, rising and falling and echoing through the corridor, just as it does in my worst nightmares.

Hissing.

Fifteen
Round the Prickly Pear

ll right, I tell myself. *Calm. Think.* Somehow willing myself to think only makes the hissing louder.

I lift the torch and scan the ceiling. It's comprised mainly of poles of all sizes, running parallel with the corridor. They're of all colors—red, blue, black, silver—and continue along the length of the corridor, disappearing into the darkness. No, not poles. They're pipes. I'm not sure what the others are for, but there were black ones of the same size in the laundry room. I raise the torch higher, and it casts a shadow of the pipes on the stone far above them. There appears to be at least a little space between the piping and the ceiling.

I force the torch into Fern's hands and wade through the muck to the old skeleton of a cart. I try to wheel it, but it doesn't move, so I yank it up and it creaks in protest but follows. "Come here, Fern," I yell. She breaks from her statue pose and hops her way through the water with the speed and grace of a dolphin, then begins climbing onto the cart before

I can even tell her to. It groans and rocks some more, but I hold it steady for her so she can get her footing. Once she is standing on it, the water is only up to her calves. She looks at me, confused. "See if you can climb up. Over those pipes."

She looks up, grabs a pipe and tries to wiggle herself up. Squeezing the torch in the armpit of my bad arm, I grab hold of her leg and hoist her up. She slides up easily, and I hand her the torch and follow behind her. There isn't much headroom; lying flat on my stomach with my chin on a pipe, the back of my head scrapes the ceiling. But we are safe. The hissing continues for a bit, the glossy outlines of the creatures winding through the black waters below, making small ripples. "Okay," I say, still trying to catch my breath. "So, there are scribblers down here."

"What do we do now?" she asks, looking past her toes at me.

I thrust my chin down the corridor. "We crawl. That way."

We can't even crawl, really; the best I can do is wiggle. Fern can lift up onto her forearms and knees slightly and manage a low scramble with her legs slightly separated. She moves ahead of me like a little spider. After a few moments, she calls back to me, "I think I would rather be spending time with Finn."

"Is it bad out there?"

"He's horrible!" she squeals. "I don't know what got into him. He is the one who told Ana not to feed me when I lost the shovel."

I bite my tongue hard. He knew the shovel wasn't lost. He knew I had it. My blood starts to boil.

"And he was the one who had the idea of having a competition to win Tiam's spot. He killed the twins."

I gasp. What *has* gotten into him? Something tells me he's taking this idea of survival of the fittest a little too far. "Both of them?"

"Uh-huh. The competition was between Mick and Finn. Finn won, but he wouldn't stop kicking Mick. And when Vail tried to step in to stop him, Finn turned on him. Everyone was saying that Wallow was a bad leader, and they all wanted Finn. Well, Finn is worse! People are starting to get scared of him." She shudders. "And then I heard Ana talking, and she says there are only four hundred of us left. Can you— Oh!"

She'd been gradually inching over to the left, until the last time she brought her knee down, it slipped on the leftmost pipe. What happens next occurs in a heartbeat. Balancing the torch in my good hand, I watch helplessly as her midsection, then her chest, then her blond head follows. When I finally manage to cast aside the torch and free my good hand, I reach over and grab strands of her hair and her bony wrist.

"Oh! Oh! Oh!" she screams, her sticklike legs flailing beneath her. "Don't let go, Coe!"

"I won't," I say. But without another arm, it's impossible to lift her up. She's forty pounds of dead weight, and I don't have the strength in my good arm. "Calm down, try to pull yourself up."

"I—I can't," she moans.

She's looking down. The hissing is louder. The once-calm water is frothing below her. I can see the outlines of black bodies of scribblers as they slither beneath their next meal. "Fern, look at me."

She doesn't look up, she just squeals and cries, hysterical. "Fern!"

She turns her head to me. He eyes are wide and fearful.

"Fern, I will not let go," I say to her calmly. "I've always thought of you as my sister. Do you know what a sister is?"

She shakes her head vigorously.

"A sister is someone who will protect you, no matter what. And I am not letting go, do you hear me?" I say. "Now, you can do this. The wall is right behind you. If you kick against it you can pull yourself up."

She looks over her shoulder, then bites her lower lip, propels her feet behind her and launches herself up so that her elbows are resting on the pipe. Then she manages to squirm the rest of her little body up to safety.

All the fear I'd had to keep in during those tense moments, while pretending to be the strong one, spills out of me. I start to cry. "Thank goodness," I breathe into her ear as we lie there across the pipes, panting. "I don't want anything to ever happen to you."

She gives me a small smile. "Now I *really* would rather be with Finn. But I'm happy you're with me."

I pick up the torch and we continue on. Fern moves with determination, like a person who wants to be anywhere else. The pipes are hard and uncomfortable to lie on, much less move over, so I find myself lagging behind. Concentrating hard, I dig in and really leap forward, froglike. I find my face pressed against the black bottoms of Fern's tiny feet. "Why have we stopped?"

"There's a wall here."

"Oh." Great. I poke my head down and see another door on the left wall. I can just make out the *L* and the *Y* on the plaque beside it. Thank goodness. "He's here. In this room."

"How do we get in there?"

"We crawl down and open the door."

"But…the scribblers?"

"They've stopped hissing." I figure we can get down in there and inside the room before they come at us again. Maybe. Of course, once I open the door, all the water will come rushing into the laundry room, and will I be able to close the door before the scribblers come? It's not the greatest of plans.

Fern senses my apprehension. "No. Way. Coe."

"Okay, okay," I say, trying to peer around her in the dark. "Scooch over so I can get up there."

She moves on her stomach to the side, and I slide in next to her. Straight ahead of us is a wall of stone. It looks as if it's the end of the passage. That's where the pipes come to an L-joint and veer off to the left. Predictably, they disappear into the wall, right above the laundry room. I inspect the place where the pipes meet the wall. It's too dark to see but it seems as though it's not watertight. Did someone carve through solid stone in order to fit the pipes there? I press my finger against the wall there. It's spongy. Not stone. Decayed wood, I think.

"Hold on," I say, drawing my head and shoulders back and

bringing my feet in front of me. I bring my heel to the soft section of the wall, and push with as much might as I can muster in such a small, enclosed area. It budges, just an inch. Fern catches her breath. I do it again and again. Each time, the wall moves out a bit, until at last it falls away, and there is a hole large enough for us to climb through.

"You did it!" Fern exclaims, holding tight to the pipes. She shivers. "Hooray. Let's get out of here."

"Hold on." I don't want to dash her glee by bringing up the horrible creature Tiam and I fought the last time we were together in this room. The creature that puts the ferociousness of the scribblers to shame. I haven't heard from Tiam in much of a tide; he could have fallen victim to one of them and be lying dead on the floor right now, a hideous, bloody sight. I motion for her to give me the torch. "Let me look."

I swing the torch out into the room and peer over. The room looks even more enormous from this angle. There are piles of crates everywhere, but the light doesn't stretch out far enough to see the door to the laundry chute or the place where I'd left Tiam. "We'll have to go down," I tell her.

I turn onto my stomach and drop down feetfirst, then motion for her to do the same. When she falls into my arms and looks around, she sighs, relieved. "Yay. It's dry in here."

"Tiam?" I call out. No answer. I call his name louder.

"Why isn't he answering?" she asks, following behind me.

She starts to gravitate toward a crate, so I pull her back toward me. "Stay close."

She raises an eyebrow. "Why?" She looks around and then says, "What is that noise?"

I freeze and listen. I hear it, too. Whispering. Gulping, I yank her toward me. "Tiam!" I yell, urgent.

The light stretches forward, and I can see the chute in the distance. Before it, though, there is a lump... Actually two... No, three shapeless masses lying on the ground. Holding in my breath, we step forward, ever so slowly, until the torchlight illuminates the forms. The first thing I see is black blood, pooling around it.

Not Tiam. Please, not Tiam.

Then I see the fur. Masses and hunks of fur curled around blood. Claws and fangs. A black button eye, staring forever at nothing. No human parts. There are three of them. So, Tiam must have had a run-in with two more. But where is he?

A second later I realize my toes are wet and sticky. We're standing in the blood.

"Agh!" Fern yelps. "Gross. What are those?"

"I don't know. They're not very friendly, though."

Her body tenses like a board. "Where is Tiam?"

"I don't know." We step around the massacre, and I wave the torch ahead of us. There are footprints in the dust, his footprints, heading in the opposite direction and disappearing around a stack of crates. Of course. Leave it to Tiam not to stay in one place for very long. "I think we need to follow those."

She nods and hugs herself, rubbing her bare shoulders. It's freezing. "What has he been doing down *here?*"

I don't know how to explain it without giving away Tiam's secret about being afraid of closed spaces, so I just shrug and answer, "Exploring. You know Tiam."

She laughs nervously. "He's funny. He should explore some-place with*out* creatures that want to make him their dinner."

I can't help but laugh, too. "You're right. Let's find him and tell him that."

I stop when I come to the candle, lying in the middle of the passage. It's considerably shorter than it once was. The hair on my ears bristles. If it *is* his, then he's down here, without any source of light. And that's impossible.

At the end of the room I think we can go no farther, but then I spot a small corridor in the very corner, in the shad-ows cast by the crates. Tiam must have done the same thing, judging from the way his footprints hit the wall, turn and then head off in that direction. When we get to the opening, there is a big sign above it, but the letters have been scratched out. Over it, I can make out the words, scratched very faintly: B MT ENT.

It must be a passage to the palace, maybe a secret door to and from the building, used for emergencies. Maybe Tiam found a way out and is roaming the island now, trying to lie low and avoid Finn and the other commoners. If so, it makes total sense why he hasn't been answering me. After all, he did say he would find his own way out, and for as long as I've known him, Tiam has always accomplished whatever he sets out to do.

I feel silly for spending all this time worrying and planning to help him. He doesn't need me. Never has. It was foolish to think that maybe, for once, he did.

I turn my attention to the sign on the wall. What is B MT ENT? It feels as if I've seen the letters before, somewhere. Maybe in my book, but if so, I can't place what part of the book it's from. That's strange, considering I have most of it memorized. I sigh, realizing I can't even flip through the book since the ink is bleeding everywhere. But where else would I have seen those letters? Maybe I'm just dehydrated and hallucinating.

And then I realize what about those letters is familiar. The letters are wobbly, strange, not like the way Kimmie and Cass wrote. I think of letters, drawn in the sand, washed away by the tide. That was how he taught me to read and write. His *B,* especially, was very different. It was a vertical line, astride two perfect circles, stacked on top of one another. So as I gaze at the markings scratched into that wall, I can't help but feel a little weak. I might be wrong, but *it looks very much like my father's handwriting.*

No. That's impossible. Buck was a fisherman. He's never had a reason to be down *here.*

We creep on. It's so dark that I can no longer make out Tiam's footprints in the dust. The passage begins to angle downward, then two even narrower paths branch off to the right and the left. They look like cracks in the walls, mistakes, instead of actual pathways. They're so narrow we'd have to walk single file. And as creepy as this place is, those pathways are even more so. I wave the torch down each and see nothing but blackness; no plaque announcing its purpose, no indication that it was meant to be traveled by humans. A giant black spider spins a web in the upper corner of the crevice, uninterrupted by our presence. I shudder, then continue down the wider middle passage. The safer passage.

We walk another ten feet or so before it breaks off again. Two more narrow passages. Then, twenty feet later, it does so again. Each time, we seem to be descending farther and farther underground. It's so cold I see my breath billowing out ahead of me, something that only happens every once in a while at night on the island. I can hear Fern's teeth chattering. That's when I begin to hear the dripping. Not a good sign. The black walls glisten. The dusty floor turns to mud. Suddenly we're splashing through water.

"Oh, no," Fern whispers. "Not more water!"

We walk on another few feet, slowly descending until the water is up to our knees.

"Let's go back," Fern whispers, clenching her teeth.

I shine the torch ahead of us. "I think the path starts to rise up there," I lie. I can't see anything at all. "Tiam must have gone this way."

"How do you know? Maybe he's…" She doesn't say it, but I know what she's thinking. It's the same thing I was thinking, something I thought and wished Fern was too innocent and hopeful to believe. Maybe he's dead. No, I'm not going to consider that again, not when I wasted so many tears on it before, only to find out he was fine. So I just press ahead in silence, and we go lower, lower, lower, until I have to raise my good arm to keep the light out of the water. He's got to be safe. He's got to be okay.

Fern's squeal plays on my eardrum. She's up to her chin in water, her neck stretched as high as it will go, teeth clenched. I can't carry her, so I know she's right. We'll have to go back. I wave the torch ahead of me one last time, hoping to see some evidence that Tiam was here, but there's nothing. Then I sigh and lead her back the way we came.

"Maybe he went down one of the other passages," she offers as I squeeze the water from my tunic. She mimics me, shaking her head so that the water from the ends of her long hair sprays everywhere.

"I guess," I say. She's right again. Tiam wouldn't give up. He'd come here and find that this way was flooded, and then he'd check every other avenue until he'd exhausted them all. And that's how we'll have to be. We'll check everywhere until we find him, alive or... *No, don't think it.*

I'm suddenly aware Fern has stopped walking. She's standing, frozen, in midsqueeze, with her wet tunic in her white hands. I follow her eyes up the passage, to where the water meets dry ground. There, above the waterline, are four sets of eyes, glowing red, watching us.

Sixteen
The Eyes Reappear

"**O**h, Coe," Fern moans, inching beside me and grabbing my hand, "I'd *really, really* rather be with Finn right now!"

"It's okay," I say, just as much to calm myself as her. I wave the torch in a figure eight at them. "They don't like fire. Or... water. See how they're not coming near us? As long as we stay here, we're safe."

"But, Coe, we can't stay here forever."

"Well, of course. But we can take our time figuring out our next move. That's a good thing."

Just then, there's a splash. The red eyes are closer. They're testing the water. They creep toward us cautiously. So they don't hate the water as much as I thought. Wonderful. With each step, Fern clutches my hand tighter and moves so near that she's standing behind me. I don't blame her. I'd give anything for something to hide behind, too.

We inch back until we're in water up to my chest and Fern's

neck again. It's so cold I can't feel anything below my waist. My breath billows in front of me, blurring my view of the bloodthirsty creatures. No, we can't stay in here forever. But the creatures don't know that. All they know is that they've got us trapped, and they want to finish us off now. They've gotten used to the water. They wade in as far as they can, and then they start to swim.

I study the walls, the ceiling, for something for us to grab on to and hoist ourselves up. There isn't anything this time. This time, I'm about to drown in my helplessness. I try to breathe, but the air isn't making it to my lungs. I try to think, but my head is thick and empty all at once. My entire body is shutting down; the only thing I can do is move farther along the corridor, my feet heavy and numb, as if I'm walking to my own execution.

And then Fern looks at me, with that innocent sweet face so twisted in terror. I got her into this. Me. But even if I hadn't, I would do anything to take that fear from her. To see her safe. Anything. I pull her up, onto my shoulders, piggyback, and wade until the water is up to my own chin. When I'm about to start treading water, a sudden loud crash rips the air, and a high, screaming squeal pierces my ears.

"What's that?" Fern whispers, her hands tightening around my neck enough almost to choke me.

I turn. There are only three now, swimming with their noses in the air. Were there four before? Yes, I was quite sure there were.

Another animal yelp. This time, I see something glinting in the firelight as it whistles down on it, again and again, plunging it beneath the water in a great splash. And then there are two.

I squint through the darkness and make out a blond head. Tiam. He does away with another creature with a deep, guttural "oof." "These things are really getting on my nerves," he grumbles. His voice is the sweetest sound I've ever heard, even if his tone is angry. Now I see him, easily dispensing of the last one with a swift blow of the craphouse shovel, as if it's a weak, defenseless little insect and not the same creature that had nearly ripped a hole in his neck two tides ago. He's obviously gotten to be quite an expert at killing them.

I slowly wade from the water, sink to my knees in the soft mud and sob.

"Hey, hey, hey, what's going on?" he says, and I feel his hand on my shoulder.

I want to pour myself into his arms and stay there for a very long time, just feeling his warmth against my body. I am so starved for it that having him near and knowing it's not possible is enough to drive me mad. If I look up, though, if I look into his eyes, I know I will crumble, weak, pathetic. So I wipe the tears from the back of my hand and, with every last bit of strength I have, say, very nonchalantly, "You came right on time."

"I noticed their whispering always gets louder when they find their next meal," he explains. "I could hear them all the way down the passage."

I bring myself to my feet and try to ignore the quivering of my ankles as I motion around us. "Where does this passage lead?"

"I think it's the way out," he says, brightening my mood. A back door, a way out of the castle, is exactly what we need. But my heart sinks when he says, "But it's like a maze. I've been all over the place, but I can't find the way. There are words on the walls, though."

"I saw the plaque in the entrance to this passage. It says B-M-T-E-N-T. I don't know what it means."

He rolls the sounds over his tongue for a moment. "They're not words?"

"I don't think so. Just letters."

He scratches his chin. "Did you find another way in here?"

I nod. "But it's no better than the way you came, I think. We had to climb through another narrow passage. And there are scribblers out there."

His face falls. "We have to find a way out through here. It's here. I know it is." He seems so sure, I wonder how he can believe that so deeply when our luck has been so bad, when nothing has indicated there's another way out at all.

Fern shakes her head, her face stone. "I wouldn't go back the way we came, *ever*, in a zillion tides."

I look at him and nod. "It was *that* bad. Plus, I've made more enemies. I was stupid. I brought the honey up with me and dropped my bag, and they saw it. Now they think the princess and everyone who works for her is hoarding the stuff. Things are breaking down. They're in the castle now. I think they're going through the stores. It's scary."

He doesn't say anything for a moment. Then he exhales. "Wow. Do you think they followed you here?"

"No. The stores are immense. I think there are rooms and

rooms, and they're not all empty, like we thought. Tiam, do you think the king and princess were hoarding it all? The princess says she never went down—"

"That was always the rumor," he says. "But Wallow and Star probably didn't know half of what's down here. If the stores managers kept quiet, they were rewarded with whatever they wanted." He shakes his head. "Burbur never did look hungry."

I nod. That's the truth.

He looks behind me, as if expecting someone else. "Where's Star? Didn't she come?"

"She wouldn't come," I say softly.

His eyes narrow. "What? But she's in serious danger! You said they're in the castle now. The first thing they'll do is go after her." He runs his hands through his hair, angry. "Hell, Coe, didn't I tell you to find her?"

I'm shocked. Tiam has never been one to raise his voice. But then, this is his princess, his love. "I did! She thought I was trying to trick her. She wouldn't come with me. She's under this delusion that she's safer up there and that the two of you will get married and live happily ever after. I couldn't pick her up and carry her!" I cry, so defensive my words tumble out on top of one another. "Then we went back to find her after formation, but Finn was already in the castle. I knew he'd go crazy if he saw me! I doubted she'd come with me, anyway! She's easily the stupidest and most obstinate person I've ever met! But in a way, she's right. There's no place on the island that's safe for her."

"Down here it's safe," he says softly. "I would keep her safe if she were with me."

"What? You expect her to live down here?" I mutter, catching my breath. "Besides, she would never come down here. It's beneath her. And *you* wouldn't go up there."

"I'm sorry, Coe. You're right. It is my fault. I'm an idiot. I wish I could…" He speaks in such a wounded way that I can't help but feel as guilty as he does. "I'll need to get to her."

I clench my fists. I want to shake some sense into him. How he could be so blindly led by that beautiful, silly thing is beyond me. Instead, I change the subject. "How can you see? Did you find another torch?"

He shakes his head, and with a sudden click the room is bathed in pure white light, a thousand times brighter than the fire. I stare at the thing he's holding in his hands, mesmerized. "There are boxes of them. Up near the chute. All you need to do is shake it. Watch this."

He weaves it around, making a pattern on the wall most dizzying. Then he puts his hand in front of it and doesn't pull away. It should be burning his hand but it's not.

Fern applauds. "Wow. Can I try?"

He hands it to her, and she flashes it around the corridor, her face bright with glee. It illuminates the face I never thought I'd see again, only minutes ago. I think about those creatures and cringe. "Can we go someplace warmer?"

"Oh. Sure. You cold?" Tiam leads us back up toward the laundry chute. I notice as we walk that a lot of the crates have been opened, the contents have been rifled through. At the base of the chute, the crates have been arranged into a nice, safe little bunker. We climb inside. He's laid out a little bed for himself made of shredded packing materials and a cloth blanket, and he has two or three of those portable lights stacked by a pillow, the can of honey and various other things I've never seen before and don't have names for. Truthfully, it looks a lot more comfortable than the sleeping compartment. No wonder he's not too excited to get back up to land. He finds a couple of cloths and hands one to me, then drapes one over Fern's back, rubbing her shoulders vigorously. She plops down on his mat and he covers her feet. "You feeling better, Bug?"

She grins and nods, then starts to dive in to his open can of honey. "Yum. This is the best place ever. Let's never leave."

So funny how food, a few warm blankets—and Tiam—can make a dreary place a whole lot nicer.

"One bad thing about these…" He shakes the light at us, then sits beside her. "They don't give off heat."

She's not paying attention. She's rummaging through her bag. From it, she produces her wand, which she gently brings to his wound. It looks as if he might have succeeded in breaking the end of the scribbler nose off, somehow. He has wrapped some dingy fabric around his shoulder, but the blood is seeping through. "You are healed," she says, with great flourish.

He smiles. "Hey. It feels much better."

"Did you…break off the end?" I ask.

"No. Just filed it down some. It's good. Can hardly feel it," he says, but he winces a little as he speaks, as if just the memory hurts.

"You can't leave it like that. It's got to come out, right? It'll get infected."

He doesn't say anything for a long time, just stares at it. "Maybe."

There's an odd noise coming from above, in the laundry chute, something that rises and falls eerily, like a woman crying out in pain. I listen, unable to keep the concern from my face.

"It's the tide. High tide," he explains. "That's the water you're hearing, Coe."

"Oh."

Fern sits up, trembling. "The craphouse! I didn't clean it. Ana will be so mad."

"I'll take care of that," I tell her, patting her knee. "Don't worry."

Tiam says, "You look tired, Coe. You should rest for a while. Then we can go look at the signs I found."

I look for a place to lie, but there isn't any room, unless I lie down right beside him. The thought makes my skin tingle. He sees my hesitation and moves over, leaving plenty of space for me. We can fit another whole adult between us. Which is just how I like it. And just how I hate it.

Not long later, Fern is snoring away, her cheek pressed against the portable light, cradling it against her heart. For all the horror she has experienced, she is so resilient. I wonder how often a person can bounce back before they begin to crumble.

"I have to get to Star, and quickly," he whispers to me. "When the tide goes out, I'll do it. I'll go up the chute."

"Are you sure?" I ask.

"I have to…" he says, then gives me a sheepish look. I don't mean to, but it's hard to stop my eyes from rolling and my body from cringing at her mention. "Coe, I told you, I promised the king I would look after her. And she was good to you."

"She was good to me because you told her to be."

He sighs. "She might be silly and naive sometimes, but she's not a bad person."

"She almost had us killed, Tiam. And she hardly cared at all when she thought you were dead," I argue. At that moment, I want to hurt him. I want to make a hole in his heart as big as the one he's created in mine. "She could care less about you."

But his response only makes me feel smaller. He nods as if he's known that all along, and says, in a small voice, "Maybe so."

I look away, feeling guilty and stupid for being jealous. Over what? It's not as if I have any claim over Tiam at all. He belongs completely to Star.

The next few moments of silence only serve to make me feel worse and worse about what I'd said. So I'm relieved when he starts to speak again. "Look at this," Tiam says after a while, handing me something. "I found a whole crate of them. Guess it's some kind of weird food they used to eat."

I inspect it. It's a long flexible brown stick, covered in red plastic. I read the words. TRUNDLE'S BEEF JERKY. "Did you try it?"

He shakes his head. "It looks a little…questionable."

Suddenly it hits me, why he's showing it to me. The piece of plastic that he'd wrapped around my wrist all those tides ago. My bracelet. I smile sadly. That's exactly the kind of bracelet I'd get. It makes sense. If Star is worth a pearl, I'm worth that. Whatever it is. Its red plastic is meant to adorn only weird, questionable things. I put it aside and close my eyes.

It suddenly grows very quiet, and just as I'm certain Tiam has turned away to let me get some rest, I open my eyes. And he's staring at me.

Holding a pile of shimmering pearls in his hands.

He's threaded fishing line through each one, into a long string. I wonder how he managed it. It must have taken him forever. I can just picture him, sitting here by torchlight, carefully making the tiny holes. "They're beautiful."

"They're yours."

He waits for me to extend my hand, to take them, but I won't. There's some mistake. Or they're not real. I'll touch them, and they'll disintegrate into dust. I bite my tongue. "But you need to give them to Star."

"To Star? Why? These are for you."

"For me? But I can't wear pearls. Why would you…"

He swallows. "I know. I mean, I was hoping…" He takes the pearls away and shoves them hastily into his pack. "You deserve nice things," he whispers. "I wish I could give them to you."

Oh, now it becomes clear. He's trying to pay me back for rescuing him that night he'd been hurt. It's a nice gesture. So fair. So very like Tiam. I suppose it's been killing him all these days being in my debt, with no way to repay me. "They're not practical for me," I say, very businesslike. "Give them to your bride."

"Oh. Yes," he says absently, beginning to chew on his thumbnail. There seems to be something he wants to say. I hold my breath, hoping we can share some tender moment, until I remember that he is focused only on our survival and nothing else. He doesn't know what tenderness is. "I don't feel like Star is my soulmate," he mutters.

I roll over onto my elbow and stare at him. He had heard. He'd heard the story of Sleeping Beauty I'd told to the princess last night, when she'd climbed into my bed. "You...what?"

He shrugs. "If it is true that another person can hold the other half of my heart, then there is no question who that person is."

My mouth opens, but it's useless. My elbow gives way, and I have to catch my head from smashing against the floor. "What?"

"Well, you and I have always been together. You're the one who stands next to me in formation. I know our spaces were assigned, but I swear to you, Coe, there is no one on the island I'd rather be next to. I always felt like it was the two of us, against everything and everyone else. And I'd thought you felt the same way. After all, you're the one who came to my rescue. Not Star." He shrugs, embarrassed. "I know. It was just a story. Forget I said anything."

"But, no..." I say gently. I want him to continue. I don't want to scare him away.

"No. I'm marrying Star. I gave my word. I shouldn't do

this." He clenches his fists and places them solidly against his thighs. Then his face hardens, and he becomes Tiam the Survivor once again, leaving me to believe the past few moments of conversation were only in my head.

"No. Really. It's okay," I urge, trying to draw him back. I want to reach for him, do something to bring him back to me, but I can't bring myself to move, to touch his skin.

He clamps his mouth closed. I think I've scared him. But at this moment, I'm more scared than ever. Scared that I'm going crazy. Scared that I'm not. And I know in my head that it's better if he stays on his side of the wall, while I stay on mine. Even if my heart has other plans, anything between us is wrong. "What I said before, about Star not caring about you," I confess, my voice soft, "that was a lie. She loves you. You're all she has left."

He nods, a small smile playing on his lips. "I know. But what do *you* have?"

I look away and tell the biggest lie I've ever told. "I don't need anything."

After a few moments, it's as if the tide washed everything away. He stands and brushes himself off. "Let's check out the signs," he says.

"What about Fern?" I nod to the little girl, sleeping without a care.

We walk outside the bunker, and he pushes a crate against the opening. "She'll be safe." Then I follow him to the maze of passages. He shakes the portable light, and it easily illuminates things I hadn't seen before, like the nests of cobwebs suspended from the black tangle of pipework on the ceiling.

It makes Tiam's skin look almost white, angelic. He's lost a bit of the sun's glow he used to have. In a moment the black letters B MT ENT come into view.

The silence begins to get uncomfortable. It's as if he doesn't want to talk to me anymore, for fear of saying too much again. "Star said we used to play a game where we would try to guess what these words said. That you thought it was a code to a secret treasure," I say to break the tension. "Do you still think that?"

He nods as if it's obvious. "I know it."

"And what would you do with a secret treasure?" I ask, trying to be playful.

"The treasure is not a treasure in the common sense," he explains, taking another step past the sign. His voice is toneless and cool, and his movements are aloof; he doesn't look back to make sure I'm all right, just keeps pressing forward, into the frozen passage. "Something more valuable than jewels or gold. Something that all of us would kill for. Something I've always wished for...but never thought it might actually exist."

I wrap my arms tightly around myself and breathe in the frigid air. "What is that?"

"An escape."

My teeth stop chattering. "You mean..." And then it hits me. Is that possible? So all this time, he's been talking about a way out... Not out of the castle... *Out of this island?* "You're talking about an underground tunnel. To somewhere else? That's crazy."

"Coe, think about what you read to me. In that diary. That girl wrote about a castle with room after room. And a giant door in the mountain. People were *hiding in the mountain.* When you read that to me, I knew it was more than a legend, which is why I've been staying down here, trying to find it," he answers, shining the portable light down the small crack of a passage. "King Wallow told me. He has known about it for some time, but until you read that diary to me, I thought it was just the ramblings of a dying man. The way out isn't by ocean. It's been under our feet all along."

Seventeen
Trembling with Tenderness

"Y**ou're crazy. Why would he stay here if he knew the way out?"

He raises his eyebrows at me. "Think about it." I know immediately what he means. The Wallows' lives here have forever been perfect. They have been waited on hand and foot, their every desire catered to. They had enough food to last them for seasons and seasons. Here, they are important. Who knows how they'd be treated somewhere else? They have no reason to want to leave.

"That's why Star was talking about leaving. She kept saying she was going to gather her things and go...." I exhale, hold my head between my arms and squeeze it like a vise. "I thought she was crazy. But if Wallow always knew, then that means..."

I can't even wrap myself around the idea, it's so hideous. That the man who I thought kept us safe all this time was in fact just keeping us. Like prisoners. It's such an odious idea it makes me shake. All the things we've seen. All the terror we've been through. This life that is more like death… Because he wanted to feel important? I think of my poor father. "So…what about the Explores he commissioned?"

"I think he always knew they were pointless. He commissioned them because the people were looking for a way out, and he wanted them to see him doing *something*. He wanted to show them he cared."

A sharp pain stabs at my heart. I can't erase the image of my father, shipping off in his raft, promising to see me again. "He didn't care. He knew my father would die."

"Your father volunteered for that mission, Coe. He—"

"He wouldn't have gone on it if Wallow had shown us the way out!" I scream in a voice I never knew I had. I want to run far away, just collapse somewhere, alone, and sob myself dry, but I don't know where to go. So I just stand there, in front of him, tears sliding down my cheeks. He watches me, confused, as if he wants to help but doesn't know what to do. I know this is frustrating him beyond belief—he is Helpful Tiam, after all. That is what he does. Our lives have always been about being strong, about showing no weakness. It's funny that even the great Tiam, who can do everything, is completely helpless when it comes to tenderness.

I wipe the tears away with the back of my hand and peer into the first small opening in the passage. "Did *our king* give you any idea where the exit is?" I can't keep the bitterness out of my tone as I say this.

"No. He doesn't know. But a long time ago, before we were born… Coe."

But I'm not listening. I'm drowning in my own tears. Because Wallow sent my father, the only person who ever cared about me, to certain death. Buck Kettlefish meant to do good, to be helpful, and instead, he was sentenced to die.

I'm stopped in my tracks by Tiam's cool hand on my bare shoulder. My whole body quivers. I look down at his hand, then back into his eyes. "Coe…" he begins, but he's baffled. He doesn't know how to act or what to say. But I know he's fighting for it, I know that he wants to do something to make me feel better, and that's all I need.

I move against him. "You could hold me," I whisper. "Like this."

I lean forward, open his arms and slide inside. His arms are first stiff, then slowly envelop me, wrapping me completely in his warmth. I press my ear against his firm chest so I can hear the *thud thud thud* of his heartbeat, and I feel his breath on my cheek. This is the thing I've been missing, I think. We've all been missing this. I never want to let go.

"I feel better now. Thank you," I say, when I finally, reluctantly, pull away.

His expression is peculiar, as if he's lost in thought, trying to solve a riddle. He looks as if he's still trying to figure out this maze of rooms. My cheeks flush madly. He didn't want it. He didn't even enjoy it. When he opens his mouth to speak, his voice is very businesslike. "Was *that* a kiss?"

I blink, surprised. "No. A kiss is when your lips, well… touch, I guess."

"Oh." He nods, but then his face wrinkles again. "Like how? Show me."

"What?" I burst out, turning all shades of red now. "Oh, no. I couldn't. Your bride should. It's supposed to be, well, special. And it's not something… I've never done something like that…."

Before I can protest any further, he reaches for the back of my head, tangling his fingers in my hair before pulling me to him. "Like this?" he murmurs, brushing his lips against mine.

"I…I don't know…." I breathe, trying to keep my knees steady, my heart from tripping out of my chest. I can't help myself. I reach around his neck and pull him to me, then we kiss, and we kiss, and we kiss. Or maybe it isn't kissing. Maybe it's just our lips and our bodies melting together as if they belong this way. Whatever it is, there can be no better feeling. He presses his body so hard against me until I can feel every part of him I've ever gazed at with longing for so many thousands of tides. I've never wanted so much to have my other hand. I run my only hand feverishly over the smooth, muscled skin of his back, wanting it to memorize every inch of his flesh because this is a dream and it will never happen again. And I can't stop. At times I can't even breathe and I don't care because I just want more and more and more of him.

"Oh, gods, Coe," he says when he comes up for air. He nibbles a trail down my neck, to my shoulder. "Oh, gods."

He doesn't have to say anything more. I know.

Suddenly he whimpers. It's a sharp, girlish cry I've never heard from him. I pull away and stare at his face. He's wincing. "My…"

He's pointing at something at his middle. His wound. How stupid can I be that I forgot that? "Oh, I'm so, so—"

But he clamps his mouth over mine in another kiss, this one even more consuming than the last. I think about how I've lived my entire life not knowing that this existed. This perfect thing. This alone could make tide after tide worth living. I think about Star's stupid assumption about a kiss reversing the tides. Before I'd thought it was idiotic. Now I'm not so sure. Oh, gods. Star. I reluctantly nudge him away. "We've got to stop. Star."

He gazes at me, breathless, murmuring, "Coe. That was amazing. What was that?"

I shake my head, dazed, as if I don't know the answer. But I do. I know exactly what that was.

That, my Tiam, was *life*. And now more than ever, I know it's worth fighting for.

Eighteen
Life

We walk to the first crevice and peer inside. "Were you in here?" I ask him, my knees still wobbly from the thought of kissing those lips of his. Already I want to do it again, but then I remember Star and want to die. Die, or just run away with him and never come back. But I know Tiam would never do that. He made a promise to our king. And that is something he would never break.

Tiam nods. "I went down a ways, but it gets narrower and narrower and, well…"

He looks away. He doesn't need to say any more. I get it. Closed spaces.

"And, yes," he says. "To answer your question. There is a map. Part of a map. It's not complete. It was drawn a long time ago."

"By whom? How did the king even know it existed, if he's never been down here before?"

"Wallow told me that many tides ago, before we were born,

an amazing thing happened. A strange woman was found wandering the passages. She was dressed strangely and looked different, spoke a different language, even."

"An outsider?" I gasp. For all our time, our population has always been dwindling. We've never had outsiders. Not for as long as anyone or their parents could remember. Because we've lived so long without any contact from the outside, we'd always assumed we were alone in the world, the only survivors. "That's not possible."

"It is. The king and some servants were the only ones who knew of it, though. The ones who didn't, when they saw her, thought she was a ghost. The Dark Girl."

"You mean…" I shake my head. "There *really was* a girl who lived in the castle and had dark hair and pale skin? I don't understand. Where did she come from?"

"From somewhere below. A city underneath us. She'd gone for a walk and gotten lost. She was very sick and delirious, so she didn't know where she came from, only that it was underground."

My body trembles at the thought. "How did we never hear about this?"

"Because the king kept her in his tower. He could never let the world know about her, because he knew they would storm the palace and rip it apart, looking for the escape. With the king's help, she spent day after day trying to find the way back, for thousands of tides, and she drew a map as she did."

Map. I catch my breath. "Oh, my gosh. A map," I sputter. "I saw it in her room, in one of her drawers. I knew that

B–M–T looked familiar. It was on the map that Star has in her room!"

He rubs the back of his neck, exhaling slowly. "Which is why I've got to get up there."

"You? You knew about this all along?"

He nods. "That was the plan. Star wouldn't leave until her father was dead. Wallow knew he was on dangerous ground, but he was too ill to make the journey. He knew his daughter wouldn't be safe here. So the plan was to leave when Wallow died. Me, Star and *her lady-in-waiting*. And I always planned to come back later, and show everyone the way out."

I raise my eyebrow. "Her lady-in-waiting?"

"I convinced her that the journey would be long and hard and that she'd need someone to carry her bag." He smiles.

"Why would you do that?" I stare at him, waiting for an answer, but I think I already know. King Wallow had made arrangements with Tiam to protect Star when he was gone. My father did the same. Tiam had made a promise to my father to make sure I was safe. "You gave my father your word?"

He nods. "But, Coe, I would have done it anyway. I promise you that."

And he never breaks his promises. "That's why you fought with Finn."

"Of course. Do you really think I'd *want* to be the last king of Tides? I'd gladly do what everyone else wanted and let Finn have the throne." He shrugs. "But I knew I could save us. All I had to do was agree to marry Star. And then they would give me the map. And a way out. For everyone."

"How long have you known about this?"

"Not long. A few tides." He smiles. "You know how easy I am to figure out. Do you really think I could keep a secret as big as this for longer than that?"

I smile back, my heart melting at the way he's looking at me. It's the way I always dreamed of, and that's when I think of Star and immediately feel guilty. To stop myself from wanting to kiss him again, I break eye contact and look at the laundry chute. "I can make it up there easy."

He startles when he realizes what I'm talking about. "No way. I'm not letting you go. Not with Finn up there." He contemplates the chute for a moment and then exhales. "You know how we got into that argument. It wasn't about me ruling Tides so much as it was about you."

I nearly choke. "Me?"

"Yeah. Well, I got that impression. Your name came up more than once. He wanted me to stay away from you."

"No. He's jealous of you. It wasn't because of me," I answer, remembering how Finn had said that every time he did anything, Tiam would come in and do it better. I think of his words, *If I were king, I'd want you to be my queen,* and shiver. "But that's okay. I don't have to see Finn at all."

"How?"

"I'll climb up the laundry chute and wait for the tide to recede. As soon as it does, I can go out, get the princess and the map, and be back here before the rest even leave the formation."

He crosses his arms in front of himself. "That's too dangerous. I should be doing it."

"But it's not a big deal. I can do it quickly. I've had practice," I say, amazed at how certain my voice sounds. "I just hope she's still there."

His lips press together, and he clenches his fists and shakes his head.

I smile at him reassuringly. "Look, you've done enough. You just saved us from those things. And everyone has things they're afraid of. It's okay."

"You're not afraid of anything," he whispers.

I snort. "Are you kidding? I'm afraid of just about everything."

"But not so much that it stops you from doing things. You take on the things you're afraid of. You don't cower in a corner like a baby. Like me. I should be over it by now. I know that. But I'm…" He brings his chin to his chest.

I narrow my eyes. "Over what?"

"During my sixth season, I was locked in a drinking jug and tossed out into the ocean. Someone's idea of fun. I was in there for three days, until I washed up on shore and Buck Kettlefish found me. If it weren't for him, I'd be dead." He sighs. "But ever since then…I don't do so well in closed spaces."

I figured it was something like that. "You don't have to explain yourself."

"Well, I just wanted to tell you that. Anyway, that's what started it. When the king found out I survived that, he thought it was a sign from the gods. That I was destined to be king." He laughs. "At least that's what he told me. He's been watching me ever since then. Crazy, huh?"

I shrug. "Well, he *did* wear those crazy pink robes, so we

always knew he wasn't all there," I say, thinking of the other sign that guided us, lit hope under us. Star. She was a sign from the gods, too, that we would be all right. Maybe the gods were right.

He starts to laugh some more, but quickly catches himself. "I wish I was as brave as you are. I don't know how you do it. You're fearless, Coe. They threw you in so many times. And yet you kept coming back. That night when I was chained in the castle, you went into the ocean to save me, even after—"

I'm lost. "Wait. What?"

His eyes widen. "They threw you into the ocean. Three or four times. No one else had survived that. But you were only a child, and every morning, there you'd be. Alive. You lost your hand, yes, but still you lived. They thought you were a demon. That if Star was sent to save them, you were sent to punish them." He stares at me. "Are you telling me you don't know this?"

"No, I—"

"Right. You don't remember a lot of it. I forgot. I'm sorry."

"They thought I was a demon?" I ask, but of course it makes sense. The way they look at me. The way they've steered clear of me all this time. But how had I done something so impossible without remembering it in the least?

"Well, you did drown in the ocean, only to come back the next day. Nobody survives the ocean."

"And how did I do that?" I wonder aloud, thinking about yesterday, when I'd been in the stores. I'd hit my head, lost consciousness, and yet, after the room swelled with water and drained, I woke, perfectly fine. And somehow, I'd managed to conquer the oceans, oceans no human has ever survived, as a small child.

Tiam watches me, gauging my reaction. "Coe. What are you thinking?"

I let out a snort. "I'm thinking something's seriously odd about me. Maybe I *am* a demon? Or maybe I'm immortal?"

"You are *not* a demon," he says with a small smile. "And don't ask me to hit you with the shovel to prove you *are* mortal. I won't do it."

Just as I start to laugh, his face turns serious. "But one thing I do think about... The girl with the dark hair and pale skin." He reaches over and gently wraps a tendril of hair around his finger, making my breathing quicken. His eyes trail to my lips, and I know he is wanting to kiss them as much as I want him to. "Like yours."

Suddenly, a high-pitched scream echoes through the cavern, making my eardrums quake. Fern.

We rush back to the bunker as fast as we can. Fern is sitting up in the little bed, eyes wide. "Where were you?" she asks as I climb beside her and pull her into my lap. "I thought you left me alone."

"I'm sorry," I say, stroking her hair. "I'm here."

The strange swishing noise we'd heard earlier from above has dissipated. I know what it means. The tide is going out. Tiam eyes me suspiciously. I know it will take every ounce of his strength to swallow his pride and let me go up the chute. I flash my most confident smile. *It will be easy,* I mouth to him. His muscles tighten, his jaw sets and he nods. *Be careful,* he mouths back.

And then I climb to the door of the chute.

Nineteen

This Hollow Valley

I t's precisely one heartbeat after I wiggle myself back into the chute that I remember. This is anything but easy. I vaguely recall telling myself the last time that I would rather drown or be devoured by scribblers than do this again. And yet here I am. Part of me thinks I am being too much of a pushover with Tiam; that I should have forced him to go instead of me. But then I remember the way his mouth felt on mine and there is no choice but to keep scaling the slick walls.

I climb until I'm weak, until my shoulders are buzzing with pain and my legs are numb. Sweat leaks into my eyes. I make it to the top and pry open the grate while the castle is still weeping, the water still swirling through the drains on the floors. I slide myself onto the stone floor with a great splash and, after massaging my sore limbs and taking in the cool, fresh air, crawl into the corridor. As expected, it's empty.

I hurry through the hallway and up the steps, taking them two at a time. If I can persuade the princess quickly enough, we may be able to make it down the chute before the last of the water drains from my quarters. Simple.

At the top of the tower steps, I pause to rap on the wooden door, softly but firmly.

No answer.

"Princess. It's Coe. Let me in."

Nothing.

I reach down to twist the doorknob, but I don't need to. The door is open a crack and creaks when I push. My eyes begin to water as some sickly sweet odor twists my stomach. Everything is a mess. Her bed is ripped apart, sheets strewn everywhere. The armoire of beautiful dresses is overturned, its contents spread over the stone floor in a sad rainbow. All of the desk drawers have been spilled. Her jars of perfumes have been smashed. And the princess is nowhere in sight.

I creep across the wreckage, wincing as the small bits of glass prick the soles of my feet, to the doorway to the king's room. I don't know why, but I shiver as I peek inside. Maybe it's because the king died there. Maybe it's because no one is allowed here. Or maybe it's because I've come to hate the king so much, after what he's done to us. The room is enclosed, stuffy and warm. There is a bit of a stench there, the sweet decay of death I've come to know so well. No windows at all, as if he wanted to keep us invisible to him. I gasp. Every wall is covered with pink seashells. They bulge from the walls unevenly, making the chamber look like the guts of some dead animal. But that's not what holds my gaze.

There is a bed that a dozen people could lie across comfortably in the center of the room, the enormous headboard of which is also adorned in seashells. The mattress looks so soft and luxurious. I imagine his frail frame sinking into the center of it as he took in his last breath.

It is the bed from my dreams.

How is that possible? No one has ever been into the king's room, save for the guards, the medic and the princess. And yet everything is exactly the same, down to the last detail, although perhaps not as enormous as I'd once pictured. How can that be, if I've never been here before?

I know the answer: I *have* been here. A long, long time ago, I'd lain across that bed, happy, carefree. It wasn't a dream.

It was a memory.

I'd been in the king's private quarters. But why? Why would he have allowed me there? I may have once been Star's playmate, but I was also a demon. That's what Tiam said they thought I was. Why would I have been granted access to a place for only the most privileged people?

I tear my eyes away from the bed and peer around the room. "Princess?" I whisper, losing all the confidence I'd had when I told Tiam my plan.

I retrace my steps to the princess's quarters and in that moment remember the map. I rush to the desk and rifle through the items that have been scattered around the floor, spilling her container of stick pins and picking through a pile of delicate silk and lace scarves. It's not there.

Helpless, I look out her window, at the balcony. The red flag that has always flown there, tattered and faded, flaps in the wind loudly, as if to taunt me. *You're too late.* Past it, the cement formation stands, the ocean around it slowly receding.

From here, the sight is so pitiful and strange. No wonder his room had no windows. I don't know how anyone could have gazed at it every day and been okay with knowing that *he'd* put us there. Bodies crush together at its surface so tightly I can't make out a single one. Star could be among them. She could still be okay. But even as I think it, I know it's unlikely. Silly girl that she is, she'd probably sooner drown than surround herself with commoners.

Now what do I do? Everything I came for is gone.

For a moment I think I'll go back, explain to Tiam that she's gone, and I've done all I can. But he'd never settle for that. Not for a mere theory that she's dead. He'd need evidence. He'd try to find a way back up to the surface to ensure that there's nothing more that could be done. As I'm thinking, I approach the balcony and see a flash of something in the very corner of my eye that makes me jump.

The pink that could only be the king's robe. Finn.

He's standing on the balcony, arms crossed, surveying the scene. My stomach drops. Sweat blooms on my forehead, immediately running down my temples and stinging my eyes. I slowly turn to leave, my movements unhurried and careful, so as not to alert him. But at that moment he throws a lock of his hair back behind his ear and catches sight of me. Rage engulfs his face. He's inside before I can break into a run, and he latches on to my stump. No one has ever touched me there, and I howl, more from fear than the pain. "Coe!" he shouts, wrenching my arm as I fight to free myself, like a fish on a line.

"Let me go!"

"Tending to the princess, were you?" he breathes. He succeeds in catching my other arm and pulls me to him, then wraps his arms around my waist as I kick and flail. But it's no use. He's easily as big as two of me. His grip doesn't loosen until I stop kicking, and when he speaks again, his voice is calmer. "You have to come with me."

I know that I, like Tiam, have aroused suspicions one too many times, and people who act suspiciously cannot be allowed to live in Tides. It has always been that way.

He presses his hot, damp hand against the back of my neck and firmly guides me down the stone staircase. We splash down to the second floor. Out the window, the formation is beginning to disperse. I can't feel my feet beneath my body. Each step feels closer to my last. The water is still knee-deep on the ground floor. I wade through it and push the heavy front doors open, squinting in the bright light. After all that time inside, the light stings my eyes worse than ever. The townspeople have begun scurrying down the long ladder and ropes attached to the formation edges. The first to see me gaze in disbelief, as if I'd just washed in with the tide. Then the shouts begin. "She's here. Over here!"

Blinking furiously, I realize that Finn has taken a spear from his back. It's a metal spear, the kind only the guards used to have. He jabs the point into my rib cage, as if I'm any match for him. "Coe," he shouts, loudly enough for everyone to hear. He is putting on a show for them, as their king. "People are worried. You have to explain yourself, right now."

"Where is the princess?" I ask, trying to keep my voice calm, but my knees are shaking. All my life, I've been virtually ignored on the island. And now every one of the four hundred people on the island seems to be staring at me.

By now two guards have come to his aid, and now they're jabbing their spears at me. I don't know what has given them the sudden impression that I'm so dangerous, when I've always been the weakest person on the island. Finn crosses his arms. "Coe. I will ask the questions."

A moment passes with us both standing, frozen in a staring match. Maybe he wants me to bow. He finally leans in beside me. "Coe, what do you think you are doing?" he says, almost gently.

"I want to ask you the same thing. Is it true you killed the twins?"

His lower lip trembles, flashing a bit of guilt that disappears as soon as he juts his chin forward. It's very regal on him. "Coe, that is the way you survive in this world," he tells me. "You dispose of the threats. And *you* are starting to look like a threat."

"You *know* I am not one," I seethe.

"I don't know that. I don't know what you are up to. You and I could have ruled this kingdom together," he mumbles. "But now..."

I grit my teeth. "I don't want to be queen. Not to a king who is a murderer." I whisper, "Please, Finn."

He narrows his eyes. "Coe, you know what I told you. It's not my decision. The king needs to do what the people want in order to remain king," he whispers, his eyes intense on mine. "You've disappeared now for three tides, only to come back from the castle each time, perfectly fine. So that leaves us all wondering, since the rest of the world is under-water, *where you have been spending your time.* We know you weren't in the tower. Coe, nobody trusts you. *They think you are up to no good, and want you dead.* So what are my choices?"

The guards' spears graze my side. I can feel the cold metal through my tunic. "I know. I don't know what to say."

"You can start by explaining yourself," he says. "Where have you been?"

I don't know how to answer, so I say nothing.

He motions to "his" men, whom I am sure were the king's men only a few tides ago. They grind their metal spears into the sand as they grab for me. I try to jump back, but their arms come from everywhere, and they clamp their rough hands on my arms and legs and yank me in the direction of the sea.

The sea. I try to kick, but their grip is unforgiving.

No, he wouldn't do this to me. He wouldn't throw me in the sea with the scribblers. He promised Buck he'd protect me.

"Wait," I shout. "Wait."

They don't wait. If anything, they move more surely.

The waves crash in front of me. The sea sprays my face. The white of the sand and black of the ocean swirl together in my vision, and I know that me surviving all those sea-sons ago was just luck. It had to have been. I was just a small child. I've heard stories about people lasting quite a while in the water, being shoved back in by the guards' spears. But most of them last moments, heartbeats even. How long will I last this time? Is it hissing I hear, or is it just my imagination?

"Drop her."

Suddenly they toss me. I feel myself flying through the air, and I hold my breath, waiting for the inevitable splash and for the world around me to turn dark and murky. Instead, my body falls against sand, damp, soft sand. It's only then I realize my face is wet with tears.

The sand clumps in my eyelashes. I wipe them and see Finn staring over me, chewing on a piece of seaweed. The men are, once again, pointing their spears at me, poking me with them, laughing. I scramble to my knees, feeling shameful already. I've spent every tide thinking about my death, and I always hoped I'd face it with dignity. But somehow I think I knew that when the time came, I'd turn into a weeping mess.

Finn crouches beside me. He's still chewing noisily on that scraggle of black seaweed. It hangs out of his mouth like a long black serpent tongue. "If you don't talk, next time, they *will* throw you into the sea. I cannot stop the people from doing what they see fit. And don't think you will be so lucky as to survive, the way you did when you were a child."

He plucks a lock of black hair that had fallen into my face, and I flinch. He trails his finger to my cheek, wiping the sand from it.

His eyes soften as he gazes at my face. "I never believed those stories about you being a demon. Just as I never believed Tiam was the savior. Those things were said to keep us living in fear, to stop us from questioning. But we *are* questioning now. And we think you have some answers."

I can't meet his stare. I think of how Tiam said I was unafraid of everything. What a lie. My whole body is shaking so hard I can barely get the words out. "I—I don't."

"Burbur gave us a little tour of the stores," he says, to which

I exhale deeply and squeeze my eyes shut. "We found some very interesting things down there. Besides the honey. But I get the feeling you know all about that."

"I didn't. Not until a few tides ago," I say honestly.

One of the guards comes forth, holding the journal and fairy-tale book I'd carried. In all the commotion, I hadn't realized they'd stripped me of my bag.

Finn picks the materials up, turning them over in his hands. "What the hell are they?" His eyebrows raise in question.

"Books," I explain.

He opens the journal and turns the pages, landing on Cass's map. He lets out a quick breath. "This map is of the stores." I'm sure his hands are trembling as he runs his fingers along the smudged lines. "Aliah," he whispers.

It's a word that means nothing. And yet, I get this strange feeling that maybe it meant something to me, once before. "You got this from your father."

It's not a question. He knows. "What is Aliah?"

Somewhere, I hear seagull squawks, punctuating the word. He closes the book and dismisses the men. They lower their spears, and he puts the books in my bag and hands it to me. He grabs me by the arm and leads me toward the base of the platform, until we're out of earshot from the rest of the commoners. "I thought you would tell me."

"I've never heard that before," I say.

"Your father told me something before he left on his Explore. He said he had to leave, that he had betrayed the king in the worse way possible and this was his penance. He said he'd always hoped that one day, Aliah would return and show us the way, but that never happened, and he needed to try something else."

"Aliah? I don't know who or what that is."

"He talked in his sleep a lot. One thing he said, I'll never forget, is 'Aliah has the map.'" He motions to the bag. "Is that the map? That's the only map I've ever seen."

I think of the map in the princess's room. I shake my head. "He gave this map to me. Not Aliah, whoever that is."

"Coc, there have always been rumors. Far-fetched tales that there is an escape tunnel to a land of paradise under the castle. That those stories of ghosts and evil under the castle were meant to keep people from poking around too much. I always figured it was just the crazed ravings of people like Xilia, who can no longer tell real life from fantasy." He stares at me and sucks in a breath. "You know what I'm talking about, don't you? That they're not just rumors?"

I just stare at him, afraid of what he'll do.

"Your father was the highest ranking guard of the Wallows, once. Before you were born. Did you know that? He had a coveted spot in formation."

"I— What?" This news comes as complete shock to me. "He was just a fisherman."

"Many tides ago, after Star was presented as a sign from the gods, the rumor of the escape route being under a castle somehow festered, and the people were clamoring for Wallow to look into it. Wallow agreed to send someone on a search. He let the people choose their best, most fearless and trustworthy man to investigate."

"My father?"

He nods. "But no escape was found. The mission was a failure. The ghosts and demons changed him somehow, so much so that he was unable to speak about what happened there. Your father was cast out to the outer edge of the formation. The king was deeply disappointed in him. I can only assume that was the betrayal your father spoke of. Didn't he tell you?"

"I—I don't know anything about this," I say, but suddenly I remember the scratched letters on the plaque in the laundry room. They had been his, after all.

He studies me. "People don't believe you. They think that he gave you information, and that you know more than you're letting on."

"If I did know a way out, I would let everyone know," I whisper.

He smiles slightly, and then looks up at the sky and shakes his head. "They don't believe you. Not anymore. You need to convince them. Take us where you've been for the past few tides."

I exhale. Of course I knew he'd say that. "They listen to you. It's not so much that they don't believe me. *You* don't believe me. Admit it."

He nods. "All right. You're not being truthful, Coe."

"Neither are you," I counter. "Fine. I'll take you down there. Tell me where the princess is first."

"Persistent, aren't you?" he groans, spitting the piece of seaweed onto the ground. "We have not seen her. We thought she was with you, but since you don't know, we can only assume she's dead."

It's not as if I'd expected anything better, but I wonder at that moment if I could have saved her. If I am capable of saving *anyone*. My insides tighten so much I think I'm in danger of passing out. I never wanted to hurt anyone. But Star, Fern, Tiam… I have a feeling I may have just brought doom upon us all.

Twenty
The Descent

I walk slowly across the wet sand toward the entrance to the castle, all the while squinting in the sun and trying to avoid the prick of Finn's spear. The rest of the towns-people have gathered around us, and they separate for us as we walk. I wish I had a plan. I wish I could be like Clever Gretel and come up with something that would get me out of this mess. But my mind swirls with thoughts of Fern, little Fern, and how she deserves so much better. Of Tiam, and the feel of his mouth on mine, his breath in my ear. Of how our first kisses were probably our last.

I think of how completely pathetic I'd acted when they'd almost thrown me into the water. I thought I was stronger than that. I thought I was prepared for death. Instead I'd squealed and fussed like a child. After everything I've been through, after all the times I almost met death! Thank God Tiam wasn't there to see that, after he'd gone on and on about how fearless I was. Maybe he's the reason why I acted so pathetically in the first place. Because only a short time before, I'd finally found something that made life worthwhile.

"You're stalling," Finn grumbles. I lurch forward and start moving faster this time, to the doors. One of his guards holds them open, and we pass through.

Not having any other bright ideas, I lead him and two guards to the door to the basement. I fumble for the key in my bag and finally produce it and unlock the door. "It's down there," I explain.

"I'm following," he says, nudging me along.

I step down until I arrive at the map at the bottom of the stairs. I study Cass's drawing, as if it really does tell me exactly where the exit is. "We go this way," I say, turning toward the honey room. I clutch the key in my sweaty palm as the guards light a torch to blaze the way.

Then it suddenly occurs to me. I have Star's key. But the only other person with a key is Burbur. If I can somehow separate from them, lock myself in the honey room… I can make it down to the subbasement before they can follow me. But… how? There are three of them and only one of me. Six hands versus one. The two guards tower over me, broad-shouldered and burly, and Finn is no lightweight, either.

The light from the torch dips and sways as the guard holding it moves. It appears he is having a hard time balancing both his spear and the torch because his armor keeps getting in the way. He grunts and groans and then curses as a few sparks land on his hand. All of this begins the wheels turning in my head. Soon, I have a plan.

We walk on past the honey room. I've never been this

far before, so it's not much of a stretch when I look to Cass's drawing for help. We pass the canned vegetables room, and the roots room, whatever that is. Then I find one that seems fitting. CANNED MEATS. I use my key to open the door. "It's in here," I explain, not looking at them.

Finn scratches the scars on the side of his face, then points to the plaque beside the door. "What does this here say?"

"This is where they store the canned foods," I answer.

"You can understand those markings?" Finn asks. The guards mumble to one another, probably suspicious. They follow me inside. It's just more crates, most of which appear empty. Finn looks around, tossing things over carelessly with the end of the spear, letting the soft packing material scatter across the stone floor. He moves ahead into the room while I hold back. The guards flank me, but I'm focusing on the guard with the torch to the right of me. I swallow, take a deep breath and tell myself it's time.

In a blinding flash I reach out and grab the torch, throwing it to the ground. Finn whirls and lunges for me, but instantly the dry paper packing material is ignited, throwing a huge wall of fire between him and the rest of us. The guard who lost his spear is on fire, spinning in tight circles, squealing and screeching much the way I did on the beach. The hair of his beard is engulfed and he's swatting helplessly at it as if trying to kill a fly; it's just making the flames curl down his chest. The other guard jabs his spear at me, but I squeeze to the side just in time to avoid it. Then he throws himself at me, hands clawing at my neck. I fall to the ground, kicking, screaming, thrashing all three of my good limbs until he

lurches back in pain. I reach for the torch, then climb halfway to my feet, stumbling to the door. As I do, I catch sight
of Finn struggling to unfurl the cheerful pink robe from his
neck, the bottom of which is now on fire. I grasp the handle,
pulling with all my might, until it's about to click shut. But
four black, burned fingers snake their way out.

"Don't you dare, Coe!" a voice screams in my ear, shaking the walls.

I pull frantically, as hard as I can, until it shuts out Finn's
voice. I try to turn the key so that it locks, but my hand is
slick with sweat, making it useless. Finally I grab on to it
with my teeth and twist it around, tasting the metallic sting
on my tongue. I move back to the other wall and just stare
at the door as they pound and claw. I wonder if it will hold
long enough for me to stay and catch my breath.

I don't wait around to find out. I rush to the honey room
and as my shaking fingers are trying to fit the key into its
opening, the pounding stops, and I hear something else coming from the faraway door. Something much more controlled.

Metal against metal. The turn of a key in a lock.

And I know that Finn has Burbur's precious key.

Twenty-One
The Last of Meeting Places

My hand feels numb on the metal, and it's as if the keyhole isn't there. I can't seem to press it through. Down the hallway, in the darkness, something creaks. The door. They've opened it. I finally lean against the wall and take a deep breath to steady myself, then push the key through on the first try. I turn it, throw myself into the room and slam the door shut just as Finn's shouts echo through the corridor.

He has a key. And yet another reason to hate me.

I hear the key scraping around the metal door outside. It occurs to me that while they may have a key, they don't have the torch. But they do have flint, and there was enough fire in that room to start a light. I rush to the metal disc in the floor and suddenly I realize…I can't lift it on my own. It was Fern who lifted it before. This whole plan had failure on it from the start.

But as the disc comes into view, I notice that it looks like two. One shiny metal, one black and endless. As I come closer, I realize it's not two... Someone has already opened it. It's open!

I squeeze the torch between my chin and chest and climb down as quickly as I can, then struggle to pull the cover over me. When it closes tightly, I breathe deeply with relief. They might not even know I'm down here. And if they do, they're big men with much pudgier fingers than I have. I'd like to see them open it.

I remember the scribblers and am just about to see if I can climb over the pipes when I'm startled by a sound. Not hissing, as I expect. A voice. A human cry.

I whirl around, still clutching the top rung of the ladder. But I think the sound came from below me. "Who's there?" I ask.

There's splashing underneath me, so I shine my torch down as a voice says, "Coe...is that you?"

I exhale when I see the figure, sopping wet and clutching the ladder only a rung beneath my feet. She still manages to look pretty and poised, even drenched and shivering. "Princess!"

If she's glad to see me, I wouldn't know it. "Help me out of here at once," she sobs. "This is not the place for me!"

"I'm sorry, but we must be quiet. Finn is above and he's not happy."

"Finn? Who is that?" She narrows her eyes. "Another stupid commoner."

I ignore her. "What happened to you, Princess?"

"I knew they were coming, so I vacated during the last

high tide. I hid in the waves until they consumed the castle and then came back here."

I stare at her, incredulous.

"Oh, do not look at me that way. I am not as helpless as everyone thinks," she says.

"How? The scribblers…"

"I can easily outswim them. I'm a royal, remember?"

I raise my eyebrows. Nobody has every claimed to be able to outswim scribblers. And in all her tides in the tower, has she ever even *touched* the salt water, much less had the chance to learn to swim? "And the door? How did you get in, when I had your key?"

She nods. "I gave you *my* key. The king had a key, as well."

"But you could have drowned," I whisper.

She laughs. "Oh, that's not possible for royalty. Now, you said Tiam was down here? I need to see him. It's disgusting and cold down here, and I am catching a chill. This is no place for a princess."

"Yes…" I say, a smile spreading on my face despite her coldness. My heart swells with happiness. Now Tiam won't have to go looking for her. Now I can bring her to Tiam, and they can be… They can be what? Suddenly everything inside me deflates. How can I feel so overjoyed and disappointed all at once? "He's this way."

I show her how to climb up to the pipes, and she stares aghast at me, wrinkling her nose. "Whatever for?"

"There are scribblers in the water. Surely you've seen them?"

"No, I have not. I'm not accustomed to wriggling around like a lowly worm," she snorts.

She's spent all of her life in the tower, away from the oceans. She has no idea how cruel the scribblers can be. But then again, for someone with no familiarity with the ocean, she certainly did a good job swimming here once she was forced from the tower. It's nothing short of a miracle that she's here. Maybe as a gift from the gods, she has their protection.

She reaches her hand up. I suppose it is up to me to pull her the rest of the way. Though she's wearing a soaked gown that itself must weigh more than Fern, she pushes her feet against the ladder and is up in no time. As I pull her up, I recognize the gown. It's her wedding dress. It's dirty and sopping and not exactly in the shape she'd hoped for.

I tell her to follow me, and we proceed the way I'd come with Fern. This time, though, the company is a little less... engaging. This time, I have to find something to tune out the mutters of annoyance and shrieks of disgust that keep emanating from behind me. I always, always go back to the kiss with Tiam. It works well to distract me, but then I realize I'm torturing myself. It was just practice for him, after all. Or maybe it was more... But does that matter? I tell myself to stop thinking about it. It's over. It can never happen again.

"There's a spider the size of my hand here," she whimpers, followed by the sound of ripping fabric. "Oh! My dress!"

She has the folds of her dress lifted up to her waist and is looking down at it. "Why don't you rip the rest of it off?" I suggest. "It will be easier to move."

"It's my wedding dress," she says, and sighs. Then she

reaches down and pulls the skirt from her waist, casting it aside. Underneath she is wearing a small white slip that clings to her thighs, but at least it is easier to maneuver around. "I look like a perfect wreck. Tiam will laugh at me. Looking like one of his own!"

"He won't laugh," I mumble, my voice tinged with bitterness. Tiam care about a torn dress? For one so convinced he is her soulmate, she doesn't know him at all.

We climb on for ages until arriving at the section of the door that I'd kicked in earlier. I stop and shine the torch through, but I can't see anything. "Tiam?" I whisper into the void.

There is no answer. Again, Tiam has disappeared. Probably out scouting for the exit. I don't know what about his past actions made me think that he'd stay around and wait in the bunker with Fern for me to return with the princess and the map. I wonder how he'll react when he sees that I've gotten only one of the two things I've set out to find. I wonder which of the two he values most.

The princess crawls beside me. "Is he in there?" she asks, wrinkling her nose and wiping her brow with a piece of fabric from her ripped dress. "Oh, dear. Another dark, damp place."

She bunches up the cloth and begins to tuck it into her cleavage when I notice something very interesting about it. There's a *B* on it. Is it really fabric from her dress after all? Her dress has a bluish tint, and this cloth is yellowed, old. "What is that?" I point at it.

"Oh, this?" She pulls it from between her breasts and waves it in front of me. "Nothing. A handkerchief."

I grab it from her and open it up, trembling, unable to contain the glee. On the top it says B MT ENT. Underneath there is a map. A maze of boxes, and a thin, dotted red line running through them. The map! "Do you realize what this means? This is the map to the exit. The way out."

She squints at me, then grabs the map. "Ridiculous. There is no such thing."

"No," I say. She has to be bluffing. "I know about the map. Tiam told me—"

"Tiam?" Her eyes blaze. "He *told* you?"

I bite my tongue. Suddenly the weight of all I've said hits me with force. Of course she knows about it. But it's a royal secret. Only intended for a select few. I wasn't to know. And now I've made things awkward for Tiam.

She sighs. "You weren't supposed to be told about it until we were well on our way. It's far too dangerous to let commoners know. I suppose this was to be expected, considering how *close* you two are. I will need to speak to him about this. Who else knows?"

"Well, um, Fern, the little girl…and…" I stop short. Finn. He knows. He'll keep looking, because the alternative is death. It's only a matter of time before he finds us. Not exactly a good thing. But he doesn't have a map. Maybe he'll get so hopelessly lost that finding us will be impossible. At least, one can hope. I mumble, "Just Fern."

She sighs. "Well, we'd better hurry. Lead me to Tiam."

I climb into the room and help her as she lowers herself down beside me. "Careful," I say. "There are vicious creatures here."

"Oh!" she moans when she sees the remains of them lying in the center of the path. She buries her face in my shoulder. "That's atrocious! I will be glad to be out of here. Surely nothing in this new land can be worse than here."

"So, it really does exist?" I ask.

"My father often spoke of it to me. He had never been there, before, though. I imagine it can't be very beautiful."

I swallow. "Why do you say that?"

She nods. "Well, it's under the castle. Dark, dank, moldy." She waves her arms around. "Like this. And the people there... Well...they're different."

"Different?" A sinking feeling blooms in the pit of my stomach. "Different how?"

"As in, not the same," she snaps, clearly getting annoyed with my questions. "I don't know. He never liked to talk about them."

"Oh." I have a thousand questions swirling in my head, so I wish she'd be more accommodating. Gently, I venture another. "Did he say...how it came to be under your castle?"

"My father told me it was a city built in the antediluvian times. For protection against any disaster that might befall the human race. Thousands of people were sent there to live, but there were millions of people in the world at that time. Only the most important people were allowed."

"A city underground!" I marvel. "How odd. How do people survive there?"

She shrugs absently.

"What? You've never even been curious?"

She looks around, shivering. "No."

"And your father wasn't? Not once?"

Star bites her lip and looks at the ground. She doesn't speak for a long time. "No. Why should he have been?"

"Why?" I ask, wanting to grab her by the shoulders and shake her. "Out of curiosity, if nothing else! There's a whole world under your feet and all you Wallows want to do is hide in your tower."

Her eyes narrow. "I hate dark, damp places."

"But your kingdom is dead! Think of how many people might have been saved if they'd known there was an escape. My father, for one!"

She ignores me and continues walking forward. After all, who is my father to her, but another lowly commoner? "Tiam!" she suddenly shouts, then whirls around to me, accusation blazing in her eyes. "You said he was here. Why is he not answering?"

I give up on her and look around. It's eerily quiet. Up ahead is the bunker and the entrance to the laundry chute, but Fern and Tiam are nowhere. "They've got to be here, somewhere," I say. I call out, "Fern? Tiam?"

Nothing.

We take another few steps toward the chute when I notice something. Daylight, streaming down the opening, making a tiny square of white light on the floor. Was the chute open? Could I have been so silly as to not peel the grate back into place? I try to remember back to when I'd climbed up there, and realize I have no recollection of ever closing it. At the time, I'd thought I'd quickly be able to retrieve the princess and the map and return to the chute before the rest of the world left the formation.

My throat goes dry. Until now, I hadn't felt the chill of my wet clothes against my skin. When the tide comes, the water will come through. And closed, nobody could see the opening. But with the grate on the chute peeled back, if someone were searching for us, it would be all too easy.

Stupid, stupid me.

"Tiam?" I whisper again, a little less surely this time.

We round a large pile of crates and the B MT ENT sign comes into view. A white gleam from Tiam's portable light dances in the distance, bobbing up the passage toward us. I hear his voice, soft and soothing, saying something to Fern likely to calm her fears.

"Coe?" he calls out. "That you?"

I sigh, relieved. The sound of his voice is like clean, pure water after a long walk. I knew he'd never leave me alone. When he comes closer, his eyes on me, I find myself blushing. I hope the light isn't strong enough for him or the princess to see. "Hi," I say shyly. Then I curse myself. Could I possibly say anything that screams *I kissed you and I can't stop thinking about it* any louder?

Fern rushes to me, burying her face in my tunic, and as I stroke her hair, I'm glad to have something other than Tiam's lips to concentrate on. The princess doesn't seem to notice my problem. She rushes to Tiam, exhaling dramatically, draping herself over his shoulder. "Oh, am I so glad to see you!" Tiam smiles at her, then his eyes trail to me, and he winces. I can't tell if it's because he regrets what we did or if it's because she's pressing into his injury. She pulls away from him and inspects him. "My goodness! And I thought *I* looked a wreck. What happened to you?"

"Long story," he mumbles, sticking his chin out bravely. She didn't seem as concerned the night she forced us from the steps of the tower as the tide approached. I start to roll my eyes but catch them halfway when Tiam suddenly turns to me. "Did you find the map?"

Star holds it up for him. "I didn't know you were going to tell *her*," she says, pouting.

"We have no choice, Princess," he says softly.

"And why didn't *you* come to rescue me?" she asks. "I thought my father put you in charge of me?"

I lift Fern onto my back and pretend not to be involved, but it's not possible. I can almost see Star's words tearing into him. Tiam swallows and looks away. I know how heavily this weighs upon him, how much he wanted to make good on his promise to the king. "I'm sorry" is all he can say. The way he says it, I can't tell if he's speaking to her...or to me.

"Let's look at the map," I say after a long silence, choking on Fern's hair, which seems to be everywhere. Star unfolds it. "Where do we go?"

"How should I know?" Star says. "I've never studied it for any length of time, and it's so dark here I can barely see a thing."

"Let me get some more of those lights, just in case. You go on. I'll be right back," Tiam calls over his shoulder, already halfway up the corridor.

I drop Fern to her feet and yank the map from Star's hands.

It's not exactly easy to decipher. There are no words, save for the B MT ENT at the top, and it's difficult to see where we are in relation to where the red line begins. Where it ends is just the tip of an arrow. There's nothing else. The beginning of the line is surrounded by what looks like a thick, wide corridor, which goes straight for some time. There the line becomes dotted. Then it becomes a thick red again, snaking through a maze of turns, and there it looks as if the corridors become smaller and smaller. "I think…I think we just go straight," I say.

Star hesitates. "Perhaps we should wait for Tiam."

I exhale loudly, annoyed. "We'll just go on a little ways."

She doesn't move, just looks down at the ground. "It will do no good to follow that map," she says. "We can't all make it."

Maybe it's because I'm so busy trying to prod her into action that I'm only half listening, because the meaning of her words is lost on me. "What?"

"The passage. The map. It's a very treacherous route," she says. I'm about to tune her out, as I'm so tired of her snobbery, when she says, "Only royals may pass."

"What? Is the passage guarded?"

"I don't know. I'm just saying what my father told me. All I know is that he told me that only certain people have the ability to make it through. I assume he meant royals, people of supreme worth."

It's so ridiculous to think that a passage could be open only to royals. After all, despite Star's claims of her importance, I've known some commoners who were twice her worth. And yet it still plants a seed of doubt. Could she be right? "Well, let's just see about that."

Fern pulls on my hand. "We're going straight?" her voice is mouselike. "Down there?"

I nod.

"But…" Fern's voice quivers. "That way… We tried to go that way before."

It hits me as I take another step. The map is leading us directly to the place where those horrible monsters cornered us. Where the corridor was flooded. Impassable.

Star begins to tremble, clutching her hands together in front of her. There is something else she hasn't told me, and if it's anything worse than what she's already said, I am not sure I want to know.

Fern squeals, "We're not going *that* way, are we?"

I massage her shoulder. "Yes, we are," I say. "It's better than where we're coming from. I'm afraid things will be very bad for us if we stay."

Fern shakes her head. "But the path…it's…"

"We'll find a way around it." We take a few more steps, until we're ankle-deep in the dank black water, and the path begins to descend sharply. I wade out until I'm waist-deep, until the iciness of the water makes it impossible to feel my toes, and study all the corners, but there's no trick door in the wall, and not even an inch of breathing room at the top of the passage. It's most completely blocked. I don't think any royal would be able to find anything different. "This can't be the way," I say, studying the map again.

Star wades out toward me, and the back of my neck prick-les. At first I am not sure why, but then I realize there is something strange about her expression. After a moment I realize it's because she's not grimacing or shuddering or squealing about the freezing water. She's just walking, arms out, ever so gracefully, her face completely serene. As she nears, I think that she'll peer over my shoulder at the map, to help me figure out where we're going. Instead, she pulls the map from my hand and whispers, "I most definitely think it is the way." Then I feel her hands, cold and silken, on my shoulders, a sudden, enormous downward pressure there...and then I am plunged fully underwater, where the world swirls green-gray.

Twenty-Two
Sunlight on a Broken Column

Immediate panic. Immediate shock. It doesn't fully register that Star, Princess Star, is holding me underwater; the thought is somewhere in the back of my muddled mind, but the first thing I feel is terror. The second is the impulse to free myself, and I begin to thrash my arms at her wildly. But it does no good. Star is stronger than I ever would have guessed. The water is so cold, like a million pinpricks on my cheeks. The brine burns my eyes, and it feels oilier and thicker than seawater. She caught me so off guard that after only a few seconds I'm dying for breath. My mouth opens in a scream and all the air is forced out of my lungs. I push against her stomach, her chest, with my own body, but still she won't let go. Her hand is wound around my hair, her elbows digging into my collarbone, as if all of her own weight is atop me.

She must know about me and Tiam. Of all the ways I could have died, I never thought it would be like this. It occurs to me that for all I thought I knew about the princess, she has an infinite ability to surprise. Maybe she's right. Maybe she *is* the better class of person.

I know soon everything will go hazy, I will no longer have the energy to fight and life will leave me. I keep fighting, thrashing my arms and legs at her, but it's little help. She is solid as stone.

I wait for the end.

And I wait.

I think maybe, in my panic, my sense of time has been distorted. That though it seems as if tides have passed, it's only a blink of the eye. But soon I am quite calm, and as I open my eyes and see everything in greenish hues, I realize something. My mouth is open, and I can taste the sour water flooding down my throat.

I am breathing underwater.

I am breathing underwater!

Finally, the pressure on my shoulders releases, and I surface. I don't gasp for air. I don't need to. I am perfectly fine. I stare at her, unable to speak. Her composure is completely unruffled. That I can do this clearly isn't news to her. I wait for her to explain, but she says nothing. "How did you know?" I ask, crawling out of the water and slumping onto the ground beside Fern.

Fern's mouth is hanging open. "Coe, I counted to two hundred twelve! How did you do that?"

Fern doesn't know that she could have counted to two *thousand* and twelve, and I would still have survived. She's shivering, so I grab her hand and wait for Star's answer.

"The markings. On your ribs. I noticed them that first day

I saw you, before you had your bath. Didn't you ever notice them?"

Water is dripping down the end of my nose steadily, tickling it, so I wipe it away and clench my teeth to keep from chattering. "What markings? You mean the scars?"

"They're not scars. I don't know exactly what they are, but they let you breathe in water. And they also make you quite a fast swimmer. Have you not noticed mine?"

Though Star loved to prance about naked, I was usually too embarrassed to look at her for any length of time. But, yes, the one time I did look at her while I was bathing her, I'd noticed the lines under her breasts. Now it makes complete sense how she was able to dive from the balcony and swim to the basement. "You mean, like fish have? You mean…gills?" I ask, so stunned I start to shiver, too. "But…how? How do I have gills? Are you saying I'm part fish?"

Star whispers, "It's the mark of a supreme class of beings."

There she goes, spouting off the "supreme class" nonsense again. After this stunt, I want to leave her here, to go my own way, despite Tiam's promise, but something makes me stall. "Wait. Are you saying *I'm* part of the supreme class?"

She nods.

"That is ridiculous. Twelve tides ago I was cleaning a craphouse," I mutter. "First you say I have gills. And now you are saying I'm—"

"I always suspected," she says. "But I knew it the moment I saw the lines on your ribs. But what I find even more unbelievable is how *you* didn't know."

"But I'm not. They're scars," I insist, looking down at my

body. I never spent much time studying myself, afraid of what I'd see there. Scribbler scars everywhere. And the swell of my breasts made it difficult to see the area directly beneath them. But could it be that those lines crisscrossing the skin there were not scars, but gills? How could it be all this time that I was part fish, and I never knew it? "Buck Kettlefish is my father. My mother died when I was a child."

"Your mother did not die," she says. "*Our* mother did not die. She had to leave."

"'Our' mother? You mean we're—"

"Sisters. Of course."

"But that's— You look like a princess, and I am...strange." I look down at myself, at my dirty tunic, my scabby skin and stump. I can't believe that this girl who has spent her entire life holed up in a tower, away from me, could know anything about my life.

"We're *half* sisters, which means we share a mother, but have different fathers. You look like our mother. She had quite beautiful black hair and the palest of skin, as white as the moon. Her eyes were pink, too. Her name was Aliah."

Aliah. I think of the Dark Girl, the ghost with the darkest hair and whitest skin who had once roamed the castle. Was that Aliah? Was that my mother? Then why had she gone? Why had she left me?

Suddenly, I'm back in the seashell room, lying across that enormous seashell bed as someone with pale skin and black hair smiles above me, tickling my stomach. Her black hair, smelling of lavender, tickles my face. *Corvina... Corvina...* she calls, and her touch is like the gentlest breeze. I'm only a baby, and yet I feel safe, warm, happy—emotions I've never known before, or I haven't known since. Too soon, reality floods in, and I'm back in the cold, dank cave, with Fern and Star staring at me as I pull myself spear-straight. But now I know everything she is saying is true. Breathless, I whisper, "You've known this all along?"

"No. I was just as shocked as you are, when I learned the truth. My father only told me about the underground city when he learned he was dying. But the rest I figured out on my own. I am not as stupid as some might think."

"And why was Aliah sent away?" I ask, my voice rising.

"I do not know." She sighs, annoyed with my questions. "Why don't we find a way out of here, and then you can ask her?"

I'm distracted by a light swirling in the distance. Tiam runs up behind us, stopping short. His eyes narrow when he sees me, dripping wet and looking as if I've seen a ghost. "What did I miss?"

I'm so stunned, I don't even know how my mouth forms the words. "Oh, just something about how only royals can pass and how my mother is alive," I mutter. "Oh, and I can breathe underwater." I look at Star. "Did I leave anything out?"

Fern pipes up. "Star's your sister!" she squeals.

I nod. "Right. That, too."

Tiam studies our faces with an amused expression, which slowly fades to disbelief as he realizes I'm not joking. "Wait. How long was I gone?"

Star studies her fingernails and says, quite unimpressed, "It's true."

She explains to Tiam everything she'd already told me. But I don't hear a word she says. All I can think about is Aliah. Aliah, who is our mother. *Our mother.* I whisper those words to myself, but the more I form them on my lips, the stranger they sound. As Star speaks, Tiam's eyes search out mine, widening with surprise at times, but never once leaving mine. It is clear he didn't know, either. When she is done, he whispers, "Coe? Are you okay?"

I am too stunned to reassure him.

"Coe," he asks, coming close to me. He takes a lock of my hair and sweeps it out of my face. "Coe? Talk to me."

But I've lost the ability to speak. The only thing that registers is Star's eyes narrowing behind him. I flinch away. As much as I crave it, he can't be doing this, touching me. Not now. Not ever again.

"Coe?"

"Stop. Let's…*not* talk about this anymore," I snap. "Please." I can't let these thoughts distract me, because I know if I begin to think about them, I'll likely be consumed by them. Finn may be coming here any moment, and I need to concentrate on the task at hand. "We have to get out of here."

Tiam reluctantly nods and turns his eyes toward the dark corridor, shining the light as far as it will go. "Is this passage…"

"It's blocked by water," I say.

"It's not a problem for you and me," Star says. "We can swim it."

Swim it? I survey the black water. It looks so uninviting, I'm shocked Star would even agree to attempt it. But she did manage to swim in the ocean, with scribblers and a heavy undertow. Compared to that, this will be easy. "It's too dark."

Tiam reaches down with his light and places it underwater. "Look. The fire doesn't go out," he says.

"Okay. I think the passage is only flooded for a short way," I say, pointing at the map. "The dotted line is where the water is. But over here, maybe it's dry. So I'll swim out and see what it's like."

Star doesn't argue. Tiam opens his mouth, but clamps it closed again, clearly frustrated. Again, it's not as if he can take my place.

"I'll be fine. Fern, when I go under, you start counting," I tell her, smiling to hide my nerves. "I'll be back in a little bit."

I wade out as far as I can, then signal to Fern to begin and slide under the water. The light illuminates a short distance ahead of me, so I push off the bottom and start swimming. I don't notice that I'm moving any faster than a scribbler might, but then, I've never actually challenged one to a race. In the water, without an undertow, even without a hand, my arms propel me forward through the green water, so quickly that everything blurs and fades around me. I open my mouth and drink the water in; it's salty and vile, but it has no power over me. I cannot believe that I spent all my life in fear of the ocean, when it never controlled me.

Up ahead, at the top of the passage, I see a light. And suddenly the path begins to curve upward. I swim until I am standing, and straighten my body. I am in the frosty air once again. The walls of the passage look much the same as they had on the other side of the blockage. I'm not sure how much time has passed, so I quickly reverse direction and go back.

When I surface, Fern applauds. "One twenty-three!" she says proudly.

"How was it?" Tiam asks.

"Fine. Not bad at all. I couldn't see much when I got to the other side. But that's got to be the way."

Star wrinkles her nose but doesn't say anything.

"So half of one twenty-three is about sixty. You can definitely make that," I tell Fern. "You can count past a hundred."

Fern says, "But I don't know how to swim!"

"I know. I'm going to swim with you." I turn to Tiam. He's putting on a brave face, but I can tell he doesn't know what he's going to do. "Star can swim with you."

He clears his throat. "I can make it on my own. You guys worry about yourselves."

I don't know what he's thinking. He can't do it alone. Swimming comes naturally to me, for some reason I still can't understand or believe. It's not so easy for Tiam and Fern.

I wade closer to him. "Let me take Fern and Star first. Then I will come back for you," I whisper.

He shakes his head. "I can't. I can't go down there. It's too closed in. I'll never make it."

"No, you will," I say. "It's not too far. The corridor never gets narrower than where we are now."

"No, but the water. It makes everything feel tighter. And did you look at the map? After this, the passages get smaller and smaller." His hands tremble. "Look, just go without me."

"I'd never do that. If you don't go, I don't," I say. "I'm

coming back for you. All you have to do is hold your breath and keep your eyes closed. All right?"

He closes his eyes for a long moment, then nods, swallowing his pride. "All right."

I take Fern by the hand and wade out with her. Star follows, and I hand her the light. "Breathe big," I tell Fern, and she does as she's told. Then we all sink under, and I start to pull Fern through the circle of light that Star is shining ahead of us. It's easier than I thought; Fern is practically weightless. As I swim, I count to myself. *Thirty-two-one-thousand. Thirty-three-one-thousand.* I look back at Fern's face, her cheeks bulge, but her expression is relaxed. *Fifty-nine-one-thousand. Sixty-one-thousand.* I look up but cannot see the light at the end of the tunnel yet. Am I counting faster than Fern had been? I turn back again; her brow is beginning to crease with worry. I push farther, kicking my feet furiously. *Seventy...*

And I see it. The light.

Sighing, I pull Fern until she's standing in water up to her neck. She takes in such a large breath that she begins to cough. I push her toward the shore, and she paddles clumsily until she's sitting on its edge. She wipes her nose with the back of her hand and grins. "We made it! That wasn't so bad. Tiam will do it, easy," she says, surveying the cavern. Star shines the light ahead, and it's more of the same. Dark stone walls, filled with crevasses that might or might not be passages.

I take some breaths to calm myself, then bid them farewell and head back through the passage again. I'm hoping that after two more trips, I'll never have to travel this route again. When I surface, Tiam is standing there, feet in the water, hands on hips. The look on his face is troubled. "You've come back for me again," he mutters.

"Of course I did," I say.

"I don't think anyone else in Tides would. They'd have given up on me by now."

I shake my head. "You always told me not to listen to people when they called me Scribbler Bait. I wouldn't be here today if it weren't for you."

He smiles at me, cupping my face in his hands and pulling my mouth to his. I give in for a moment and then try to push him away, but the desire to draw him close wins out. "No," I say, but my voice is weak. "We can't."

"Coe, I've been thinking," he says breathlessly, running his lips down my jaw to my neck. "If I make it through this…"

"No if. Of course you will. It will be easy."

"I'll tell Star. When we get to this new place, if it exists, I'll let her know. It's you I want. If I'm what you want, that is."

I gasp as he nibbles on my shoulder, wondering how he could even ask that question. This is what I've always wanted. I feel as if I've entered one of my perfect dreams. "Star will be so upset," I whisper.

"Let's not think about that right now," he groans, kissing me again, this one so deep and long I nearly forget who and where I am. He traces a finger on my lips. "You never get out of breath when I kiss you."

"Star says I have royal blood," I whisper. "Isn't that crazy?"

He laughs softly into my ear. "No, Your Most Grand and Benevolent Majesty," he says, making me giggle. I know this is a dream. I don't think it is possible to be this happy awake.

If I could, I would stay in this moment forever. It seems as if everywhere else, danger waits for us. Only here, with him, I feel completely safe, safer than I ever have. He must sense it, too, because he says, "What are you thinking about?"

"About the new land. I'm wondering how it will be."

He nods. "I know. Me, too."

"It's underground! It must be so strange. I wonder how they even breathe. Star says the people there are different. Do you think they will accept us?"

He shrugs and squeezes my hand. "I guess we'll find out." He pulls it to his mouth and kisses my knuckles. "Coe. It's like all those wishes I made… Those crazy, stupid wishes… They're all coming true."

I smile through my tears, tears of happiness and relief. "I know."

We separate, the inches between us feeling like miles as the chill from the air begins to settle on my skin again. Then we wade down the passage together, to our waists. Tiam pauses, preparing to take that final breath, and in the silence of that moment, a heavy, uneven pounding sounds in the corridor behind us. At first I wonder if it is just the new tide coming in, the ebb and flow of the waves above us. But as it gets louder, I recognize it. Footsteps. Many of them. An army, maybe.

We both whirl at once. Orange firelight reflects in the black water. Someone is coming, coming up fast. I tighten my grip on Tiam's hand. "Tiam. I made a horrible mistake. I left the grate to the laundry chute open," I say.

He cranes his neck to see in the dark, but it's only outlines. I know who leads it. The new king of Tides.

"Let's go. Just close your eyes, okay? Think positive thoughts, and I'll do the work."

"Right." He takes a deep breath and as the light in the corridor grows more intense, I grab his trembling hand and pull him under.

And we swim. Even though he weighs more, I have less trouble pulling him along as he's stronger and faster than Fern. He moves beside me as if he, too, were made for living underwater. As this is my fifth trip, everything is familiar. The stone walls, coated in green moss, the bits of rock and rotted wood planks at the floor of the passage. I open my mouth and let the water flow through me, and though my only thought should be getting to the other end, getting free, in a small flash at the back of my mind, it occurs to me that the water swirling through me is washing away all trace of Tiam on my lips.

And maybe that's why I go slower. I falter. I still can't see the light up ahead, so I know we have far to go. This is no time to panic. I look back at Tiam for reassurance. At my hand on his. Our hands fit perfectly together, the ridges and folds conforming to one another, two halves making a whole.

I think about the new world, thrilling at the thought of us, together. Of him wanting me as much as I've wanted him. It seems almost impossible to believe that these dreams of mine could come true. And yet here we are. So close.

His eyes are closed, his face strangely serene despite his fear. He looks as if he is sleeping. I wonder what thoughts are going through his head, what positive thoughts he's thinking to calm himself. I wonder if he's thinking about me.

His eyes flicker once, then open wide, wider. I try to smile at him, to motion to him to calm down, but it all happens so fast, and by then there's no return. His face is pure terror, something that's so foreign on him, I quickly begin to feel it, too.

All at once I'm aware that my grip on his hand is loosening, and then I feel only his fingertips on mine. And then he slips away.

Twenty-Three
Falls the Shadow

"Tiam!" I open my mouth and scream but it's drowned out by the water rushing through my body. The light sinks slowly to the ground, landing in the soft dirt. I kick off the mossy wall, propel myself downward and pick it up, shining it feverishly in all directions. There's nothing behind me, nothing farther down the corridor. The light only illuminates a small green-tinged circle around me, but he's nowhere. Vanished.

Panic. He can't live underwater for much longer. Not the way I can. And without light it's impossible to tell up from down, or which way is out. He can't survive like this.

Nononono, I scream in my head, kicking idly in circles as I swing the light around. How could I have let him go? Why couldn't I have held on tighter?

I can see the opening to the passage behind us, hazy through the water, lit by orange torchlight. It must be Finn and his men. In the blackness, without light, that's the only thing Tiam would have seen. We're too far from the end of the passage, where Star and Fern are waiting. His only chance is if he went back toward the torches. I have no other choice. I have to go back, too.

I swim back to where the floor rises, then walk along the floor until my head is on the surface. I blink the water from my eyelashes and see a figure standing in the water, his smile a nasty slit, his metal spear glinting in the torchlight. Finn.

I turn away from him and see Tiam at his feet, hunched over and defeated. He's breathing hard, chest heaving, dripping hair matted against his eyes. He grabs his side and coughs again and again, but doesn't attempt to look at me.

Finn slowly saunters up to me. He's with two lanky men I recognize as fishermen, not the same guards he was with earlier. It takes me a moment to realize that his two hefty guards would never fit down the small chute, but it doesn't matter; each fisherman has his own spear. There are several other bodies in the background; the light glints off of their spears. In the torchlight I can also see that Finn's face is dark and raw in spots from the fire, the once sun-streaked stubble on his chin now crisp, a chunk of white skin hanging loosely off his nose. It doesn't seem to bother him. "So, this is where the exit is," he says.

"There's no exit," I mumble, helpless.

"I've had enough of this, Coe," he growls, jabbing the spear into my ribs. "It was a surprise to find that Tiam was alive after all this time. But it explains perfectly where you've been. You've been lying to us all along."

I turn to Tiam. But I have no other plan. No ideas. I point

to the flooded passage, all the while hoping Clever Gretel will provide me the inspiration I desperately need. But my mind is blank, my body tired and wasted. "It's not that way. We just tried it. Flooded."

Tiam finally speaks up. "Leave her alone, Finn," he growls, still breathless.

Finn scowls at Tiam and presses a spear against his neck. "Or you'll do what?" But Tiam's eyes are focused on me, intent, unblinking. He's trying to tell me something. But what? I take a tentative step forward.

"Coe, your light was flickering. Let me fix it," he says, his voice stilted. He motions to my portable light.

I'd almost forgotten I was carrying it. I hand it to him, wondering what he has in mind. I don't remember seeing it flicker, so I can only hope this is part of a grand plan to save us all. He crouches down, reaches into his bag and begins working on it. Then he screws the top on it again and hands it to me. "Should work better now."

"What are you—" Finn starts.

"Relax, they're just lights." Tiam takes one out of his bag and hands it to Finn, who lowers his spear and does just what I did. He inspects it for a while, turning it over in his hands, trying to figure out how the damn thing works without emitting any heat. And in that moment, Tiam mouths something to me.

Help Fern and Star. Don't worry about me.

What is he talking about? Is it possible he doesn't know that I've spent precisely every moment between every tide worrying about him?

Finn smiles, still taken with his new gadget, oblivious to the change in Tiam. The muscles in Tiam's chest and shoulders tighten, his jaw sets. His eyes dart between Finn and my own eyes. Finally, they settle on me, almost lazily. "Coe," he says. "R-U-N."

I stare at him. And maybe it's that all this time I've had this image of us going to the escape together, but my knees suddenly buckle. *Don't worry about me.* He wants me to go. Without him. I shake my head, but he doesn't relent. Before I can open my mouth to protest, his voice echoes through the chamber, full of fight. "Now!" he shouts, and lunges for Finn.

It all happens so fast, I stand there, frozen. "No," I say, over and over, as he and Finn topple to the ground, Tiam delivering punch after punch to Finn's already raw face. But immediately, the other guards are on him. And I know the odds aren't good.

I want to help him. I want to tell him that I'll wait for him, that I would never go anywhere without him. I couldn't. And yet I know what he's thinking. He's thinking he tried it, and it's impossible. He can't make it through the flooded corridor. But there is one way for him to feel useful again. And this is it.

Just then, two of Finn's guards charge me. I'm no match for two of them. Either I run now and live, or let them take me and die. I know those are the only choices. And so I take the light, run down the hallway and plunge into the black water.

Twenty-Four
Not with a Bang but a Whimper

Everything about this feels wrong. What am I doing? As I swim, I look over my shoulder until the light of the torches disappears. He's gone. I left him. There were a dozen of them, only one of him. And I left him. Why? I could have helped him fight.

But we were outnumbered. And I know what Tiam would say if he were with me. *Keep going. Don't look back. Better just one casualty instead of two.*

I don't know how I keep pushing forward when everything—the only thing—I want lies behind me. My vision blurs, and I'm sure it's because I'm crying. My body trembles as I move through the cold, taking the water in, letting it flow through me. Washing every trace of Tiam away. Only heartbeats have passed, yet I already know that this was the most important decision of my life, and I made the wrong choice. I already know that as long as I live, that will be the moment I replay time and time again in my head, wishing I had the chance to do it over.

When I arrive at the shore, Star and Fern are sitting there, huddled together, studying the map. I crawl out and collapse beside them, sobbing.

"I left Tiam," I whimper, and once the words are out I know that I will never see him again. And I know that Tiam was wrong to let me go alone, because the moment I left him, my world ended. We both died.

Fern's sweet face goes white, and her lip trembles. Star squeals, "What do you mean?"

I don't answer. I can't bring myself to talk about that horrible moment. I just lie there on the ground, wanting it to suck me in and bury me forever, in the same passage where Tiam will meet his own end. At least that would be a fitting final chapter to the story of Tiam and me. *Together, apart.*

"We have to get him! We can't leave him!" Star shouts, malice in her voice.

I don't want to move, but somehow I pick myself up from the soft mud and say, "Finn and his men. I don't think they can make it through. But in case they can…we need to go."

"Leave him? Just like that? But he's my beloved!" Her face is twisted, giving her an ugliness I never thought possible. Her breath comes out in short bursts, and tears form in her eyes. "We can't go. Not until Tiam is with us."

I'm too tired to fight her. "Then you go back for him. But they'll kill you. There are a dozen of them. If not more."

She contemplates the flooded passage for only a second before slumping onto the muddy ground. "We're done for," she moans between sobs.

"What are you talking about?" I whisper, my voice flat and

toneless. "The map goes on for a while, but we can make it. We just follow it. And if Finn and his men come through, they'll never be able to find their way without the map."

"You don't understand," Star moans. "He was to be my husband, my protector. I love him. I *need* him."

I look at the ground. She makes it seem as if she's the only one. As if I don't need him. As if I discarded him on the other shore like a piece of seaweed. Maybe it stings so much because she's right. I spent all my days wanting him, and yet I just left him. Too easily.

I take Fern by the hand. Fern. She is all I have to live for now. She is the reason I must go on. I squeeze her close to me as we walk, not wanting to ever let her out of my sight. Star points the way with her own light, and I follow with Tiam's. It makes a strange rattling noise as I move, in time with our footsteps. We continue through a maze of doorways, on and on, but Star doesn't falter. She doesn't speak, and I wonder if it's possible she could be feeling as terrible as I do. We're sisters, after all. Even if we are so very different. We'd been raised in completely different circumstances. But maybe we have more in common than I know.

This is my family. And I'll protect them with all that I am, because I know Tiam would have done the same.

I cannot say much about the rest of the journey. I crawl inside myself, just a walking, breathing corpse.

Just as Tiam had predicted from the lines scraped into that map, the passages narrow considerably. We stop to rest twice, or three times, but even rest does not revive me. There are many wrong turns, even with the map, scrapes and bruises from the rocky, craggy walls, frightening, ghostlike sounds and movements in the darkness that prove to be only our imagination. With every obstacle, I am reminded of what Tiam would have said or done to make things better. A thousand times, I hear his voice in my head, feel his lips on mine.

And then…

"The map ends here," Star says softly, awakening me from my daze.

We come to a giant slab of thick, solid metal. I think of the opening that Kimmie wrote about in the journal—big, steel, carved into the side of the hill. There is a small door to its side, and words scratched into a plaque nearby.

BLACK MOUNTAIN
EMERGENCY CONTAINMENT UNIT II
ENTRANCE
PROPER ID REQUIRED

I read the words to Star and Fern.

"Oh, my goodness," Fern whispers, squeezing closer to me. "This is it?"

I nod. I try the door. It opens with a creak, grinding on its hinges as if no one has ever opened it. But someone must have, thousands and thousands of tides ago. Aliah. Our mother.

I peer through the darkness. There's a light glowing in the distance. Someone is there. Star walks forward, ahead of me, making her way through the dark passage. Toward light. Toward a new world.

Behind her, I take a deep breath, all the while feeling cold and distant, as if watching this amazing moment in the history of our people happen to others, not me. Because I guess in my heart, without him, I'll always be on that island, waiting for the end. Tides was never where I belonged, and it never belonged to me. *He* was my world, and I abandoned him. Before, the thought of escape sent a thrill through me. But now my heart is still. Dead.

As if it senses the fact, my portable light suddenly goes out, casting me into darkness.

I shake it, and it rattles noisily. The light does not return. It's rattled ever since Tiam "fixed" it. Curiously, I turn it toward the ceiling and unscrew the top, the way he'd done. And then I reach inside.

Behind the dead bulb, my fingers brush against something strange. Tilting it over, I scoop out a handful of milky pearls. The stones are warm from the light, and they melt pleasantly into my palm.

Tiam's pearls.

My pearls.

I pool them in my fist and press them against my heart for a moment, then follow Star into the new world.

★ ★ ★ ★ ★

Acknowledgments

My sincerest gratitude to the following people, who helped make *Drowned* happen.

Mandy Hubbard, thanks for being the first to say that this crazy idea might actually work.

Rhonda Stapleton, Lynsey Newton, Jennifer Murgia, thanks for reading my drafts and for your insightful comments and cheerleading. If it wasn't for you guys telling me that you couldn't forget this story, even months after you read it, I'm sure I would have. And to the Debs, who so many years later still give me sanity.

Thanks to Jim McCarthy for never giving up and always patiently answering my inane questions.

My deepest appreciation to the entire wonderful team at Harlequin TEEN, especially Natashya Wilson, for seeing the potential in my story, and my editor, Annie Stone, for the amazing read-throughs and insightful comments.

Thanks to my family, who indulges me.

And last, but certainly not least, none of this would be possible without you, the reader. Thank you for allowing me to tell you this story. I hope you enjoy it.

Questions for Discussion

1. Coe is a unique protagonist for a variety of reasons, but not least because of her wide range of strengths and weaknesses. What do you think are the most important strengths that set her apart from her fellow citizens of Tides? How does she offset her weaknesses, and would you say that she thinks of herself as a strong or a weak person?

2. Through her family's journal entries, Coe learns of the events that created the reign of the Wallow family. Why do you think the people of Tides were willing to follow the Wallows' leadership, even as it became corrupt? Basing your answer off the events of the novel, do you feel that people naturally gravitate toward having a leader, or do they wish to rule themselves?

3. Tiam and Finn are set up as opposing claimants to the throne. How do their goals for the island nation differ?

In your opinion, which of them is better suited to be king, and why?

4. Despite their history as childhood playmates, Star and Coe are raised very differently, and have starkly different beliefs about the world around them. Yet in some ways their goals and desires are very similar. What do you think their biggest differences are—and do you think these differences are inborn, or a result of their differing upbringings?

5. How does Coe's belief that her world will soon come to an end affect her actions and her relationships? When do you feel Coe begins to truly have hope for an escape from their island home?

6. Coe copes with her father's absence by trying not to think about the fact that he'll likely never return. What are some other coping mechanisms that characters in *Drowned* use to deal with the harsh realities of their lives?

7. Coe thinks of Tiam as the strongest person on the island. In your opinion, is he? Why or why not?

8. "Creeping normality" refers to the way a major change can be accepted as the normal situation if it happens slowly, in unnoticed increments, when it would be regarded as objectionable if it took place in a single step or short period. For example, the ruin of the Easter Island civilization came about because of gradual deforestation, though it seems strange, in hindsight, that the inhabitants would not have recognized the loss of a resource so

important to them. What are some beliefs the people of Tides have slowly come to accept that may be hindering their chances of survival?

9. Interestingly enough, history has shown us that societies most vulnerable to collapse are also the ones that are most creative and technologically advanced. *Drowned* offers up one reason why a mighty society might collapse: environmental change. What are some other reasons a society might collapse? Why do societies succeed?

10. The chapter titles from *Drowned* are from T. S. Eliot's famous poem "The Hollow Men." In what ways are the people of Tides hollow? How are they not?